"If you kiss n   makeup."

"I'm willing to take that chance."

"We have a job to do." As hard as it was to push him away, Kendra knew it would be impossible to go through with her plans if she let him make love to her now.

"Spoilsport. You know I'll have to beat the men away with a club, don't you? Nervous?"

"Of course I am." Scared spitless would be closer to the truth. They were posing as a man-and-wife security team for a powerful and deadly criminal. Anything could go wrong. "I'd be a fool not to be."

"I'll be nearby at all times," Rafe promised. "Ready?"

"As I'll ever be."

"Then let's get this over with. Remember one thing," he said as they started down the hall. "All night long I'm going to be peeling that dress from your body in my mind. So if you want something to really worry about, think about what's going to happen when we have to share that bed later on."

Dear Harlequin Intrigue Reader,

The days are getting cooler, but the romantic suspense is always hot at Harlequin Intrigue! Check out this month's selections.

TEXAS CONFIDENTIAL continues with *The Specialist* (#589) by Dani Sinclair. Rafe Alvarez was the resident playboy agent, until he met his match in Kendra Kincaide. He transformed his new partner into a femme fatale for the sake of a mission, and instantly lost his bachelor's heart for the sake of love....

THE SUTTON BABIES have grown in number by two in *Little Boys Blue* (#590) by Susan Kearney. A custody battle over cowboy M.D. Cameron Sutton's baby boys was brewing. When East Coast socialite Alexa Whitfield agreed to a marriage of convenience, Cam thought his future was settled. Until he fell for his temporary wife—the same wife someone was determined to kill!

Hailed by *Romantic Times Magazine* as an author who writes a "tantalizing read," Gayle Wilson returns with *Midnight Remembered* (#591), which marks the conclusion of her MORE MEN OF MYSTERY series. When ex-CIA agent Joshua Stone couldn't remember his true identity, he became an easy target. But his ex-partner Paige Daniels knew all his secrets, including what was in his heart....

Reeve Snyder had rescued Polly Black from death and delivered her baby girl one fateful night. Polly's vulnerable beauty touched him deep inside, but who was she? And what was she running from? And next time, would Reeve be able to save her and her daughter when danger came calling? Find out in *Alias Mommy* (#592) by Linda O. Johnston.

Don't miss a single exciting moment!

Sincerely,

Denise O'Sullivan
Associate Senior Editor
Harlequin Intrigue

THE SPECIALIST
DANI SINCLAIR

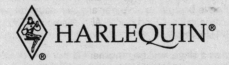

TORONTO • NEW YORK • LONDON
AMSTERDAM • PARIS • SYDNEY • HAMBURG
STOCKHOLM • ATHENS • TOKYO • MILAN • MADRID
PRAGUE • WARSAW • BUDAPEST • AUCKLAND

If you purchased this book without a cover you should be aware that this book is stolen property. It was reported as "unsold and destroyed" to the publisher, and neither the author nor the publisher has received any payment for this "stripped book."

Special thanks and acknowledgment are given to
Dani Sinclair for her contribution
to the Texas Confidential series.

ISBN 0-373-22589-X

THE SPECIALIST

Copyright © 2000 by Harlequin Books S.A.

All rights reserved. Except for use in any review, the reproduction or utilization of this work in whole or in part in any form by any electronic, mechanical or other means, now known or hereafter invented, including xerography, photocopying and recording, or in any information storage or retrieval system, is forbidden without the written permission of the publisher, Harlequin Enterprises Limited, 225 Duncan Mill Road, Don Mills, Ontario, Canada M3B 3K9.

All characters in this book have no existence outside the imagination of the author and have no relation whatsoever to anyone bearing the same name or names. They are not even distantly inspired by any individual known or unknown to the author, and all incidents are pure invention.

This edition published by arrangement with Harlequin Books S.A.

® and TM are trademarks of the publisher. Trademarks indicated with ® are registered in the United States Patent and Trademark Office, the Canadian Trade Marks Office and in other countries.

Visit us at www.eHarlequin.com

Printed in U.S.A.

ABOUT THE AUTHOR

An avid reader, Dani Sinclair didn't discover romance novels until her mother lent her one when she came for a visit. Dani's been hooked on the genre ever since. With the premiere of *Mystery Baby* for Harlequin Intrigue in 1996, Dani discovered she not only enjoyed reading this genre, she loved writing the intense stories, as well. Her third novel, *Better Watch Out,* was a RITA Award finalist in 1998. Dani lives outside Washington, D.C., a place she's found to be a great source for both intrigue and humor!

Books by Dani Sinclair

HARLEQUIN INTRIGUE
371—MYSTERY BABY
401—MAN WITHOUT A BADGE
448—BETTER WATCH OUT
481—MARRIED IN HASTE
507—THE MAN SHE MARRIED
539—FOR HIS DAUGHTER*
551—MY BABY, MY LOVE*
565—THE SILENT WITNESS*
589—THE SPECIALIST

*Fools Point

HARLEQUIN TEMPTATION
690—THE NAKED TRUTH

Don't miss any of our special offers. Write to us at the following address for information on our newest releases.

Harlequin Reader Service
U.S.: 3010 Walden Ave., P.O. Box 1325, Buffalo, NY 14269
Canadian: P.O. Box 609, Fort Erie, Ont. L2A 5X3

The Confidential Agent's Pledge

I hereby swear to uphold the law
to the best of my ability; to maintain the
level of integrity of this agency by my
compassion for victims, loyalty to my
brothers and courage under fire.

And above all, to hold all information and
identities in the strictest confidence....

★★★★

CAST OF CHARACTERS

Rafe Alvarez—The chameleon; known for his charm, sex appeal and sense of humor, he'll need the latter to deal with his new "partner."

Kendra Kincaide—The beautiful computer whiz has a deadly secret and an unknown enemy.

Mitchell Forbes—As head of Texas Confidential, he agrees Kendra's skills will help their latest mission; he just isn't sure he trusts her.

Penny Archer—She may be Mitchell's right-hand woman, but is the left hand hiding a secret crush on Rafe?

Stephen Rialto—The oilman hires only brilliant, attractive, upscale people to work at Rialto Industries—perhaps to hide his other less than legal activities?

Marcus Slade—The man for hire will do anything Rialto tells him to—even kill.

Cody Gannon—The youngest Texas Confidential agent and the only other bachelor left is about to see his past unravel right before his eyes....

For Angela, Tashya and my fellow "confidentials."
What a great group to work with.
And always, for Roger, Chip, Dan and Barb.

Prologue

Silence stilled even the chirp of crickets. Whicker suddenly lifted his head and stared into the darkness. The creak of leather cracked the silence as Rafe Alvarez sat up straighter in the saddle, coming fully alert. He stroked Whicker's sleek neck and whispered softly, instantly quieting the massive gelding.

For months the rustlers had seemed to know exactly when and where to strike. They either had the luck of the devil, or they had inside information on the placement of the ranch hands.

Rafe set his jaw. The possibility festered in all their minds. After what his fellow Texas Confidential agent Jake and his wife Abby had gone through because of a mole inside the FBI, tension was heightened for all the agents at the Smoking Barrel Ranch. This was, after all, the headquarters of Texas Confidential, a quietly secretive government organization. Protecting the cattle around the clock on a ranch this size was impossible, especially since the Smoking Barrel was being deliberately and systematically targeted. No doubt Tomaso Calderone, the drug lord they'd been trying to nab for months, was behind the problem, but that begged the question—who else was on his payroll?

Backing his horse into a stand of scrub pines Rafe waited, his hand hovering over the rifle stock. He welcomed this instant rush of adrenaline after the tedious hours of waiting and watching. Rafe liked being a working cowboy, as well as a Texas Confidential agent. So did his colleagues. And none of them liked the strain they'd been working under lately. Rafe welcomed action at this point—any action that would result in the capture of the men responsible for the systematic raids and bring them one step closer to Calderone.

Any moment now, the rustlers would break out over the ridge and be silhouetted clearly against the cooperative moon before the encroaching clouds could darken the landscape once more.

The sound of a hoof striking rock gave him final confirmation. Whicker took several mincing sidesteps, sensing Rafe's tension. He, too, was eager for action. Rafe soothed him silently as they waited.

A horse and rider abruptly broke the ridge in an easy, almost sanguine canter. Rafe frowned. Rider singular. And this would-be rustler was entirely too confident. Rafe watched him come to a stop at the top of the ridge, pausing to survey the cattle below as if he had every right to be there. The man sat tall, his hat pulled low. With the moon at the stranger's back, Rafe couldn't make out any features, but he did catch a reflection beneath the brim. The man wore glasses.

The wind abruptly shifted. The rustler's paint picked up Whicker's scent. The smaller horse whinnied a greeting, alerting his rider. The man swiveled to peer at the lone stand of pines.

Rafe dropped his hand from the rifle butt and gently kicked Whicker into a gallop. The well-trained cutting horse gathered himself without effort and sprang forward, even as the rustler whirled, urging his horse into a reckless plunge back down the incline.

Was the fool trying to kill himself?

The rustler had the advantage of the lead, but Whicker's training and much longer stride made the outcome a given. The smaller paint didn't stand a chance of outrunning him, though his rider tried. The distance between the two horses closed quickly. It was obvious that the other rider wasn't going to stop as the two horses thundered dangerously down the embankment, right toward the grazing cattle herd.

A cloud drifted across the moon, darkening the night as Rafe pulled alongside the other rider. The rustler twisted around for a look just as Rafe came abreast. Rafe kicked free of the stirrups and lunged. Like a choreographed movie stunt, momentum carried both of them to the hard-packed earth in a bone-jarring fall. Hats went flying as they rolled several feet before coming to a stop.

Rafe found himself lying full-length along the other's skinny form. His hand had come to rest inside the intruder's open jacket front. He was stunned to recognize the softly rounded curve beneath his hand for what it was.

"A girl?"

She gave him a shove. "A woman," she corrected with haughty disdain.

Her voice flowed over him like warm brandy as she tried to adjust the glasses that were hanging half off her face.

"Rafael Alvarez, I presume?"

Stunned, Rafe could only nod.

Her mouth tightened in a line of anger right before her fist landed against his jaw with enough force to hurt more than his pride. She scrambled out from beneath him, rising to her feet.

"Next time, watch where you put your hands." She regarded him with narrowed eyes and began dusting off her jeans.

"Who *are* you?" he demanded.

"I'm Kendra Kincade—your new partner."

Chapter One

Rafe rose slowly, rubbing his jaw. He was going to have a bruise! In fact, she might just have loosened a couple of his teeth—but he'd be hung before he'd admit that out loud.

"My partner, huh?" He surveyed her lanky, boyish build beneath the dark jacket she wore and the no-nonsense glasses that still hung askew on her narrow face after their tumble. Rafe suddenly found himself wanting to grin. Whoever she was, she was no rustler.

"Darlin', most women who want to be my 'partner' use a slightly different approach."

Her lips thinned in prissy rejection of his attempt to tease. "Not *that* sort of partner."

"Well, I'm not into rustlin' cattle, darlin'," he offered.

"I'm not a cattle thief!"

"Well certainly not the sort I was expectin'," he agreed watching her closely. It was difficult to tell in the dark, but he'd swear she was blushing. Now when had he ever seen a grown woman blush? Was she so naive she didn't realize the risk of running around the countryside in the middle of the night by herself?

"What are you doing out here at this hour, darlin'?" He took a step in her direction. Instantly, she backed away, almost stumbling over a rock.

"Stop that!"

Rafe halted. He was used to a much different reaction from the women he met and he found himself unaccountably irritated by her angry response and this entire crazy situation. Somebody needed to teach Ms. Kendra Kincade that there could be consequences to foolish actions.

"No call to be shy, darlin'. There's only you and me and the cattle out here." He swept his hand to indicate their isolation and caught a glimpse of Whicker munching contentedly on some grass a few yards away.

"Shy? Why you arrogant—" She fumbled for words, obviously at a loss. "Male," she finally spit at him.

Rafe rubbed his jaw where her fist had connected. "Guilty."

Her eyes glinted in the moonlight reflected off the unattractive glasses she wore. Any minute now, like a cartoon, steam would pour from beneath the open collar of her jacket. She was too annoyed to be frightened, but she should be frightened. Didn't she see the risk out here in the predawn morning hours?

Rafe closed the distance between them. This time, she held her ground. Overhead, clouds parted to let the moon highlight her features.

Thirtyish, at a guess, though her age was hard to determine for sure. Her brown hair was long and stringy. The ends looked as if she'd taken dull scissors to them. No jewelry, not even a ring. He continued his assessment, waiting for her reaction. Dark jeans hugged a surprisingly nice pair of legs, and a light colored, button-down shirt that he'd already discovered harbored nicely rounded breasts. Her feet had been stuffed into a pair of boots that looked suspiciously new. She had surprisingly small feet.

"If you're through with the inventory, you can hold it right there, buster."

She might not be much to look at, but she did have spunk, he decided.

"Buster?"

She set her jaw, planted her fists on her hips and glared at him. "Your name is Rafael Alvarez," she snapped out, "but you're called Rafe. Six feet one inch tall, brown hair, green eyes, half Spanish and half Irish," she recited. "And all baloney," she added defiantly.

"Baloney?"

"Your parents died in a car crash when you were an infant. Your grandparents raised you until your freshman year of college. Tragically, they died along with a lot of other people in that fire on board the cruise ship *Althea.*"

His amusement dissolved at her recital.

"Their deaths left you alone, but financially secure," she continued. "You went back to school where you got in with a rowdy crowd. Your sophomore year culminated in your drunken arrest for grand theft auto. A friend boosted another friend's car before picking you up along with several young females after a party. All of you were drunk and there was beer in the car."

Rafe flinched at the memory.

"Fortunately, the police stopped the driver before anyone was hurt. You spent a full night in jail and hired a high-priced lawyer to avoid serious criminal charges. Apparently, you wised up after that. You dropped your former associates, changed your major and went on to study law, though you never took the bar exam."

How did she know all this?

"That's enough." His soft voiced tone would have warned off anyone who knew him. Kendra never batted an eye.

"Next, you applied to the police academy, but you were too much of a maverick for all their rules and regulations. You dropped out almost right away. Or maybe they suggested you leave. Either way, you did some research of your own. I'm guessing you stumbled over the very quiet, very private organization known as Texas Confidential.''

Rafe drew in a breath, his body vibrating with sudden tension. ''Who *are* you?''

''We already covered that. Then—''

He grabbed her shoulders in a punishing grip. Instantly, he relaxed his hold because she felt astonishingly delicate beneath his broad hands. While he wanted to scare her enough to interrupt her recital, he didn't want to hurt her. Her eyes widened behind her glasses giving her a frightened, baby owl appearance.

Rafe gentled his hold even further when she licked her lips nervously. He followed the motion of her tongue, annoyed to notice that she had very nice lips—when they weren't pursed in disdain.

''I want to know who you are.''

''I told you,'' she stated boldly, ''I'm Kendra Kincade.''

He crowded her until she was pressed along his jacket. The action defined her slenderness against his much larger masculinity. He watched her eyes widen in final acknowledgment of his size and gender and their isolation. Nearby, a cow snorted at a patch of ground.

''Who is Kendra Kincade?'' he asked softly.

She lifted her chin a little higher, though she flinched when he took the back of his hand and ran it down the side of her face. He felt her body quiver. The softness of her skin took him by surprise yet again. Her long, unstylish hair tumbled messily about her shoulders while a beguiling scent of shampoo filled his nostrils. She wasn't his type by a long shot. Still, he found himself aware that she was definitely a woman. That firm round curve of flesh he'd held so fleetingly had left an indelible impression.

Some of her assertiveness drained away as he continued to hold her shoulders now. She licked her lips once more and planted her hands on her hips. ''I told you I'm—''

"My partner," he finished for her. Time for her to comprehend the risk she was taking. He trailed his fingers over the curve of her cheek, sliding them along the slope of her neck to where the V of her open jacket revealed the cotton material of her blouse. "But if you know so much about me, you know I prefer selecting my own—*partners.*"

Rafe didn't feel the least bit sorry for using his own brand of intimidation. The woman was playing a dangerous game of some sort. A game that could have serious consequences if she tried this approach on the wrong man. He let his fingers slide beneath the top button of her blouse in a subtle warning caress.

For a moment, neither of them moved. The abrupt prick of the knife tip against his exposed throat came as a complete shock.

"Back up, Alvarez. I mean it." There was nothing teasing in her tone.

While it would have been a simple matter to take the knife from her, Rafe was more curious than alarmed. This was not the effect his legendary charm generally had on women. Of course, he wasn't exerting a whole lot of charm right now. Still, no other woman had ever caught him so totally off guard as this skinny handful of a female with the glittering eyes.

Rafe dropped his hand and took a step back, watching her intently.

"Do I make you that nervous, darlin'?"

"No, you annoy me that much."

The knife disappeared with a speed that made him pay attention. She was not what she seemed.

"And stop calling me darling!"

His lips curved at the corners. "Whatever you say, sugar."

Kendra Kincade looked like she wanted to stomp her booted feet—preferably in the region of his face. Rafe found his lips curving in a reluctant smile that disappeared almost as fast as it had come. He rocked back on his heels, hooked his thumbs in his belt and studied her.

"I assume you're going to explain why and how you know so much about me?"

Kendra shook the hair out of her face and kept from sighing her relief out loud. Thankfully, he'd finally given her some breathing space. She wasn't used to being crowded—and he was a very large man.

"Your life is an open book," she told him.

"Is that right?"

She told herself she was edgy because she didn't appreciate the way he studied her like some tasty morsel waiting to be sampled. The truth was, she'd been totally unprepared to meet Rafael Alvarez in the flesh.

He looked deceptively relaxed as he nudged his hat further back on his forehead with a knuckle and regarded her. He was toying with her, darn him. The knowledge annoyed her.

"It is for anyone who knows how to operate a computer keyboard," she affirmed.

"And you do."

"It's what I do best."

"Now that," he said suggestively, sweeping her body once more with his gaze, "is too bad. There are lots of better things a woman like you should do best."

The moonlight allowed her to see his gently mocking expression. She'd studied his computer image for hours. She'd thought she knew every nuance of his features, but nothing could have prepared her for the sensual reality of the man himself.

Rafe Alvarez was bigger, more masculine, and far sexier than any picture could convey. His suave, rumbly voice slipped inside her mind like a phantom lover's caress.

She wasn't supposed to be feeling this pull of attraction,

yet her skin still felt the path his hand, then his fingers, had taken down her face and below. Her heart still hadn't settled back to a regular rhythm. This would never do. The key to handling a man like Rafe was to keep the upper hand. He was baiting her, but two could play at that game.

"I know everything about you and Mitchell Forbes and his Texas Confidential agents," she asserted. "I even know your next assignment." She watched his body tighten. "You're going after Stephen Rialto."

She dangled the name between them in the silence of the night, disturbed only by the distant shuffle of the herd of cattle.

Rafe's eyes narrowed dangerously. A shiver traced its way down her spine at his new expression. Despite the sensuality that practically radiated from him, this was not a man to trifle with.

"What do you know about Stephen Rialto?" Rafe asked softly.

"More than I want to know." She knew he saw the small shudder she couldn't control. "He's lower than a snake and far more deadly. I intend to help you see that justice is served."

Rafe studied her in silence. The sweeping glance of his eyes was disturbing, making her uncomfortably aware of herself in a whole new way. Until this moment, her lack of attractiveness had never bothered her one whit. She'd take brains over useless beauty any day.

Rafe, on the other hand, was gorgeous—in a purely masculine way. He was cocky with the self-assurance that came from being handsome and confident in who he was. When she'd decided to use him, Kendra had made a complete study of the man. He loosed his lethal charm on any unsuspecting woman that came within range—an ingrained habit on his part no doubt.

But she was supposed to be immune.

"Let me guess," he said quietly. "You used to work for Rialto."

"Hardly."

"A jilted lover?"

"Of course not!" She shuddered at the very thought of letting Stephen Rialto touch her for any reason at all. Stephen Rialto had climbed over the bodies of the people he'd killed to become Tomaso Calderone's number one henchman here in Texas. Kendra squared her shoulders. "I'm not going to stand here and spar with you. My motives don't come into this. All you need to know is that I'm going to help you destroy him."

The moon darted behind another cloud. Rafe didn't so much as twitch at her words. He watched her in unnerving silence while the dampness of the grass they had rolled in soaked its way through her jeans to chill her skin uncomfortably. She had to remind herself that she'd left behind the safety of her computers for one reason and one reason only. Rafael Alvarez was going to help her achieve her goal—whether he wanted to or not.

"I think," he said softly, "this conversation requires a different setting. Would you like to ride back to the Smoking Barrel Ranch with me?"

She released the breath she hadn't been aware she was holding.

"I hadn't planned…"

"Hadn't planned what?"

She pushed back her uncertainties. "On meeting you tonight."

"But you did plan to meet me, huh, darlin'?"

"Not the way *you* mean."

"Really."

He ruffled her anger all over again with the simple arrogant inflection of the word.

"Yes, really."

"Then what were you doing out here at this hour?"

"I was enjoying a quiet ride."

"At four o'clock in the morning?"

"Yes!"

"On posted land."

"I wasn't here to steal any of your precious cattle."

"Perhaps not, but you do realize you could easily have run into whoever is."

"It never occurred to me that anyone would have the temerity to steal from the Smoking Barrel."

"No? Your computer didn't give you that little fact?"

He was trying to provoke her again. "Has anyone ever told you that you can be real annoying?"

"Yes, as a matter of fact, Penny tells me that on a regular basis."

"Penny Archer?" She was Mitchell Forbes's indispensable right hand.

"Do you know her?"

"We've never met. I know of her."

Rafe's jaw clenched, but he inclined his head. "You do have a lot of knowledge."

"I told you, I know all about the setup here."

"So you did. Then you must know that you and Penny have a lot in common. She has a sharp tongue, too. I think you should come with me and meet her for yourself."

Kendra hesitated. What would he do if she refused? Would he force her? A shiver of something that might have been anticipation but was probably fear, worked its way down her spine. She shrugged off the sensation. After all, she hadn't come out here to play word games with him. She'd planned to reconnoiter the area before approaching the ranch later this morning.

"I'm tempted, but thanks to you, my horse took off."

"No thanks necessary," he said wryly. "Fortunately, my horse is better trained. He won't mind if we ride double."

"Maybe he won't, but I will." Get on top of that big horse he'd been riding—with *him?* No way.

"It's a long walk."

"So go catch my horse for me." She saw the flash of his teeth as he smiled and she tried not to clench her jaw. She'd spent so much of her life talking to computers, she was finding it more difficult than she'd expected to deal with a man like Rafe face-to-face.

Rafe whistled, startling her. His horse lifted its head, whuffed and trotted over obediently. Kendra was impressed despite herself.

"How'd you train him to do that?"

"Charm," Rafe replied. "You ought to try it sometime."

She refused to let him see how that stung. "Charm only works on susceptible females."

"Nope, he's a gelding."

"Very funny."

Rafe took up the dangling reins and swung himself into the saddle with grace and an economy of movement she had to admire. He was incredibly sensual without even trying.

"I'm not riding double with you," she said defensively.

"I believe I mentioned the long walk."

"Settled Sue can't have gone far."

"Settled Sue? You rented one of Chet's broken-down ponies? She'll be halfway to Ash Pond by now."

So he recognized his neighbor's horse, which meant he must realize Kendra was staying at Chet Thilgarde's dude ranch several miles away. Kendra watched as he reached for his saddlebag and withdrew a cell phone, quickly punching in a series of numbers. The call must have been answered immediately because he began speaking almost at once. "Hey, beautiful, what are you doing awake at this hour? Oh. Sorry. Does that mean you're still in bed? Want to describe what you're wearing? Something black and sheer, I hope."

His rumbled chuckle resonated right through Kendra

along with a stab of something that felt suspiciously like jealousy.

"Ah, Penny." Rafe lowered his voice. "And here all this time I never thought of flannel as particularly erotic."

Kendra realized that while he was speaking to Penny, he was actually watching Kendra from beneath long sooty eyelashes a woman would kill to possess. She tried to keep her face impassive, but it was more difficult than it should have been.

"You wound me, darlin', but I'm afraid we'll have to postpone that conversation for another time. I called to give you a heads up. I'm on my way in with company. Nope. I'm afraid Ms. Kendra Kincade assures me she isn't a rustler, but she does pack a rather wicked six-inch knife."

He flashed Kendra a grin and listened some more.

"Hey, what can I tell you? A man like me simply isn't safe guarding the range anymore. Apparently we've got women hiding behind every shrub out here. Next time I pull guard duty you'll have to come along and guard the guard. What's that? Why, Penny, shame on you. But that reminds me, you might want to alert everyone who's on watch to keep an eye out for a riderless paint by the name of Settled Sue. Yeah, one of Chet's. She spooked when I jumped her rider." He listened for another minute and his devilish grin widened. "Why Ms. Archer, you have a dirty mind. Why didn't I think of that? We'll be there in about twenty minutes."

With a chuckle, he clicked off the phone and reached a hand toward Kendra. "Come on."

When Kendra didn't take the offered hand, he lowered his voice to an intimate level. "I only bite when I'm invited."

Several responses leaped to mind, but Kendra was determined to maintain control if it killed her. Reluctantly, she took his hand. She found herself on top of his massive horse before she could change her mind. Rafe was stronger than he looked. His horse had to be seventeen hands high.

"Hold on, darlin'."

"To what?"

He reached back, took her hands, and guided them around his waist. "Me."

Kendra resisted the desire to shove him out of the saddle. For a moment it was sorely tempting but she had the distinct feeling he knew exactly what she was thinking. His lips quirked again in subtle amusement.

"Hang on tight." And Rafe prodded the animal into a long, loping canter.

Reflexively, her hands closed around his waist, finding no purchase on the slick dark leather of his jacket. Instead, she gripped lower, where the jacket ended and the rough feel of denim met her touch.

"As much as I could really enjoy this," he called back to her, "if you drop those fingers a few inches lower darlin', I'll have to assume you really are planning to become my partner."

Instantly, her hands let go. He captured one and placed it against his belt. Her cheeks burned at the intimacy and his knowing chuckle. She gave more serious thought to knocking him out of the saddle. Only the knowledge that she needed him stilled her impulse.

She was glad he couldn't see her expression. With her face pressed against his broad back, and the scent of man, horse, sweat and leather filling her nostrils, they plunged across the uneven ground while her wayward mind churned with all sorts of thoughts she shouldn't be having.

Penny Archer met them at the front door of the large white house. Despite Rafe's comment about flannel pajamas, Penny was fully dressed in loose slacks and a blouse with a baggy sweater overtop. Her stylish glasses gave her an efficient look that went with the sharp intelligence in her gaze.

"Ms. Kincade, welcome to the Smoking Barrel. I'm afraid it's a bit early even for Rosa or Slim, but may I offer you—"

"Nothing. Thank you. I didn't intend to drop in this way. Especially not at this hour. I'm sorry Rafe got you out of bed."

Penny Archer raised cynically amused eyebrows in Rafe's direction. "Yes, that isn't his general sequence with women."

Rafe put a hand to his chest. "Another wound to the heart."

"It would take a cement truck," she assured him dryly. "How can we help you, Ms. Kincade?"

"I'm afraid Rafe spooked my horse. I need a lift back to the dude ranch where I'm staying. The truth is, I was hoping to speak with Mr. Forbes later today, but I'd planned to call first and ask for an appointment."

"Kendra knows all about our setup here at the ranch," Rafe put in.

Penny's expression didn't waver. "I'll tell you what, why don't you rest here until Mitchell wakes up? I'll see if he can meet with you after breakfast."

"Oh, but—"

"It's no problem, really. We keep a spare room ready for unexpected guests. You can rest until Rosa starts breakfast. You'll be welcome to join us then. Come with me."

"But—"

"Cody is on his way in," Penny informed Rafe as if everything was settled. "I believe he has something he wants you to see."

Rafe nodded seriously, then added a teasing smile. "Ah, Penny, here I was hoping *you* had something to show me."

"Dream on, Rafael," Penny replied dryly. "See you at breakfast."

Kendra watched the easy exchange with interest. It was strange to finally meet and observe how these people interacted. Penny was as efficient as Kendra had expected, but her deft ability to handle Rafe's teasing was interesting and unexpected. Kendra allowed herself to be led up the large winding staircase to a bedroom at the front of the house. Sturdy oak furniture graced a room done in neutral tones of beige and green. Penny Archer indicated the adjoining bathroom and left her there to "rest."

No key turned in the lock. That did surprise her a bit. These people weren't fools and they had no reason to trust her. She suspected she wouldn't get far if she stepped out into the hall. Making use of the bathroom instead, she discovered it connected to another room. A third door probably led into the hall. Judging by the few items neatly stowed in the vanity, she shared the bathroom with Penny.

Kendra returned to the guest quarters and flopped down on the queen-sized bed. She was tired, but too keyed up to sleep. While things weren't exactly going to plan, she was here, inside the headquarters of Texas Confidential. Now she must convince them that she could be an asset to their plan. It would have been better if she had her laptop, but in the end, it wouldn't matter. When Rafe entered Rialto's world, she would be with him—one way or another.

Kendra smothered a yawn and closed her eyes. Maybe she could nap for a few seconds after all.

INNOCENCE SHATTERED at the first dry popping sound. She tasted the dry-edged fear that left its metallic flavor lingering in her mouth. Part of her knew it was hopeless, yet she tried to call a warning to the young girl slowly counting to twenty out of sight beyond the kitchen.

From inside the bottom of the linen closet at the top of the stairs, she had a commanding view of the steps, the main hallway, and part of the kitchen. The pretty blond woman stepped away from the stove and answered the brisk knock on the front door.

"Why, hello. We...weren't expecting you."

The shadow man entered, big and burly in his heavy winter coat, snowflakes melting against the dark material. There was a popping sound. The woman crumpled to the floor. At the kitchen table, her husband started rising from his seat. *"What the—?"* he began, only to slump back down in his chair as two more popping sounds came. His outflung hand struck a glass of cola, spilling the sticky contents across the tabletop. The liquid began to drip, drip, drip against the clean, white tile floor.

In her head, she screamed a warning to the young girl who stopped counting and suddenly entered the kitchen from the dining room, innocently unaware.

Pop. Pop.

She fell like a broken rag doll. The shadow man stepped over her body and into the dining room.

In the closet, she drew herself into a tiny tight ball and closed her eyes. She wished she dared close the closet door all the way, but the metal would make noise. He would see her if she made a single sound. Suddenly, he bounded up the stairs, pausing to check each of the three bedrooms before moving straight for her hiding place.

She held her breath in terror as the closet door groaned open all the way. He rummaged on one of the upper shelves. She opened her eyes, hardly daring to breathe. A blanket fell to the floor in front of her.

She waited in an agony of fear for him to bend and pick it up. Because then he would see her and the popping sound would come again from the strange gun with its long barrel. But he left the blanket, and a towel that landed on top of the blanket, lying there. He turned and pulled off his glove for a moment. The gun hand disappeared from her line of sight. His left hand fell to his side as he stood silently for a moment.

A pretty red stone sparkled in the heavy gold ring he wore

on his left hand. She stared at that stone until he pulled his gloves back on and went downstairs again, disappearing from view.

She heard him moving noisily in the basement. He thought he was alone in the house. Silently, she uncurled her body and crept down the stairs. When she paused in the hall she jumped as the woman's eyes fluttered open.

"Next door," she whispered. "Get Mr. Lee. Hurry! Run!"

And she heard the shadow man start up the steps from the basement level.

She ran into the living room, ducking behind a chair so he wouldn't see her. Fear made her chest feel all hard and tight. Her stomach hurt. She was so scared. He would shoot her if he caught her. But he never looked toward her hiding place. Instead, he gazed down on the woman and fired his gun again.

She wanted to scream. She wanted to hurt that horrible shadow man with every fiber of her eight-year-old body, but all she could do was huddle beside the chair, consumed with hate for the man and his shiny red ring and his long, ugly gun.

He strode into the kitchen. She pictured him checking the others. There were no more pops from his gun. Were they dead? Was she the only one left alive inside the once-cozy house?

Then he was gone, out the front door. She rose on legs that trembled violently.

A strange smell had begun filling the house.

She decided not to investigate because he could come back at any minute. She turned to the sliding glass door in the dining room and struggled with the bar lock until she got it open. The smell was stronger. It made her feel really sick. She opened the door and stepped outside, closing the door behind her in case the man came back.

It had started snowing again, she discovered. Big fat white flakes that made her shiver. She wished she had her coat— and her boots. The snow was deep. She was going to ruin her shoes. Stupid thought. That didn't matter. She had to hurry. She had to go next door. She started running across the pristine expanse of white.

And the world exploded at her back, destroying her life forever.

Chapter Two

Brushing aside the haunted shadows of her dream, Kendra let the aroma of coffee and bacon draw her downstairs. She had slept longer and deeper than she would have guessed possible. The silence of the house unnerved her. Where was everyone?

"Buenos días, señorita."

Kendra smiled back at the short, plump woman with the cheerful smile and the graying hair pulled back in a bun. This would be Rosa Chavez, the Smoking Barrel's cook, she decided.

"Buenos días."

The following spate of dialogue was more than Kendra's tiny bit of Spanish could follow.

"I'm sorry I don't understand. *No comprende."*

"She wants to know what you'd like for breakfast."

Kendra's stomach gave a lurch. She twisted to find Rafe leaning nonchalantly against the door frame leading to the front room. His worn denims and open-necked shirt invited a woman's gaze to linger appreciatively. Her impression hadn't been wrong last night. Rafe was dangerously sexy.

"Thank you." She offered him a polite smile. "I'm not real big on breakfast. Would you tell her juice and toast will be fine?"

His eyes swept her from head to toe. It was all she could

do not to blush under that perusal. She was uncomfortably aware of her thinness beneath her slouchy clothing, and her finger-combed hair. She pushed her glasses tighter against the bridge of her nose and waited for him to make some remark. Instead, his expression remained neutral, neither approving nor condemning. He spoke rapid-fire Spanish to Rosa who frowned and nodded, hurrying back out to the kitchen.

"We don't stand on ceremony around here. Everyone eats in the kitchen."

"Fine. I don't like ceremony either. And I can get my own juice and toast. I don't need to be waited on."

Rafe came away from the door frame in a sinuous movement of pure grace. "No choice with Rosa manning the kitchen. Come on. I haven't eaten yet either. I'll join you."

Kendra tried not to let her consternation show. With him sitting beside her, she'd likely spill the juice or choke on the toast. She knew it was ridiculous, but Rafe made her unaccountably nervous.

"What about the others?"

"This is a working ranch. Everyone else ate hours ago. Penny checked on you, but you were sleeping so soundly she didn't have the heart to wake you. You'll be happy to know that Cody found Settled Sue last night. He returned her this morning. Chet was relieved. He was a little annoyed that you took her in the middle of the night without permission."

Kendra didn't respond. She had no defense for the subtle accusation. Instead, as they stepped into the brightly lit, spacious kitchen, she focused on her reason for being here.

"When can I meet with Mitchell Forbes?"

"One o'clock suit you? He's tied up until then."

"Yes, of course."

"Have a seat." Rafe seemed to glide forward, holding out a chair and waiting.

Kendra didn't think she'd ever had a man hold out a chair for her. The action made her feel awkward, and foolishly feminine at the same time. The long table could easily seat fifteen or more. So why did Rafe have to pull out the chair beside hers and sit down? She was already far too aware of him.

"Tell me what you know about Stephen Rialto," Rafe said.

Kendra wished she could look away from his penetrating eyes, but she couldn't. "He's the lowest form of human slime. He uses his legitimate oil company as a cover for all sorts of illegal activities."

"For instance?"

"Murder, drugs, money laundering, gun running—whatever Tomaso Calderone wants him to do."

Emotion came and went in Rafe's expression at the mention of the other man's name.

"So you also know about Calderone."

"He's a high-priced gangster who thinks he's untouchable."

Rafe nodded. "Close enough. What's your stake in going after Rialto?"

"I want to see him pay for his crimes."

"Why?"

"It doesn't matter."

"It matters very much." He lifted her hand from the table, stroking it gently in his much larger, rougher hands. Working man's hands. She felt the hint of calluses against her skin.

When she tried to pull free, he released her at once. But his suggestive smile caused her stomach to flutter. She had to stop letting him get to her like this. She was here for a purpose. Keeping that firmly in mind was proving difficult.

"Mr. Alvarez—"

"I think we've gone past formality, don't you?"

"Rafe then. I…what's this?"

Rosa plunked down two platters of bacon, eggs, homefries and toast. Rafe watched, openly amused.

"I told you to tell her toast."

Rafe shrugged. "You got toast."

"And an entire meal."

"Rosa tries to fatten everyone up. We've never been able to explain the dangers of cholesterol to her."

"But I only wanted toast and juice."

"Juice, *sí,*" Rosa beamed as she deposited glasses of fresh-squeezed orange juice in front of Kendra and Rafe.

"*Gracias,* Rosa," Rafe told her with a beaming smile. The woman returned it and bustled away before Kendra could find the wits to thank her as well.

"But—"

"Don't fight it. You won't win." He forked up a mouthful of scrambled eggs.

Kendra stared from him to her plate, wondering if he'd deliberately told Rosa to bring her this huge meal. She couldn't eat it all, but to ignore it seemed churlish. She was an unexpected, unwanted guest here. Kendra picked up her fork.

"Now tell me why you personally hate Rialto," Rafe said.

Eggs fell from her fork to land back on her plate with a splat. "I never said—"

"Not in words, but your tone says it each time you say his name."

If Rafe could read her so easily, she was going to have trouble lying to him.

"He killed some people I—cared about."

"You mean he had them killed."

"They're dead and he's responsible." She leaned toward him, seizing the chance to push home her point. "I know a great deal about Rialto. I can help you get to him."

"Thanks, but I don't need any help."

"I can make your job easier. Take me along as your personal assistant when you get the security chief's job."

Rafe stopped chewing. For a long second he simply stared at her, then he swallowed slowly, took a sip of his dark, strong coffee and shook his head. "No."

The finality of his tone shocked her. She blinked and set her jaw. "This isn't negotiable."

"Nope. It's not."

"I *am* going with you."

"I told you, the only sort of partners that I have—"

She aimed her fork at him. "If you don't take me along, I can and will blow your cover completely. You'll never get near Rialto again, but *I'll* find another way inside."

Anger darkened his eyes, though his expression remained calm. "I've never cared for threats."

"You aren't leaving me any choice. You've written me off without even knowing what I can do."

He leaned toward her suggestively, but there was only hard appraisal in his expression. "What is it, exactly, that you can do?"

Kendra refused to be intimidated. "I can help you get hired—or I can make it impossible. I know computer systems better than anyone you're apt to meet. Once we're inside, I can pull information from his computer files that you'd never get any other way. Information that can help you get not only him, but Calderone as well. I promise you, I know what I'm doing."

Rafe sat back, picked up a piece of bacon and bit down, chewing and swallowing before he spoke. "And if I don't take you along, you'll blow my cover, is that it?"

"Yes."

"What would you gain from that?"

He was so smug.

"Satisfaction?"

Rafe continued to stare at her. She shifted, uncomfortably under that hard appraisal.

"Your ego could use a pin or two," she added.

Rafe leaned so close to her that she could see the angry flecks of color in his dark eyes.

"You don't even know me."

He was trying to intimidate her. Well it wasn't going to work.

"That makes us even, so stop trying to write me off before you hear me out. All I want is a chance."

Without warning, his hands framed her face. Her breath caught somewhere in the back of her throat while her heart began to pound wildly. His eyes went from glittery to dark and smoky. His voice deepened erotically.

"What sort of chance, Kendra? This?"

From somewhere she dredged the will to pull free before those tempting lips could settle over hers. "No!"

The corners of his lips tilted in amusement.

"No?"

She would not let him bait her. She would *not!*

"I see 'no' isn't a common word in your vocabulary. Don't worry, you'll get used to hearing it."

Was that a flash of respect she'd glimpsed in his eyes? Her glance fell on Rosa who stood across the room, watching them with a troubled frown.

"Blackmail is an ugly business," Rafe said levelly.

"Yes, isn't it? But I mean what I say. I want to be there when Rialto is taken down. And I *can* help."

Rafe sat back thoughtfully. "You must have cared about this person he killed very much."

Kendra forced down the nightmare.

Rafe stood abruptly. He gathered his dishes and strode to the sink. In a quiet, kindly tone he spoke to Rosa before lifting the handset on the telephone.

"This isn't my decision to make, Kendra. Excuse me while I make a phone call."

Kendra wondered if he was angry or just annoyed. He pushed a series of buttons and stepped into the hall. His voice drifted to where she sat.

"Hey, beautiful, how are you this morning? No, nothing like that, but I'm afraid I'm going to have to cancel our date this afternoon."

The back door swung open with a crash that sent Kendra whirling. A little girl rushed inside, giggling in glee. An older man dressed in dusty work clothes, and a woman with golden brown hair and dark brown eyes followed on her heels.

"Rosa! Rosa!"

The child stopped calling and came to an immediate halt at the sight of Kendra sitting at the table all alone.

Rosa bustled forward saying something in rapid Spanish. The little girl responded, never once taking her pretty brown eyes from Kendra. The gnarled ranch hand and his companion came to a stop as well, but they didn't seem surprised to see her sitting there.

"Ma'am."

Kendra offered an uncertain smile.

"Who are you?" the child asked abruptly.

"I'm Kendra. Who are you?"

"I'm Elena. My daddy works here. That's my mommy."

Abby and Jake Cantrell's little girl, Kendra realized.

"I'm Abby Cantrell," The woman greeted her, while her dark brown eyes assessed Kendra candidly. "This patient man is Slim Dillon."

"Hi."

"I'm going riding," the child announced. "Do you want to come and watch?"

"Uh," she looked helplessly at the child's mother, but it

was the man called Slim, towering beside her, who answered.

"Can if you want. We got a training ring set up outside. She tends to show off for visitors, but that's okay."

"Well—"

Abby smiled. "You'd be welcome to join us. It looks like you've been abandoned."

"Rafe's on the telephone."

"Lydia, no doubt," she said.

The tall man harrumphed and turned to Rosa who got caught patting her hair in a purely feminine action. Kendra wanted to smile when she saw the way Slim's features and his voice softened as he addressed her.

Abby shared a knowing smile with her and Kendra wondered if Mitchell Forbes knew he had a budding romance going on right here in his kitchen. Obviously Abby knew and approved.

Rosa beamed at the foreman and the two shared a low-voiced spate of dialogue.

"Do join us, Kendra," Abby urged. "It will give us a chance to become acquainted while you're waiting to talk with Mitchell."

"Does everyone know why I'm here?"

"No secrets on the Smokin' Barrel, girl," Slim announced turning back to them. "You ready to ride, little one?"

"Yep! Come on, Kendra! Slim says I can take Sugar Cube out for a walk today."

"Uh, maybe I'd better not leave until I see Ms. Archer."

"Penny will find you when she's ready," Abby assured her.

Casting a look through the empty doorway where Rafe had disappeared, Kendra reluctantly stood. "Well then, thank you for inviting me." Maybe the grilling could work both ways. She'd like to hear Abby's opinion of the disturbingly impossible Rafael Alvarez—and the unknown woman he was breaking a date with.

"So WHAT'S your take on the Kincade woman, Rafe?" Mitchell demanded, looking around the conference table at the assembled members of Texas Confidential.

"She's got spunk. And I suspect she could give stubborn lessons to a mule. We need some factual information on her."

"Do you think she'd go through with her threat?" Jake asked skimming a hand over his short, dark hair.

"Maybe. I'm more concerned that she might do something foolish if she's left on her own. I don't think she's faking her hated for Stephen Rialto, though I'd be a lot more comfortable if I knew why."

"Maybe he had her boyfriend or a lover killed," Cody suggested.

Mitchell frowned. "She wouldn't explain?"

"I seem to make her nervous," Rafe admitted with a shrug.

There was a discreet shuffling of feet and a couple of not-so-hidden smirks.

"Imagine that," Penny murmured.

"Charm's starting to fail you in your old age?" Brady asked with a grin.

Rafe faced his fellow agents with a self-deprecating smile. "I prefer to think that my charms simply overwhelm the poor woman."

"Yeah, right."

"Oh, brother."

Mitchell put a stop to the teasing. "We have to decide how to handle her. If she knows as much as she implies about our operation she could be a problem."

"On the other hand, if she's as good with a computer as she claims, she could be an asset," Brady put in.

"Or she could be someone whose job it is to infiltrate us," Penny pointed out.

Jake frowned. "She's with my wife and daughter." And there was still a touch of almost awed pride in those words. "Abby may be able to learn something from her."

Mitchell turned the silver lighter over and over in his fingers. He turned to Penny. "Find out if we can get any information out of Washington, D.C. yet," he ordered. "In the meantime, we'll string her along. We'll keep her here until we have more information. It's possible we can use her."

"There's a problem with that," Rafe said. "Even if she's as good with a computer as she claims, there's no way I can bring her along as my assistant. You know the sort of people Rialto surrounds himself with. Young, attractive—"

"Oh, listen to that ego," Cody teased.

"No," Mitchell said thoughtfully, tapping a thumbnail against the lighter. "In this case, Rafe's right. In the past five years Rialto has only hired female staff with a certain 'look.' Ms. Kincade doesn't fit."

"Exactly," Rafe agreed.

Mitchell set the lighter on the table. "So fix it."

"What?"

The other agents began to snicker.

"Do what's necessary to make her fit in. Clothes, hair, whatever."

"Me? Why me? Penny—"

"Hey, I have enough to do around here. Glamorous women are your department, Rafe," she said archly.

"You know they are merely substitutes while I wait for you, darlin'."

"Well while you're waiting," Mitchell growled around the end of his unlit cigar, "take care of Kendra Kincade."

"Now wait a minute, how am I supposed to do that?"

The others began gathering their stuff in preparation for the end of the meeting.

"This isn't funny, guys." They ignored him with wide smirks. He rounded on Penny. "I'm at least going to need a feminine point of view here."

"Not mine," she said firmly. "Why not ask the widow, Lydia?"

"Yeah," Cody agreed. "Now there's a lady who knows how to fill out a dress."

Penny snorted. "Bear in mind that Lydia's favorite shade of yellow definitely won't suit Kendra's coloring," she pointed out coolly. "Also, Kendra doesn't have Lydia's abundantly obvious charms."

Jake nudged Brady and muttered, "This could get interesting."

Mitchell surveyed them in silence. Rafe knew when he was licked. With an exaggerated sigh, he acquiesced. "All right. I'll see what I can do. When should I start?"

"Right after I meet with Ms. Kincade," Mitchell said. "Forgo your outside duties so you can stay near the phone lines. Our information says Rialto's appointment secretary is supposed to call the candidates today or tomorrow to set up interviews. Penny will continue to pose as your assistant, but they might ask to speak to you. I want you around if that happens."

"Does this mean I get to hang out down here and chase Penny around the conference table?"

Penny fluttered her eyelashes at him. "Be still my foolish heart."

"What about the roundup?" Cody interrupted.

"Slim's hired plenty of extra help," Mitchell promised.

"In that case," Cody said, "maybe I'll give you a hand after all, Rafe."

"You will report to Slim and find out if he needs someone to ride herd on any of the new men," Mitchell said sternly.

Cody's lips tightened at the rebuke, but he remained silent as the meeting broke up.

An hour later, Rafe was invited to join Kendra, Mitchell and Penny in the library upstairs.

"Kendra has tentatively convinced me that she may be an asset as your assistant, Rafe." Mitchell informed him as if it were the first time they'd spoken on this issue. "She has some rather impressive computer knowledge. That being the case, you need to prepare her for the assignment."

"Prepare me?" Kendra queried.

Rafe noted the way Kendra bit down on her lip. She wasn't pretty, he told himself, yet there was something naively appealing about her.

"Yes sir."

"Rafe will drive you over to Chet's to gather your belongings. I'll see you at dinner this evening."

It was clear dismissal. Kendra rose from her seat. "You won't be sorry."

Mitchell's smile didn't reach his watchful eyes. Rafe was relieved to see the older man had as many reservations as he did about this woman.

There was no chance to ask Mitchell if he'd discovered anything about Kendra during their talk. Rafe led her outside to the ranch's battered pickup truck. The drive to Chet's was almost silent. None of Rafe's conversational topics drew her out. Kendra watched the scenery and answered in monosyllables.

"You know, if you're having second thoughts, it isn't too late to change your mind," he finally told her.

Kendra twisted on the seat to stare at him. "I'm not."

"You're awfully quiet for someone who just got what she claims to want."

"What do you want me to say?"

"For starters, I'd like to know more about these people

he had killed that you cared about. Were they friends, lovers, relatives, what?''

''What difference does it make? Rialto is slime and I want him to pay for his crimes.''

Color climbed her neck. She turned mutely back to the window. The sun sent prisms of color bouncing around the cab of his truck from the crystal earrings she wore. What was she hiding? He turned the truck into the drive leading to their neighbor's dude ranch, determined to learn what was behind her animosity.

Penny had called ahead, so Chet's staff knew they were coming. Apparently, so did Chet's sister. Lydia flew out of the house, a welcome smile on her lips.

''Rafe! First you cancel our date and then Chet tells me you're stealing one of our customers away!'' As soon as he stepped from the truck she slid her arm through his, beaming up at him, her generous breasts pushing against his arm.

''Mitchell is a friend of Kendra's parents. When he ran into her this morning he invited her to spend a few days with us.'' The prepared lie rolled off Rafe's tongue with practiced ease.

''It was really too naughty of you taking Settled Sue like that. Chet was most unhappy.''

''I'll apologize when I see him,'' Kendra said. She held Lydia's gaze for several seconds before turning and disappearing inside the house.

Rafe had seen disapproval in those expressive eyes of hers, but he wasn't sure if the look was for what Lydia had said, his lie about her visit with Mitchell, or the way Lydia clung so sweetly to him.

''Are we still on for tomorrow night?'' Lydia asked.

''Uh…''

''Please don't tell me you're going to cancel tomorrow as well.''

Looking into her anxious eyes, he didn't have the heart

to sever another date. He liked Lydia, and he knew this week was especially hard for her. She was coming up on the anniversary of her husband's death.

"I plan to pick you up—"

"No, *I'll* pick *you* up. I want you to ride in my new convertible. I take delivery tomorrow afternoon. Is five o'clock too early?"

"That will be fine." He disengaged himself gently. "But right now I'd better go in and give Kendra a hand with her luggage."

"That won't be necessary," Kendra said, striding onto the front porch, a computer bag over one shoulder, pulling a wheeled a suitcase behind her. "I'm not a heavy packer."

"And it appears you never got around to unpacking."

Kendra didn't respond. She seemed surprised when he took the heavy case from her and lifted it easily into the back of the pickup truck.

"Then I'll see you tomorrow, Rafe?" Lydia asked anxiously.

Rafe nodded and Lydia visibly relaxed.

"Goodbye, Kendra. I hope you and Mitchell have a nice visit."

"Thank you. And please thank your brother for me."

Lydia's smile widened until her dimples showed. "Oh, I will. Bye, Rafe."

"I know it's none of my business," Kendra said as he turned the truck onto the main road, "but are you and Lydia…"

"Good friends."

Kendra stared out the window. "Does she know that?"

Rafe relaxed. "Now darlin', you wouldn't be jealous, would you?"

Red scorched her cheeks. "Of course not. I was wondering because of the way she hung on you."

"She normally isn't like that. Her husband was killed during a holdup near their home a year ago this week."

"Oh."

"Lydia moved back here to lend her brother a hand."

Kendra relaxed. "Chet seems nice."

"So is Lydia." Rafe liked the hard-working Chet. Once Lydia made it clear she wasn't looking for anything permanent, Rafe had allowed himself to be attracted to the tall, curvy, vivacious woman.

"May I ask you a question?"

"Ask away."

"Is there really a problem with rustlers in this day and age?"

The question surprised him, but he gave her a serious answer. "Yep. We've lost several head in the last few months. Why?"

"I was thinking back to last night. When I was out riding, I noticed a closed truck driving along this road."

Rafe nearly ran off the road, swiveling his head to look at her. "You didn't mention this before."

"I wasn't thinking about it earlier."

"Did you get a look at the truck? A license plate? See the driver?"

"No, nothing like that. I noticed the truck because it seemed like an odd time to be out and about. I thought maybe it was a vegetable farmer on his way to town with produce or something."

Rafe shook his head, drumming his fingers against the steering wheel. "Not on this road. What color was the truck? And what direction was it traveling"

"White I think. It was going east. I wasn't paying a lot of attention. You think it belonged to the rustlers?"

"I'd say it's a pretty good chance."

"Don't they use horses?"

"Sure, but they need a truck to carry the animals away

once they herd them. If you think of *anything* about that truck that might help us identify it, let one of us know. We'd really like to catch these guys.''

''I'm sorry. If I'd known it was important I'd have paid more attention.''

They lapsed into silence until they reached the Smoking Barrel.

''Are you up to a challenge?'' Rafe asked as he hauled her suitcase from the back of the truck. She clung to the computer case, he noticed.

''What sort of a challenge?''

He set the suitcase in the hall near the stairs. ''For starters, I need to see how well you can handle yourself in difficult situations.''

''I thought I was doing that rather well.''

Rafe tipped his head in rueful acknowledgement. ''We have about an hour before dinner. Are you game to show me what you can do?''

''That depends on the game.''

''Let me take your cases upstairs and I'll meet you in the basement.''

''The basement.''

Deliberately, Rafe stepped into her personal space and lowered his voice. ''It's where I take all my women.''

For an instant, her eyes opened wide behind the lenses of her ugly glasses. Then they narrowed while her lips pursed in annoyance. She shoved surprisingly hard at his chest. ''Must make it hard to get a second date.''

Rafe stepped back with a bark of laughter. ''You might be on to something there. However, in this case, the basement is the only appropriate place for what I have in mind.''

''Sorting laundry?''

''I'll show you.''

Kendra watched him carry her cases upstairs. He was up to something and she had to go along. Mitchell Forbes had made that entirely clear this morning. Anything—even putting up with Rafe's teasing—was worth obtaining her goal.

She followed him to the rear of the finished basement, surprised to find a small gym set up.

"You want me to work out?" She demanded, coming to an abrupt halt. "Sorry, I work on computers, I don't lift them."

Rafe chuckled again. The sound rippled right down her spine, inviting the listener to share his amusement.

"We'll get to that part later. Take off your boots and step on the mats." He was already removing his own boots.

"Planning to get kinky?" Her heart began pumping a little faster.

"Maybe later," he said suggestively. Then he surged to his feet. He was a large, vital man. The basement abruptly felt isolated, locking the two of them away from the rest of the world. Rosa was just up the steps in the kitchen, but that seemed a long way off all of a sudden.

Kendra tugged off her own boots, wincing at the blister forming on the back of her left heel. She should have worn the boots more often to break them in.

"Still have your knife?"

She nodded tightly.

"I want you to come at me with it."

"What?"

All traces of the humorous teasing had disappeared. "We're going into a hostile environment, Kendra. I want to see just how well prepared you are to take care of yourself."

"You don't need to worry about me."

"Prove it."

Her heart pounded faster. "I might hurt you."

"I'll take that chance."

It was the dismissive way he said the words. She set her jaw, stepped on the mat and started toward him reaching for her knife. His arm snaked out without warning. It happened so fast, the action was a blur. Rafe held her wrist in his grip, applying just enough pressure to make her fingers go numb.

"Lesson number one," he said as he took the knife away as easily as if she were a child. "Never get close enough to let your assailant take your weapon away."

"You weren't able to take it away from me before."

"No, I didn't *choose* to take it away from you before."

Angrily, she brought up her knee. Rafe deflected the action before he threw her lightly to the padded mat on the floor. He followed her down, pinning her there.

A wave of sensations swamped her while a spicy light masculine scent filled her head. Accompanying the annoying surge of awareness was humiliation at how easily he had defeated her.

His eyes were darkly kind, but it was his mouth, much too close to hers, that held her complete attention. Every hormone in her body leaped to unexpected life. What would it be like to be kissed by Rafe?

"Never had any judo or martial arts training?"

His breath whispered across her cheek, reminding her of the last time he'd pinned her like this. Then his hand had cupped her breast. Now her nipples rose in memory and she knew that he was as aware of that fact as she was.

"No formal training," she agreed totally flustered as she tried to shove him off without success.

Rafe smiled, a wickedly slow, superior sort of smile. Instantly, her temper flashed.

"But I'm a real fast learner."

And she kicked him in the shin right before she socked him in the jaw.

Chapter Three

"Kendra Kincade is exactly who she says she is," Penny informed the meeting of the Confidentials the next morning. "Twenty-nine years old, originally from El Paso, Texas, parents, Tina and Martin Kincade."

"El Paso was Rialto's old haunting grounds," Rafe muttered.

"Yes. Kendra is a computer programmer who works as an independent contractor for anyone who will pay her pricey fees and let her work from home. She must be good at what she does because she has a huge client list despite being something of a recluse."

"Like that character in the movie where they erased her life?" Cody asked.

Penny shook her head. "Not quite that bad. Her neighbors do know her. She's friendly, but she keeps to herself. She's been known to travel to meetings when absolutely necessary, but most of her business is conducted through e-mail and the telephone. Her parents moved to Arizona after she graduated college, but they gave Kendra the house where she grew up. She seems close to them even though she only visits at Christmas."

"She seldom leaves her house yet she came here," Rafe said thoughtfully.

Penny nodded. "This trip is a total departure for her. She

turned down three lucrative contracts last week, telling employers that she was going on vacation. The one I spoke with said it had never happened before. According to him, she's as good as she claims with a computer—fast and thorough.''

"What about her assertion that Rialto had somebody close to her killed?" Rafe asked worrying about the one area that truly concerned him.

"I'm working on that."

"Any other family?" Jake wanted to know.

"Not that I know of, but *I* am *not* a computer whiz. This kind of investigation takes time."

"Something we have little of," Mitchell reminded them.

"Well, as far as official records go, she's never even had a parking ticket."

"That's a little too squeaky clean for me," Brady muttered.

"Not if she seldom leaves the house," Penny pointed out.

"Keep checking," Mitchell advised, chomping on his unlit cigar.

"Try going back to her college roommates," Rafe suggested. "Maybe a roommate or a boyfriend had some connection to Rialto."

Humor sparked to life in Brady's gray eyes. "Speaking of which, how's the makeover coming?"

The others around the table shared grins. Rafe rubbed his sore jaw and shook his head. "She's a stubborn little thing, but I'll give her an *A* for determination."

"Need a referee?" Cody offered.

"You're a pal, but there's only going to be one outcome to this bout." He felt the weight of her knife in his pocket. "I showed her a few moves yesterday."

Someone snickered.

"Defensive moves," he corrected. "I'm going to take her out back today and see how she does on the firing range."

"Better clear the ranch first," Brady suggested. "No sense putting innocents in her line of fire."

"I think the only one in jeopardy here is Rafe," Cody said with a wicked grin. "And we all know innocent isn't a word we'd use to define him."

"Very funny."

"Putting an ambulance on stand by only seems prudent," Jake offered. "Rafe here seems to be the one doing the learning—the hard way."

Rafe grinned good-naturedly. "Cute. I don't think she'll shoot me until she gets what she wants."

"Excuse me, but I thought the makeover was about looks," Penny said.

"One step at a time," Rafe protested. "I'm doing the easy stuff first."

Two of the men chuckled.

"Chicken?" Cody asked.

"Absolutely. You ever tried telling a woman how to dress?"

"I place a much higher value on my life."

"Exactly."

"All right folks, we've got a lot to do, so let's get to work," Mitchell ordered.

"And speaking of work," Penny added, opening her notebook, "Mrs. Skerritt called here again. Something about two other dates you are supposed to keep in mind?"

Rafe groaned. Lydia could turn into a problem. Neither she nor her brother knew anything about Texas Confidential, and Rafe knew Mitchell wanted to keep it that way.

"I gave her the number for the bunkhouse, so do check your messages, Rafe."

Jake stretched. "The joys of bachelorhood. Personally, I'm glad all I have to deal with nowadays are ornery cows, bad weather, construction crews, a wife and daughter."

Brady shared a smile with him. "Their day will come."

"Not a chance," Rafe and Cody both vowed.

"NO!" RAFE MOVED alongside Kendra, trying to ignore the tug of awareness he continued to feel every time he touched her. He positioned his hand along her arm to straighten her stance and her wide eyes blinked up at him from behind her big ugly glasses covered by safety goggles.

Rafe shook off the distracting thought that she had very pretty eyes under all that glass. For one beat of his heart, he thought he glimpsed a recognizable spark of feminine interest before Kendra lowered her lashes and he stepped back from her.

"Remember to squeeze the trigger," he told her. "The object isn't how fast you can pull it, but how accurately you can put a bullet in someone."

"I'm not planning to put a bullet in anyone. You want to do this?" Kendra demanded, stepping away from him and tugging off the safety glasses.

"I already know how to do this," Rafe told her. To prove it, he took the gun from her hand and finished the round, firing carefully into the target. He knew he was showing off a bit, but her disdain bothered him.

Rafe wished he could stand further away from the utterly distracting scent and feel of Kendra Kincade. No matter that he kept his frequent touches impersonal, he continued to find himself aware of her as a woman.

Kendra wasn't particularly attractive and she definitely wasn't his type. She had the sassiest mouth he'd ever seen on a woman. Still, there was something appealing about her. Something that got under a man's skin.

He'd thought the gun range would be less distracting than teaching her basic self-defense tricks that might require a lot of touching, but he'd been wrong. She had an uncanny way of reducing the great outdoors to closer quarters than the basement. If only he could stop noticing how good she smelled. The light, subtle scent wasn't a perfume, yet it continually snuck up on him, reminding him that she was a woman.

Rafe set the weapon on the shelf.

Kendra raised her eyebrows. "You didn't hit the head even once," she pointed out.

Stung, he glanced at the target. "I wasn't aiming for the head." Every one of his shots was within inches of where he'd wanted them. "And neither should you. The chest is a bigger target. Remember, if you shoot at someone, you're trying to stop them from coming at you. You're not a marksman aiming for the kill."

Something flickered in her eyes. She quickly looked away. Before he could wonder about that look, the far-off rumble of thunder sent both their gazes skywards. Despite the sun directly over their heads, the sky was darkening quickly in the distance as rain swept in over the mountains.

"Maybe Abby and Jake should be building an ark instead of adding on to their cabin," she said.

"Good point. I think I'll suggest it. Let's break and clean up for lunch. We can work out inside after we eat."

Kendra groaned.

"Are you stiff?" She'd landed pretty hard a couple of times yesterday, but she never complained. As promised, she was a quick study. She already had a good grasp on quick releases and easy throws.

"Not at all. I'm sure my bones creaked like this before I got here."

"That's the spirit."

"Uh-huh." She watched him gather up the equipment. "What's the real reason behind all this training, Rafe? You don't really expect me to use any of this, do you?"

Before he could respond, his beeper went off. Rafe checked it and thrust the pile of equipment into her startled hands. "I've got a phone call. Can you bring this stuff?"

He was gone without waiting for an answer. Kendra watched him sprint for the house and tried to banish the thought that the man really did know how to fill out a pair of jeans. Her hormones had picked a rotten time to remind her that she was a woman and Rafe was an incredibly handsome man. He would never look twice at someone like her. And she didn't want him to.

Did she?

Penny met her at the back door and took the equipment off her hands. "He's on the phone with Rialto," she announced.

Excitement surged through Kendra. Finally, after all this time, her plan was going to happen.

"I have a meeting with Rialto tomorrow morning," Rafe announced, when he rejoined them in the kitchen. The long table was set with three places and Rosa bustled about the stove, humming to herself.

"I'm surprised he waited so long to do the interviews," Kendra said nervously.

"He probably needed time to run checks on all the candidates," Penny said. "Don't worry, Rafe's background will hold up."

"Are the interviews at Rialto's office?" Kendra asked.

Rafe nodded.

Rosa set plates of food in front of each of them, but Kendra barely glanced down. Rosa would scold her again in broken English, but excitement had stolen any appetite Kendra might have had. Everything was finally coming together after all this time.

"You should know about the painting," Kendra told Rafe.

He paused in the act of lifting his fork. "What painting?"

"Rialto has a large abstract on the wall behind his desk. It's supposed to be a Sylvian original."

His brow pleated as Rafe looked the question at her while he chewed and swallowed.

"Rialto was briefly interested in the art scene a year or so ago. Either he wanted some legal investments or he was looking for a criminal angle," Kendra explained.

"How come we never heard about this?" Rafe asked Penny.

"Because I'm not a computer guru?" she suggested mock sweetly.

"It wasn't common knowledge," Kendra assured them. "Rialto got conned by a dealer who sold him a couple of genuine pieces before this fake Sylvian. I'm sure you won't be surprised to learn that the dealer vanished after duping Rialto. There was a lot of blood left behind, but no body or a weapon."

Penny pursed her lips thoughtfully. "Rialto kept the painting?"

"I think it's to remind him not to get taken again. Plus, I'm pretty sure he installed a miniature camera in the picture or its frame to keep an eye on his desk."

Rafe stared at her. "How do you know all this?"

"I told you, I've made a study of him. The Dallas newspaper recently ran an article on him in the business section. He was pictured at his desk with the painting directly behind him." She squirmed a little under Rafe's scrutiny. "He also paid for the painting, and subsequently the camera, through his checking account. I could be wrong about the camera of course, but given what I know about him—"

"How do you know about his checking account?" Penny interrupted.

"I've, uh, seen his bank statements."

Rafe abruptly pushed aside his own plate. "You accessed his personal account at the bank? I thought that was impossible for an outside hacker to do."

"It is, but I did some consulting work for his bank a few

months ago.'' She shrugged uncomfortably. ''Look, the point is, if you notice the painting and tell him what an excellent reproduction it is, you're bound to impress him.''

Rafe shook his head. ''If I do that, he'll figure I know something about art, which I don't.''

''No. You point out that you know someone else who bought a fraud exactly like it from Jasper Coons. He's the crooked art dealer Rialto used. Rialto is vain. If you say it right, like you know he knows the painting is a forgery, you'll impress him. He likes people who pay attention to details. Especially the prospective new chief of Rialto Industries.''

''She may have a point,'' Penny agreed.

Rafe nodded, eyeing her thoughtfully. ''Do you have other tidbits like this for me?''

''Maybe. I've told you I made a study of him.''

''So you did. If you're finished ignoring your food, let's get back to work.''

''But shouldn't we be making plans?''

''The plans are already made, Kendra. Now we wait for him to hire me so we can put this operation in motion.''

Penny waved them off. ''I'll distract Rosa while you two make your escape.''

''You are a lifesaver.''

''So true.'' She batted her eyes at him. ''Let me know when you want mouth-to-mouth resuscitation.''

''Ah, Penny my love, I'm not sure my old ticker could tolerate that much excitement, but any time you want to practice…''

''Get out of here while Rosa's back is turned.''

Rafe squeezed Penny's hand and winked at Kendra. He was teasing, but Kendra wasn't so sure about Penny. The other woman had a wistful gleam in her eyes. Kendra and Rafe scooted down the basement steps where Rafe proceeded to work her harder than ever while asking questions about Rialto the entire time.

"No! Not like that like—"

"Touch me again and I'm going to have to break that hand," she warned him as he reached for her once more.

Rafe stood still. They were both sweating and she was pretty sure she was going to have a bruise from that last fall.

"I have had enough," she announced firmly.

"Is that what you're going to tell one of Rialto's goons when they corner you?" He narrowed the distance between them until her chest was practically touching his.

"No," she answered sweetly, "I'll shoot him. In the chest," she added for good measure.

The smile started in his eyes and finally lifted the corners of his lips. Her gaze fastened on those lips, so temptingly near. She tried to tell her hormones they were pinging after the wrong man but her hormones weren't listening. Neither was her common sense.

"You'll need a weapon," he said softly, taking another step closer.

Her heart stepped up the pace as his hands touched her shoulders. Lightly. Almost tenderly.

"Yes." The word was a faint hiss of sound. In that moment as his head lowered toward hers, she knew he felt the sensual pull between them as well. Her lips parted in silent invitation. He was going to kiss her.

At last!

"Excuse me, am I interrupting?"

Kendra would have pulled away, but Rafe's fingers tightened on her shoulders, holding her in place. He lifted his head and looked past her at the voice that had come from behind her.

"Actually, yes," Rafe said calmly. He released his hold slowly to allow her to turn.

Lydia Skerritt stood a few feet away, dressed in heels and

a canary yellow dress that would jump-start any man's libido. Her long blond hair was in casual disarray that had probably taken her an hour to arrange. She looked sexy, sultry, and ironically amused.

"We were working out," Rafe said.

"So I see. Did you forget our date? Dinner and a movie?"

Rafe ran a hand over his jaw, his expression chagrined.

"You did forget," she said.

"Guilty. Do I have time to shower and change?"

"You do. I knew this might be a problem so I came a little early."

"Okay, give me five," he rubbed his jaw, "make it ten minutes." He turned to Kendra. "You did very well. I'm sorry to cut this short. Will you excuse me?"

That look had probably melted harder hearts than hers. "No problem. I'm exhausted. One more throw and I would have cried uncle."

"You did," he reminded her.

"Ah, but that was just a trick. I was about to send you flying." She turned to Lydia before he could comment. "Thanks for the rescue. I could use a shower, too."

Rafe watched her walk away, her head held high, the slight sway of her stride momentarily confusing him. What was going on here? He wasn't seriously attracted to Kendra. He didn't even trust her most of the time. Yet he found Lydia watching him watch Kendra with arched eyebrows.

"Working out, huh?" she asked playfully. "Just what were you two working at?"

If there'd been any trace of jealousy in her tone, he would have taken offense, but Lydia simply sounded amused.

"Mitchell asked me to show her some self-defense moves. She lives alone. I'm sorry, Lydia, I really did forget our plans. Ten minutes, promise."

"Uh-huh."

But she was still smiling as she linked her arm with his

and started for the steps. Her perfume permeated the room. He'd always liked the scent of jasmine, but tonight it smelled cloying to his senses.

He left Lydia in the kitchen talking with Rosa while he walked over to the bunkhouse, stripped and showered in record time. A night with Lydia was exactly what he needed to unwind. She was witty, charming, beautiful and willing—and like him, she wanted no permanent ties. Who could ask for anything more?

So why did he keep picturing wide hazel-brown eyes and softly parted lips, waiting to be tasted?

The date wasn't a disaster, but it wasn't the escape he'd hoped for. Rafe found it hard to concentrate and more than once had to apologize for not hearing something Lydia said. He was grateful for the darkened movie theater where nothing more was expected from him than sitting there with his arm around her. He was heartily sick of the scent of jasmine by the time the evening was over.

He knew when Lydia invited him back to Chet's for the night he was going to say no. Her talented mouth wasn't stirring him tonight. He had too many other things on his mind. The ringing of her car phone changed everything.

"There's been an accident. A couple of the guests are hurt," she told him, hanging up. "I have to get back to the ranch."

"Do you want me to come with you?"

"If you don't mind. Chet thinks he might have to take one of them to the doctor's and the helicopter is temporarily grounded."

Rafe offered to go to the doctor's office with Chet so it was the wee hours of the morning before Lydia finally drove him back to the Smoking Barrel.

"I'm sorry about the way the evening turned out," Lydia apologized.

"Hey, you have nothing to apologize for. I should apologize for being so distracted."

"You can make it up to me another time."

"Deal."

Her lips clung to his, inviting him to passion. Rafe was unmoved. They broke apart and he watched her drive out of sight before turning toward the bunkhouse. The door to the main house suddenly shut firmly as someone left the darkness of the porch.

Rafe spun around. It could have been Penny, or Mitchell or even Maddie Wells, their other close neighbor and the only woman in Mitchell's life. She often stayed over, but Rafe didn't think it had been any of them. One of them would have called out a greeting to him. Rafe headed across the compound to the front door. Locked.

He hesitated only a moment before pulling out the cell phone. Mitchell answered on the second ring. Someone else picked up as well.

"Someone just entered the front door," Rafe began without preamble. "Door's locked, but you might want to check the alarms and Kendra."

Mitchell grunted. Penny's voice took over. "Her bedroom door just closed."

Rafe relaxed.

"I'll go and see if she needs something."

"I'll have a look around and reset the alarms," Mitchell grumbled.

Penny came back on the phone. "Kendra apologizes. She says she went out for a breath of air."

"At three in the morning?" Mitchell demanded.

"That's what she says. She didn't realize her actions would alarm everyone."

Mitchell muttered something and clicked off.

"Sorry for the alarm," Rafe apologized.

"No problem. I wouldn't know what to do with a full

night's sleep anyhow,'' Penny said with a yawn. ''Good night, Rafe.''

Rafe frowned. Before he headed across the way to the bunkhouse, he made an entire circuit of the house. Everything was calm and quiet. Had Kendra really only come outside for a breath of air at this hour? Or had she met someone?

He resisted the urge to demand answers right now. Morning would do. But her wide hazel eyes followed him down into sleep that night, innocently mocking.

THE SECRETARY with the pouty lips and a body designed for a man's distraction ushered Rafe into the spacious office belonging to Stephen Rialto. With a throaty invitation to make himself comfortable, she left him there promising Rialto would join him shortly.

Rafe eyed the expensive modern decor with interest as he settled himself into an uncomfortable white chair across from the wide desk. The papers and clutter on the desk top were out of keeping with the pristine neatness of the large room. Rafe stared at the expansive painting behind the desk. Kendra had been exactly right. A man like Rialto would never leave a stranger in his office unattended. He was being observed.

After a few moments of waiting, Rafe rose unhurriedly and strolled behind the desk. He never glanced at the contents. Without Kendra's warning, he might have been tempted by the stacks of papers. Instead, he studied the large oil painting. He couldn't spot the camera in the miasma of colorful splotches, but he didn't doubt that it was there.

He turned away and strolled to the large window, examining the view before returning to his seat to wait patiently. As if that was the cue, a cleverly disguised door on one wall opened and Stephen Rialto stepped inside.

Rialto wore his dark hair slicked back from his face in a

style that drew attention to his high forehead and watchful eyes. His suit was custom tailored and a large ruby and gold ring glinted on his perfectly manicured hand. Rafe knew the man was fifty-six, but anyone meeting him would understandably put him in his early forties. Rialto was a powerful man with the money to defy the aging process as long as possible.

His smile, like the rest of him, was relaxed and assured. He apologized for the delay, while assessing Rafe, giving nothing of his true thoughts away.

"So what do you think?" Rialto demanded after they were both seated.

"About the company? Rialto Industries is impressive. About the job?" Rafe shrugged gently. "It would present some unique challenges."

"You like challenges?"

"Life would be boring without them." He knew he'd scored a point. "As for your office, I'm sure you know the impression it makes. Quite spectacular." He let his gaze drift toward the painting. "Especially the Sylvian copy."

"You know art, Mr. Alvarez?"

"No, but I know someone who does." Thanks to some fast work by Mitchell and Penny this was now true.

"Most people can't tell that this isn't an original."

"I happen to know the original's owner. He's a former lover of Marissa Sylvian."

For the first time, those cold eyes warmed slightly. "You must introduce us some time. Let us discuss your background, Mr. Alvarez."

Stephen Rialto was nobody's fool. He opened a folder on his desk. His questions were pointed and tricky, but Rafe sat back, relaxed. This was familiar territory. He'd rehearsed this information until he was comfortable with everything in his phony and not-so-phony background. And he came prepared with appropriate questions of his own about the job and the company.

They parted on a first-name basis and Rafe felt pretty certain he had impressed Rialto. He was going to get the job. Now he had to do something about Kendra.

KENDRA GLARED at him. "What do you mean you arranged for a beautician to come out to the ranch and do my hair?"

"I figured it would save time. Phoebe's an old friend. You'll like her."

"I don't want to like her. If she's an old friend, let her cut your hair."

Rafe knew he should have told her about the arrangement with more tact. Funny. He never had this sort of problem with other women.

"Kendra, if you want out of this deal, say the word."

"You'd like that, wouldn't you?"

"Yes."

"Tough."

"Then you'll consent to the makeover."

Kendra's gaze swept him with anger. "Who made you the fashion fairy?"

Silently, Rafe named Mitchell and his fellow Confederates.

"I thought the plan was to punish Rialto, not seduce him," she ranted on.

Once again, Rafe admired the fire in her. She knew everyone was suspicious of her, especially after last night. Five more head of cattle had disappeared. Yet he didn't believe she had anything to do with the rustlers who were working the ranch.

"In all that research you've been doing, did you happen to notice the sort of people Rialto surrounds himself with?" he asked calmly.

"Well-educated and young. Are you implying I'm not well-educated and young?" she demanded.

He would not let her provoke him. "As my assistant you need an upscale wardrobe, hair, nails, the works."

She eyed him in silence for several long seconds. "Just whose image are we worried about here? Mine, or yours?"

"What's that supposed to mean?"

"If you are trying to turn me into a fashion statement like your friend Lydia, it isn't going to work."

"What the devil does Lydia have to do with anything?"

"Nothing. She's a nice person."

"But?"

Kendra raised her chin a defiant notch. "But she's who she is and I'm me."

"Are you saying you won't let Phoebe do your hair and nails?"

"Nails?" She glanced down at her chewed on fingernails and scowled.

"Nails," he said firmly as if she were agreeing with him. "Have you ever seen what a pair of fingernails can do to a man's eyes? They make a great set of weapons right out in plain sight."

"I don't have nails."

"Phoebe said that wouldn't be a problem."

"I am not wearing fake nails."

"If you want to be my assistant, this isn't negotiable. Phoebe's an old friend and she's willing to trek all the way out here to help you."

More than likely, she was willing to trek all the way out here for a glimpse of Rafael Alvarez, Kendra decided, but there was no point saying so. Especially not after last night. When another nightmare had brought her out of sleep she'd headed outside. She'd watched Rafe and Lydia's return like some jealous schoolgirl. The memory still stung. What had she been thinking?

Kendra sighed. She knew exactly what she'd been thinking. And she felt like a fool. The entire house thought she'd been waiting up for Rafe. As if she was a perverted stalker, she hadn't been left alone for a single minute all day. Then she heard about the missing cattle and realized there was a different reason. Did they think she'd gone out there and rustled them herself? Did they think she was hiding them in her bedroom?

"This argument is a waste of time," she said in resignation. Her hair did need a professional cut. She'd been meaning to have it done for months and hadn't gotten around to it. If a makeover meant she got on the inside of Rialto Industries, this Phoebe could cut every hair from her head.

"I couldn't agree more. She'll be here shortly."

And Kendra would take bets Phoebe was another blond bombshell like Lydia.

Lydia arrived minutes later with a picnic basket over her arm and a look of expectancy. Kendra watched Rafe apologize for breaking yet another date. She felt sorry for Lydia who took the news with a stoic lack of surprise.

"I'll make it up to you," Rafe promised.

"You certainly will." But she smiled at Kendra and shook her head, feigning exasperation with the male of the species. "I seriously doubt Phoebe will need your help doing Kendra's hair, Rafe. Do you have time to eat this lunch out on the front porch with me?" she asked.

"Uh—"

Kendra smothered a grin. Rafe had just finished eating a sizeable lunch.

"Sure, why not?"

His gaze locked with hers, daring Kendra to say a word about the meal they had just completed. To his credit, Kendra saw self-deprecating humor in his expression.

"Great!" Lydia enthused, "I hope you're hungry. We

have an entire cherry pie. Your favorite. Kendra, you'd be welcome to join us, too.''

"No thanks, *I've* already eaten. You two have fun. I'll wait here for Phoebe.''

Rafe cast her a glance that promised retribution, but they were both saved by the arrival of his friend Phoebe. Phoebe had red hair, white fingernails and a figure that surely limited her number of female friends in direct proportion to the number of male friends it probably drew. Obviously another of Rafe's conquests, the strikingly beautiful woman was dressed in form-fitting jeans, a jean jacket studded with beads and a blouse open at the collar. The flashy outfit suited her tall, nicely curved figure perfectly.

"What we want is a soft, sexy look, but easy to take care of,'' Rafe instructed after he introduced the women.

Kendra glared. Phoebe preened under Rafe's attention.

"Phoebe is a professional,'' Kendra reminded him. "I think we can handle it from here.''

"He just wants to see my computer program in action,'' Phoebe said with a flirty grin.

"What program?'' Lydia asked entering the library.

"I'll show you. Kitchen or bathroom?'' she asked Rafe.

"Upstairs. Maddie's coming over and she and Rosa are cooking some extra rations for the trail hands this afternoon. I don't think the smell of perm solution goes with beef stew.''

"Good guess.''

"I'll see if they want any help in the kitchen,'' Lydia said and disappeared.

While Rafe and Kendra watched, Phoebe spread out the tools of her trade in the upstairs bathroom Kendra shared with Penny. Once she was done, she returned downstairs and with Penny's permission, borrowed the computer in the library to set up an imaging program. Taking Kendra's picture digitally, she deleted Kendra's hair and began replacing it with different hairstyles.

"I like that one," Rafe said. "That's too short."

Behind Rafe, the audience had grown. Penny, Rosa, Lydia, and a woman Kendra had never seen before stood watching the display intently to Kendra's acute embarrassment.

She tapped Rafe on the arm. "Go away."

He blinked at her, looking puzzled. "What?"

"Go away," she repeated.

"We agreed—"

"That I would have a makeover," she finished for him.

Penny caught her eye and smiled sympathetically. "Kendra's right. She and Phoebe don't need all of us kibitzing. As fascinating as this is, what do you say we give them a chance to work? Hey, hi, Maddie, when did you get here?"

Lydia captured Rafe by the elbow.

"We're embarrassing Kendra. Come on, Rafe. We haven't even gotten to the pie yet."

"But—"

"Rafe," Kendra said firmly, "Shoo."

The room cleared as if by magic. Relieved, Kendra allowed herself to relax. In truth, she too was fascinated by her image with different hairstyles.

Phoebe knew her business. She discussed the amount of time Kendra was willing to spend working with her hair, the maintenance each style would require and other pros and cons as they narrowed the choices. By the time they went upstairs to begin her perm, Kendra found she did indeed like Phoebe Miller.

"From the laughter, I'd say you two are getting along fine," Rafe said from the doorway of the bedroom a good while later. "But I'm surprised you haven't asphyxiated from the smell. What is that stench?"

"Perm solution, nail adhesive, nail polish, take your pick," Phoebe announced.

"Never mind the smell, this is never going to work, Rafe." Kendra held up her hand to display her new nails. "How am I going to type in these things?"

Rafe captured her hand. Kendra knew it was ridiculous, but she felt the contact of his touch all the way up her arm.

"The nails look real."

"They're supposed to. Wait until you see them with the polish," Phoebe said proudly.

"Rafe, I'll never be able to type with claws like these." Kendra tried to pull her hand free, but Rafe continued to hold her, stroking the sensitive skin ever so lightly.

"Sure you will, Kendra," Phoebe said. "It's just a matter of getting used to them."

Kendra stared at her hand where it rested in Rafe's much larger one. Her fingers did look longer and gracefully feminine. She tore her gaze away to find Phoebe watching the two of them curiously.

"Where's Lydia?" Phoebe asked archly.

"She had to get back to Chet's. What's this stuff?" He picked up the plastic bottle on the dresser.

"Nail polish remover."

"Oh." As he set the bottle down his hand bumped the glass of water sitting next to it. The glass toppled, sending water cascading all over Kendra's pants.

Rafe swore as she leaped to her feet. "I'm sorry, Kendra."

He grabbed for the large bath towel on the end of the bed and began blotting at her sodden sweat pants.

Kendra pushed his hand away as he reached between her legs with the towel. "Rafe!"

"Sorry."

"Will you please—"

"I know. Go away."

"Now!" she said in sharp agreement.

"I'm already gone."

"Good. I need to put on another pair of pants."

Rafe closed the bedroom door and started for the stairs.

"Rafe!"

Phoebe's scream held an edge of terror. He raced back and flung open the door.

"Kendra, don't move!" Phoebe cried shrilly. "Rafe!"

Kendra stood before her open closet, statue still.

"Kendra?"

"There's a rattlesnake on the floor of the closet," she said in little more than a whisper.

"Do something!" Phoebe ordered shrilly. "Oh, God, it's slithering out of the box!"

"Kendra, stay still!" Rafe ordered.

"I wasn't planning to tap dance," she whispered.

Rafe reached for Phoebe, grabbed her around the waist, and swung her behind him. "Go downstairs. Tell Penny to bring a gun."

Phoebe fled. Rafe edged around the corner of the bed until he had a clear view of the closet floor. The rattler was full grown and not happy. The tiny forked tongue tasted the air while its tail sounded its annoyance.

"What did you do to spook him?"

"Opened the closet door. Get him out of here, Alvarez. I don't want a roommate."

He wanted to smile at her spunk, despite the quaver of genuine fear in her voice.

"He's no happier with the situation than you are."

"No? Well he's definitely got the advantage. If he wants the room he can have it." The snake swayed, testing the air.

"Rafe," his name was a whisper of fear.

"Señor Rafe."

Rosa and Maddie stood in the open bedroom door. Rosa clutched a broom. Maddie held out a gun. But she was too far away and they were fresh out of time.

Chapter Four

With his left hand, Rafe snatched the towel and tossed it directly at the snake. As the snake struck at it, Rafe yanked Kendra back and away.

Rafe flung them both on the bed. Rolling over, he grabbed for the revolver. He barely heard the sound of the shot over the pounding of his heart. Kendra sat up wide-eyed and shaking beside him.

"Rafe?" Maddie asked hesitantly.

"It's okay," Kendra said. "He shot off its head." Her voice was unnaturally high and tremulous. "Whatever happened to aim for the body?"

Rafe grabbed her, pulled her against his chest in sheer relief and began to laugh.

"Did you get it?" Phoebe asked, joining the throng at the bedroom door.

"Be careful," Maddie warned. "It might not have been alone."

Instantly sober, Rafe released Kendra and stood.

"Señor Rafe?"

Rosa held out the broom.

"Gracias."

While the others watched, he carefully probed the cardboard box and then the closet.

"Looks like he was alone."

"Are you sure?" Kendra demanded, still sounding as shaken as he felt. "Check under the bed."

Rafe checked everything in the room including dresser drawers. The dead snake had been alone.

"Where did it come from?" Maddie wanted to know.

"It slithered out of that box," Phoebe said with a shudder.

"Yours?" Rafe asked Kendra.

"You saw my luggage. What do you think? I'd have mentioned it if you'd just killed my pet rattlesnake."

Rafe nearly smiled. "Maddie, would you mind beeping Mitchell and Penny to let them know we have a problem?"

MITCHELL CALLED a meeting shortly after dinner. The agents sat around the conference table watching him finger his elaborate silver lighter like a worry stone, while puffing away on one of his noisome cigars. His blue eyes were dark with worry as he regarded Rafe.

"No markings on the box?" he asked beneath a thick plume of noxious smoke.

"Just your average cardboard box. They sell them at shipping places all over the country. Someone loosened the lid so the snake could get out." Rafe rubbed the back of his neck wearily.

"Who had access to the room?" Brady asked.

"People were in and out of the house all day."

"Carrying boxes?" Jake asked.

Penny shook her head. "I asked Rosa and Maddie. They didn't see anyone, but there were those minutes when we were all gathered in the library watching Phoebe set up her equipment."

"Phoebe carried stuff into the house," Cody pointed out.

"Why would Phoebe put a snake in Kendra's closet?" Jake asked.

Cody raised his eyebrows. "Jealousy?"

"Over Kendra?" Rafe snorted dismissively.

"Don't forget Lydia. She brought stuff with her, too," Penny pointed out.

Exasperated, Rafe shook his head. "A picnic lunch! Believe me, there was no room for a snake in that basket."

"Just a thought," Penny said mildly.

"You *have* broken several dates with Lydia to spend time with Kendra lately," Jake pointed out.

Rafe shook his head. "Even if Lydia or Phoebe were the jealous type, which they aren't, I've made it clear that Kendra is a family friend of Mitchell's and I'm simply helping her at his request."

"Could your cover be blown already?" Brady asked tapping a pen against the tabletop.

"I don't see how. I don't even have the job yet. Besides, the attack wasn't aimed at me."

"Something in Kendra's past?" Jake asked reasonably.

"I'll prod our FBI friends a little harder, but I haven't turned up anything yet," Penny said. "Kendra's parents are model citizens and she has no boyfriends or close associates of any kind."

"That in itself is troubling," Mitchell said rolling the lighter between his fingers.

"What about an Internet stalker or something?" Cody suggested.

For a moment there was silence, then Rafe shook his head again. "How would he get inside without being noticed?"

Penny chewed on her lower lip. "When we were all gathered in the library? Afterwards, I went into the other room and made a telephone call while Kendra and Phoebe worked in the library. Then I came down here to do some work. Someone could have gone upstairs while I was on the telephone. You saw Lydia leave, Rafe, which would have put you outside about then."

"I didn't notice anyone hanging around."

"Maddie and Rosa went back to the kitchen. They didn't see anyone either."

"None of us saw anyone inside the house," he reminded her.

"But that doesn't mean someone didn't come inside," Penny protested. "We do have a lot of extra hands hired for the roundup."

"Are any of them acting strange or hanging around the house when they should be working?" Rafe demanded of the room in general.

"I'll talk with Slim," Mitchell promised.

"It's just a thought," Brady said hesitantly. "But could Kendra have brought in the snake herself?"

For a moment, there was silence. Rafe looked at each of them in turn and found them all watching him intently. "Why?"

"A bid for sympathy?" Jake suggested. "If you thought she was in danger you'd pay her more attention?"

"If I paid her any more attention we'd be engaged," Rafe muttered, but he turned over the possibility, liking that a whole lot better than some stranger walking inside the house without anyone noticing.

Finally, he shook his head. "No. She was too scared. She was shaking all over. I can't believe she'd risk getting bit."

"After last night and today I want a much closer watch on our houseguest," Mitchell announced. "If someone *is* after her, our entire operation could be compromised."

"To say nothing of her personal safety," Rafe added.

"Maddie and Catherine are with her now," Brady told them. "If anyone can ferret out information, it's my wife."

KENDRA SAT IN the darkness of the front porch with Brady Morgan's wife, Catherine, and Mitchell's friend Maddie Wells. A former newspaper reporter, Catherine was unabashedly curious about the newcomer in their midst, but

Kendra felt sure her probing had more behind it than mere curiosity.

In one way the situation angered her. She'd nearly been the victim of a vicious attack. In fact, she wasn't sure how she was going to sleep in that bedroom tonight. If someone wanted to scare her, they'd done a terrific job.

On the other hand, these people didn't know her or anything about her. She couldn't blame them for trying to ferret out more information about her. She'd been sidestepping questions for what felt like hours now. Everyone had disappeared into the library right after dinner leaving her with Catherine and Maddie. Maddie's role seemed to be that of referee. It had taken Kendra awhile to realize that Mitchell Forbes and his neighbor, Maddie Wells, had a thing for each other. Her computer hadn't given her that little detail.

"The stew was excellent, Maddie," Catherine complimented. "You and Rosa make a good team in the kitchen."

"Oh, we both like to cook, and fortunately, we get on well together."

"Do you like to cook, Kendra?"

"Only if it comes prepackaged and fits in a microwave," she admitted. She didn't add that there wasn't much point to cooking for one.

"Well your hair looks wonderful," Maddie offered. "That style suits you."

"Thank you."

Everyone had complimented her hair except Rafe. He barely noticed the dramatic change. Phoebe had been so shaken by the near disaster that it was amazing she'd been able to finish the job. Once Rafe had taken away the snake and the box, she'd pulled herself together and showed Kendra different ways to work with her new style despite being understandably upset. Kendra was astounded by the difference. She had to admit that Phoebe knew what she was doing when it came to styling.

"Phoebe's a nice person. And she does know how to do hair," Maddie said. "I was so glad when she bought Lois's shop. That woman hadn't paid attention to new styles since 1914. I must say, I never knew Phoebe would make house calls, though."

"She and Rafe go out together, don't they?" Catherine asked.

Maddie glanced at Kendra before answering, "They have, yes."

"You don't have to tiptoe around me," Kendra assured her. "I'm not part of Rafe's fan club. Besides, I get the distinct impression that Rafe has dated most of the women in the county."

Maddie pursed her lips. "He's not a rake you know. Mostly he's all tease. But he does like the fairer sex."

"And I'd say it's pretty reciprocal," Catherine added almost fondly. "He's not as handsome as Brady, of course, but he does have a certain…sizzle. Don't you think so, Kendra?"

"He's got something all right," she muttered direly.

"Rafe's a good man," Maddie admonished. "While he is a ladies' man—and he makes no bones about that—he doesn't take himself seriously."

"Brady claims he's a prankster," Catherine put in.

"Was he the one who sent the condom balloon arrangement to your honeymoon suite with the bottle of Viagra pills?"

Catherine laughed. "That's what Brady swore but Rafe would never admit it."

"Rafe does tend to keep things hopping," Maddie agreed, "but he'll make himself the butt of the joke as quickly as one of the others."

"What about you, Kendra? Anyone special waiting for you back home?" Catherine asked, changing the subject.

"No. I'm pretty busy with my consulting business."

"Mitchell says you're a computer expert." Maddie made the statement sound more like a question.

"I'm a freelance programmer," Kendra corrected.

"Well you can't spend all your time in cyberspace," Catherine said. "What do you like to do in your spare time?"

"Actually, most of my time *is* spent on the computer. I enjoy my work."

"But you must have friends, go out and do things," Catherine persisted.

Kendra gripped the arms of her chair. "Am I being interviewed here?"

For a moment, Catherine appeared chagrined, but immediately she smiled. "Would you like to be? You know I could work up an interesting article about your business for the local paper."

"No!"

Both women stared at her and Kendra realized she'd overreacted. "Thank you," she added more softly, "but I have all the business I can handle right now. Besides, I generally lead a very dull life."

One that had never before involved rattlesnakes in the closet.

Who saw her as a threat? She didn't even know half the people wandering around the ranch. She'd only met Catherine this evening when she'd interrupted the woman kissing one of the most strikingly handsome men Kendra had ever seen. Catherine's husband, Brady Morgan, Kendra realized.

Rafe, dogging her heels, had entered the room and instantly begun teasing the twosome about how newlyweds shouldn't leave the privacy of their bedroom until they'd been married at least a year. Without releasing his wife, Brady told Rafe to stuff it since he was simply jealous. Up to that point, Kendra hadn't met Brady, but he was not only good-looking, he was nice as well.

The camaraderie she'd witnessed so far among the agents was impossible to deny. This was a group of men and women who obviously loved and respected one another. While Brady and Catherine were a couple, their friendship with Rafe and the other men was solid. Kendra had glimpsed the same thing between Jake and Abby and the others. Being couples didn't exclude these deep friendships. What must it be like to have that sort of support? In a way it reminded her of the way her parents had been before…

Kendra turned away from that thought, struck by a poignant longing she couldn't put a name to. She was almost relieved when she smelled the cloying scent of cigar smoke before she saw the approaching figure. The screen door opened and the women turned as Mitchell Forbes limped out onto the porch. His silver-tipped cane glinted in the moonlight. He walked straight to the glider where Maddie sat and settled beside her, his hand resting with comfortable familiarity on her arm. "So this is where everyone went."

"We were taking in the pretty night. Are you finished talking business?"

"For now. What about you ladies? Have you settled the issue of world peace yet?"

"That won't happen until we have a woman president," Catherine retorted smartly.

Brady stepped outside, followed by Rafe. Brady strode over to where Catherine half sat, half leaned against the railing. He slid his arm around her waist and she leaned into him with ready acceptance.

"Don't tell me you have political ambitions," he said.

"No. I just figure it will take a woman to really get the job done." She teased her husband with an affectionate smile.

"And speaking of jobs, how about getting me home? Morning comes awfully early during roundup."

"Ah, the woes of being a cowboy. Good night everyone. It was nice meeting you, Kendra."

"Yes, same here." Kendra was having trouble focusing on the conversation. She was trying to fight her overwhelming awareness of Rafe who slouched negligently against the door frame beside her chair.

The porch seemed to empty in a slow motion hurry, leaving Kendra and Rafe to face the night and each other.

"Guess I'd better head over to the bunkhouse," he said. "Tammy will be here around ten."

"Tammy?"

"She's going to do your makeup."

Kendra jerked to her feet as if on strings. "What?"

"Didn't I tell you?" He came off the wall with lazy grace belied by the glint in his eyes. "She's coming to show you—"

"Stop right there. I do not need anyone showing me how to put goop on my face! Hair and nails are one thing, Alvarez, but I draw the line at looking like a department store mannequin."

His lips curled at the corners. "A department store mannequin?"

"Haven't you ever wondered what size trowel those women at the cosmetic counter use to get all that goop off their face? No thank you. I will not look like that. Call your friend and tell her to stay home."

Rafe sighed. "How many times are we going to have this conversation, Kendra? Tammy sells Jupiter Cosmetics. She's coming out here as a favor to me—"

"Does every female for miles around owe you favors?"

Rafe stepped forward. "Just the single ones."

"That isn't funny."

"Kendra, Tammy is a nice person, trying to make a living to support herself and her daughter. This won't cost you a thing except time."

"That depends on whether she plans to travel with a pet snake as well."

Rafe stiffened. "Why don't you tell me what you think happened here today."

"What I *think* happened?" She put her hands on her hips to keep them from going for his big, thick neck. "You and I both know I'm here on sufferance because I threatened to blow your operation apart if you didn't let me help. What I *know* happened is that *someone* tried to scare me off."

He stepped close enough for her to see the moon reflected in the depths of his eyes.

"Are you implying I had something to do with that snake?"

"Let's just say I don't see you as a clumsy person."

Kendra hadn't meant to spout off, but she had thought hard about who had had motive and opportunity. The obvious conclusion was inescapable.

"You knocked over the water so I'd have to go to the closet and change. You were conveniently there to save me in the nick of time, but in such a way that I couldn't miss the implied threat. Haven't you implied all along that danger lurks around every corner?"

She had to believe the snake was an attempt to scare her away.

"It isn't going to work, Alvarez. I'm not leaving."

She waited for Rafe to explode over her accusation. Instead, his expression grew thoughtful. For the first time, she felt a sliver of apprehension crawl along her spine.

What if her conclusion was wrong?

"In the morning," he said quietly, "we'll try the gun range once more. It's supposed to rain again in the afternoon. Tammy is coming around noon. I won't leave your side once she gets here."

"That's it? That's all your going to say?"

"Nope. I will personally see to it that no one has an opportunity to put anything else in your room. And I would take it as a personal favor if you would keep your thoughts and comments about makeup to yourself while she is here.''

Kendra bristled instantly. ''Don't tell me what to do. I'll deal with your friend Tammy. And I want you and the rest of this household to remember that I am not a dog and pony show. You can wait outside while I talk with your friend. The only reason I'm consenting to any of this is because you made it a condition of my going with you to Rialto Industries.'' She aimed a finger at his broad chest and rammed home the rest of her words. ''And I *am* going with you, Alvarez. You can put snakes all over the house and throw every old girlfriend you have in my face. I couldn't care less. But if you think you're going to send me running, you've seriously miscalculated.''

Her chest heaved under the force of her anger. She'd waited too many years for this opportunity. Nothing he said or did was going to get in her way. She was finally going to put an end to her nightmares once and for all.

He grabbed her hand, startling her. His grip was firm, but not painful as he stared at her face. She tried not to react to his touch, but her heart revved into overdrive as she gazed defiantly up at him.

Without warning, his other hand rose to brush a strand of hair back from her cheek. The feel of his gentle fingers against the warmth of her skin caused an immediate hitch in her breathing.

''Get some sleep, Kendra. Mornings come early around here.''

Dumbfounded, she stood there as he released her and stepped off the porch, striding toward the lights of the bunkhouse. For a long time, she remained in the dark, barely hearing the quiet sounds of the night. Had she badly miscalculated?

She could swear she'd hurt his feelings. But if Rafe hadn't

put that snake in her closet, someone else had. And that meant Kendra had acquired a dangerous and silent enemy here on the Smoking Barrel.

RAFE WAS PLEASED at the way the target shooting went. Kendra's last round had all found their target. She was more comfortable with the weapon, if not with him. She practically jumped each time he spoke to her. He'd felt her quiver when he'd touched her accidentally.

Neither of them had referred to yesterday, but both the incident and the scene last night fluttered between them, unspoken.

"There. I think we can safely say I know how to shoot." Kendra set the empty weapon on the shelf.

"You do realize there is a big difference between aiming at a target and firing at a live person coming at you."

"Really?"

He found himself almost smiling. Kendra had spunk. Unfortunately, that could also prove a handicap.

"All right, Annie Oakley, let's call it a morning. I'm satisfied if you are."

"Praise from the master?"

"Interesting choice of words."

"Yeah? Well don't read anything into them," she warned.

"Wouldn't dare." He stopped her when they reached the back porch. "I've been thinking."

"Sounds painful."

He didn't smile. "If you didn't put the snake in your closet yesterday…"

"Me?!"

"…and I didn't put the snake in your closet, we're left with the inescapable conclusion that someone else did."

"Brilliant deduction," she snapped.

"You need to stay alert at all times."

"That was my plan," she agreed drolly.

"Just so you know, we're running a thorough background check on you to see if someone out of your past could be responsible."

For a second her eyes widened, but then she nodded. "You won't find anything," she told him confidently.

"Because you've tampered with the records?"

"Because there's nothing to find!"

"No possibility of an Internet stalker? Maybe someone you did business with who didn't like what you did?"

She started to respond quickly and paused, nudging the heavy frames of her glasses back against the bridge of her nose with a knuckle.

"I talk with a lot of people on line, Rafe. And not all jobs go perfectly, you know that. But I can't think of anyone who would have a reason to hurt me. Besides, how would they know where to find me?"

"You said you told a couple of clients you were going away on vacation. Were they regular clients?"

"Yes. And I've completed successful jobs for all of them in the past. No complaints that I know of."

"None of the individuals tried to hit on you and were rebuffed?"

"Of course n… No."

"You hesitated."

She shrugged. "The one guy I do quite a bit of work for told me he loved me and wanted to marry me, but he was only joking. He was just happy that I solved his latest computer problems."

"What's his name?"

"Oh, no you don't. He's a tease, Rafe. *You* know the type."

Rafe ignored her dig. "Let me have his name."

"No! That's crazy. No man is going to come after me. He and I have never even met."

"Nutcases are unpredictable. Give me his name, Kendra.

At the very least, let us a run a quiet background check on him to be sure he doesn't have a record.''

He thought she'd continue to refuse, but after a moment of silence, she finally gave him the name. Good. She wasn't nearly as complacent as she pretended. It also meant she didn't really think he'd planted that damn snake.

"Out of curiosity, why do you think no man would ever come after you?" He surveyed her features closely. "There isn't a thing wrong with you, Kendra." She might not be his type, but if she lost those glasses and changed her wardrobe a bit she wouldn't be unattractive.

"Get real."

"You have a low self-esteem, don't you?"

"I do not!" Red flooded her cheeks. "Have you seen the prices I charge? I'm good at what I do, Alvarez, and I'm not afraid to say so!"

"That's business. Are you as good at being a woman as you are on the computer?"

Her face tightened. He instantly regretted his words, but before he could apologize, she glared at him through slitted eyes.

"*That* is none of your business."

He stroked her arm and watched her eyes widen. "You're wrong, Kendra. Rialto's players are all self-assured, piranha types. You have to be able to hold your own on every level."

"Don't worry about me."

"I have no choice if you plan to go in—as my partner."

"Your business assistant," she corrected.

He resisted another urge to touch her. She wanted him to believe she was tough as nails, but there was a vulnerable core to Kendra that he found himself wanting to protect.

"You can't afford to get flustered when a man makes a pass at you."

"Is that what you're doing?"

"No."

"Then where's the problem, Alvarez?"

He moved closer and she held her ground—even when he reached out to run a knuckle down her cheek.

"Stop that."

He noticed the betraying shiver. Kendra wasn't as impassive to him as she'd like him to believe.

"This group eats virgins for breakfast, Kendra."

She raised her face, bringing her lips temptingly near. The light fragrance that she wore teased his senses and he had to resist an impulse to pull those ugly glasses from her face.

"Then I have nothing to worry about, Alvarez. I'm perfectly safe."

She turned on her heel and headed inside. Totally caught off guard, it took Rafe several seconds to realize what she'd said and then he had to hurry after her.

"We aren't finished talking," he told her inside the kitchen.

"I'm finished." She kept going down the hall.

"Wait a minute. If you have a lover, I need to know about him. He could—"

"I don't."

"But you said—"

"Now. I don't have a lover now." Her head turned back toward the front of the house. "Would that tall brunette coming to the front door be your friend Tammy by any chance?"

Annoyed by the distraction, Rafe followed her pointing finger and discovered Tammy of the silky short hair and the silky long legs striding toward the front door with a perfect smile in place.

"Yes."

"Don't you think you'd better answer the door?"

"This conversation isn't over, Kendra."

"It is for me."

Rafe had no time to argue with her, but he wasn't anywhere near to done with Kendra Kincade. Perversely, he found himself greeting Tammy with more enthusiasm than normal. Despite a slightly puzzled look, she responded with her usual friendliness. He'd always enjoyed Tammy's company, but he'd known that she had needs he could never fulfill, so he had stopped seeing her. They'd remained friends.

Now as he welcomed her inside, Rosa announced lunch. Tammy accepted the invitation to join them. He found Penny and Mitchell already at the table.

What was Mitchell doing inside during roundup? The older man was dressed in jeans and an open-necked flannel shirt and boots—his favorite riding attire. His left knee that he favored and referred to ambiguously as an old "war wound," had never kept him out of the saddle as far as Rafe knew. Rafe had always assumed Mitchell used his cane for show more than anything else, but it was out of character for him to be inside instead of working the cattle with everyone else. Something was up.

Rafe held out the chair beside his own for Tammy, letting Kendra seat herself across from them. Tammy kept everyone entertained with funny stories while they ate. Rafe was aware that both Kendra and Penny watched how frequently she managed to touch him during the meal. He wanted to explain that Tammy touched everyone like that, but he didn't. It did, however, serve to remind him why he had stopped calling her.

"Rafe, I was wondering if I might see you in the library after lunch," Mitchell said at the end of the meal. He set down his coffee cup and reached in his pocket for one of his ever-present cigars.

"Of course. I'll just see that Kendra and Tammy get settled upstairs."

"Thanks," Kendra interrupted, "but we don't need any help, do we Tammy?"

"None at all." She laid her hand on Rafe's arm and gave it a gentle squeeze. "You just tend to business and Kendra and I will do the same. Penny, you're welcome to join us if you like."

"I'm afraid I'll need Penny as well," Mitchell said.

Unfazed, Tammy stood up. "Well then, I guess it's just you and me, sugar. I have my war paint out in the car. Where do you want to set up?"

"I'll show you."

Rafe frowned at their departure. After yesterday's happening, he was reluctant to let Kendra go off alone with anyone.

"Cody checked the contents of her car while we ate," Mitchell said. "I went over Kendra's room myself. No one will have an opportunity to get to her today."

Rafe relaxed, but only a little. He followed Mitchell and Penny into the library. Was it his imagination, or did Mitchell lean a little more heavily on his cane than usual? He glanced at Penny, but saw no concern in her expression.

The hidden panel sprang free and the bookcase slid back, allowing them to step inside the elevator that would take them to the command center in the basement. This was the secret heart of their operation. The soundproof room was really a high-tech office beneath its hidden entrance.

"What's going on?" Rafe asked as soon as they were seated. He had to wait while Mitchell lit his cigar and leaned back in his chair, fingering his lighter.

"The FBI finally turned loose some information. Penny?"

"Kendra Kincade had an aunt and uncle," Penny announced. "Benjamin Ford, his wife, Ellen, and their eight-year-old daughter, Ginny, were murdered by person or persons unknown twenty-two years ago."

Chapter Five

"I take it the aunt and uncle had some connection to Rialto?" Rafe questioned.

Penny nodded, tapping her pen against her notebook. "Kendra's Uncle Benjamin was Rialto's chauffeur at the time of his murder. Police thought it might be a rival gang hit at first. It was a professional job, but nothing really pointed to a rival gang."

"Did Benjamin see a little too much in his capacity as a chauffeur?" Rafe asked.

"That's what homicide concluded, but conclusions aren't proof. Still, it explains Kendra's quest for justice."

Rafe pictured Kendra's expression when she announced she wanted to help bring Rialto to justice. "Twenty-some years is a long time to want such active revenge for people who weren't immediate family," he said thoughtfully.

"Maybe not," Penny argued. "The cousin was the same age as Kendra. Their murders must have made a strong impact on an impressionable young girl."

"How young?"

"Kendra was seven. Her cousin was only eight. The Fords were shot at close range, including the child."

"We've requested a copy of the file to see what other information there might be," Mitchell added. He drew in a lungful of smoke and exhaled quickly on a cough.

"You okay?"

Eventually he nodded. "Maddie says these things are gonna kill me." He frowned at his cigar. "She just might be right. On the other hand, I don't plan to live forever."

Rafe frowned. It wasn't his imagination. Mitchell didn't look well. Despite his white hair, he normally looked much younger than his sixty-five years. Today, however, there was a tired, pinched quality about his features that worried Rafe.

"Maybe you ought to give Doc Brandinger a call," he suggested.

"Now don't *you* start. Maddie's enough."

"She cares," Penny said simply. "We all do."

"I appreciate that, but I'm fine. Tired, but fine. I'm having a little allergy trouble today is all. Did you get anything from Kendra?" The last was addressed to Rafe.

"I'm certain she didn't put that snake in her closet. She thought I did it." He carefully kept emotion from his voice, even though that still rankled.

"Oh-oh, trouble in paradise?" Penny asked archly.

"Yeah." Rafe gave her a half smile. "Kendra has the mind of a mule."

"Not falling for your charms, huh?"

"Penny, my love, she could give you lessons in how to resist my wildly exaggerated charms."

"I wouldn't go so far as to say *wildly*, however, two of us striking blows at your ego at once? How *will* you cope?"

"I have some ideas—if you're interested," he leaned forward suggestively. Penny merely raised her eyebrows.

"Promises, promises."

"What else did you learn?" Mitchell said, interrupting the byplay.

Rafe sat back in his chair. "She's not a virgin."

Penny's mouth dropped, then shut with a snap. Mitchell's lighter clattered to the tabletop.

"I don't think I want to hear these details," Penny said.

"No details. I told her Rialto's crew would tear a virgin apart and she said not to worry. That means a boyfriend somewhere. She isn't the type to just fall into bed with anyone."

"I guess you would know."

"Penny, my love, is that jealousy I hear?"

"Wishful thinking on your part, Rafael."

Mitchell retrieved the lighter, but didn't reach for another cigar. "Penny, what have you turned up on her male friends?"

"Nothing. If she's got one, he's invisible."

"Did *you* get a name while you were having this conversation?" Mitchell asked Rafe.

"Nope. Someone asked her to marry him." Rafe gave Penny that name to run and added, "She claims he's a client that she doesn't take seriously because he likes to tease."

"Imagine that," Penny quipped.

Rafe ignored the sarcasm. "The point is, the guy could be a nutcase who was serious. Or she could have an ex-lover waiting in the wings who has it in for her. I can't afford to take her inside if someone is coming after her."

"No," Mitchell said slowly. "We don't want to bungle this opportunity. If need be, we'll keep her isolated until after this assignment is complete."

"In that case you'll need to contact Doc Brandinger after all. It's going to take sedation to keep Kendra out of this investigation now. And she's getting pretty good with a gun," he warned half in jest. "The one thing that woman has plenty of is spunk."

KENDRA WAS pleasantly surprised by Tammy Gordon. She'd been prepared not to like the woman, but Tammy wasn't what she'd expected. For one thing, her makeup had been applied so skillfully at first glance she appeared to be wearing only lipstick. She wasn't pushy and she had a great sense of humor as she taught Kendra several neat little tricks to highlight her features. Unfortunately, the poor woman had a thing for Rafe despite her assertion that Rafe wasn't the marrying kind.

"He's just so incredibly sexy, you know?"

Kendra knew.

"But he's real upfront about not wanting any sort of a commitment. Still, he can't blame a woman for hoping to change his mind."

"I think there are quite a few of you. Hoping, I mean."

Tammy nodded. "I know. It's depressing. Have you gone to bed with him yet?"

Kendra managed not to gape. "We don't have that sort of relationship."

"Oh, too bad. He's a wonderful lover. Nobody ever leaves his bed unsatisfied."

Embarrassed in a way she hadn't been since she was a young girl first learning about sex, Kendra sought to change the subject.

"You did a great job with my makeup."

Kendra found she meant it. The subtle transformation was amazing. Her eyes appeared larger and more attractive despite her glasses and her skin had a deceptively pretty glow to it.

"I'll never be able to duplicate what you did."

"Sure you will. Here. We'll wash it all off and you do it this time."

"Oh, no. I don't have your knack."

"Honey, you're a woman, aren't you? We're born with the knack. Sometimes it just takes a nudge or two. Come on, try it. Then we'll go for a more exotic look."

"Exotic?"

"Sure, you know—for those seductive moments."

"Oh. Right." She did not want to hear any more about seductive moments or Rafe's sex life from the bubbly, outgoing Tammy. However, under Tammy's insistent guidance, Kendra was finishing the final touches on the "exotic" look when Rafe arrived. Tammy immediately floated to his side. Rafe didn't seem to mind. It was a relief when Penny came in and announced that he had a phone call.

So much for exotic moments in makeup. Rafe had barely glanced her way.

He reappeared a few minutes later and smoothly got Tammy and her bag full of cosmetics back downstairs and out front without seeming to hurry. With the bedroom window standing open, Kendra heard the murmur of their voices. She stared at the array of stuff the woman had left behind and shook her head. Penny appeared, eyeing her critically.

"Nice, but a little heavy, don't you think?"

"According to Tammy this is for evening, when seduction is the plan," Kendra told her wryly.

"Planning on seducing anyone in particular?"

"Not me," she said firmly. "In fact, I'll be in the bathroom scrubbing this off if anyone needs me."

They both glanced toward the bedroom window as a trill of laughter wafted up from out front.

"I don't think you'll be needed soon," Penny said, peering outside. "You might even have time to read a book."

"War and Peace?"

"In German," Penny agreed.

The women shared a smile. Kendra realized it was the first time Penny had directed a genuine smile her way. She was amazed at how it transformed the other woman's features. Penny was actually quite pretty in an understated sort of way.

"Want to see what she showed me?" Kendra found herself asking.

Penny hesitated. Another giggle drifted on the air. "Sure.

Why not. Looks like we've both got plenty of time. Maybe Neil will appreciate a new me.''

"Neil?"

"A man I've been seeing. He's Maddie's nephew, actually.''

Even though Penny didn't sound particularly enthusiastic over Neil, for a second, Kendra felt a stab of envy. Everyone on this ranch seemed to be part of a pair except her. Another laugh from outside drew Penny's gaze and the corners of her lips turned down. Kendra amended her last thought. Penny might have this Neil person, but beneath all the teasing Kendra suspected it was Rafe she secretly wanted.

Kendra stood and heaved a mental sigh. She hoped not. She liked Penny and no hairstyle nor any amount of makeup was going to turn Kendra or Penny into the sort of woman Rafe was drawn to. Besides, who wanted to be part of such a vast crowd?

Rafe surprised them both by returning a few minutes later. Kendra watched the sparring between Penny and Rafe and decided her assumption was correct. The blatant flirting was a cover for Penny's interest in Rafe. Being male, he was no doubt totally unaware.

None of her business, she told herself firmly. Once Rialto was taken care of, she'd be out of their lives forever.

Rafe insisted they had time to work out for an hour before dinner. Kendra enjoyed learning various defenses she could use in the unlikely event something ever happened. And fortunately, she was past the point where Rafe's every touch sent chills all through her. But she didn't think she'd ever get past the point of being so aware of him at all times. Tammy was right. He was too darn sexy for his own good.

"Tomorrow," Rafe announced as he called an end to the session, "we're going shopping."

"What for?" she asked suspiciously. Sweat beaded her forehead. She wiped at it with a hand towel, unconcerned that most of her carefully applied makeup was now on the towel rather than her face.

"You need clothing." He put out a hand. "And before you start another argument, that call I took was from Rialto. I got the job."

Excitement zapped right through her. "That's great!"

Satisfaction made him smile in return. "Yeah. We're in. He's invited me to a party at his ranch for this coming weekend. I asked if I could bring my assistant along and he said that would be fine."

After all these years, it was actually going to happen!

"As my assistant," Rafe continued, "you need to be dressed appropriately. This is nonnegotiable, okay?"

Her euphoria lurched away. "What makes you so sure I don't have appropriate clothing?"

"I just knew you weren't going to make this easy," he muttered. "I should have told you you *couldn't* have a new wardrobe, then you'd be chomping at the bit to go shopping."

"Not a chance, I hate to shop."

"Of course you do."

Kendra blushed, aware of her baggy sweat suit. She hated that his guess about her wardrobe was correct. She'd been working at home for so long her clothing consisted mostly of sweats and jeans and comfort clothes. She did need to go shopping. She just didn't want him to take charge.

"I suppose you plan to pick out my clothes yourself?"

"Nope. Lydia's going to help us."

"No!" The thought of fashionably dressed Lydia directing her wardrobe was enough to give her a screaming fit. "Thank you, but I don't need any help. I'm quite capable of dressing myself. I've been doing it for years."

His eyes skimmed her, deepening her blush. "We'll leave by eight-thirty," he said calmly.

"Eight-thirty? In the morning? What sort of store opens at that hour?"

"This isn't the city, Kendra. Depending on traffic it will take us an hour and a half to two hours to get to the nearest mall. I'll see you in the morning."

She watched him saunter toward the steps. If she'd still had her knife she'd be tempted to throw it at his broad, manly back.

"Rafe?" She called after him. "I want my knife back."

He glanced over his shoulder. "Why do I get the feeling that could prove dangerous to my health?"

"Because you're perceptive?"

A slow grin started across face. "You'd better change for dinner. I'll see you in the morning."

"Afraid to eat at the same table with me?"

"I have a date."

Her stomach did a funny little tumble at his words. Calling on all the skill she possessed, Kendra tried for the light tone Penny would have used. "Lydia, Phoebe or Tammy?"

"Janet."

Another one? The man had a harem!

"Let me guess. Does she sell women's clothing?"

"No, she does not." But his eyes shifted guiltily and he didn't meet her gaze. Janet probably sold shoes or accessories. Or maybe her father owned the store.

"Señor Rafe?" Rosa called down the stairs.

"Coming, Rosa. I'll see you the morning Kendra. You did very well tonight."

Ha! She'd done better than he knew. She hadn't thrown anything at him even despite the unbearable temptation.

Kendra followed slowly, telling herself she wasn't jealous.

It was a great big fat lie.

RAFE INSERTED his key in the bunkhouse door, relieved to finally call an end to the very long day. He'd realized something painful on the drive home tonight. He was getting too old for a different woman every night of the week.

His social life wasn't usually this hectic. In fact lately, he'd been seeing a lot of Lydia—mostly due to proximity. But this function of Janet's had been planned a long time ago and he liked both her and her friends. Still, he was starting to envy what Brady and Jake had found. What must it be like to go home to one special woman every night? Someone he could kick back and relax with. Someone who didn't need to be entertained. Someone who wanted to share more than his company and his bed.

Whoa! That sounded suspiciously like settling down. He wasn't ready for that just yet. While Elena was a cute kid, he had plenty of time for parenting a brood of his own.

Frowning, he entered the bunkhouse without turning on the light. Cody was riding patrol duty, and the rest of the men wouldn't be back tonight. It felt odd coming in to a completely empty bunkhouse. He felt a stab of guilt for not pulling his weight during the busy roundup season. On the other hand, this was Mitchell's orders, and at least the rustlers hadn't struck again.

Rafe sat on the edge of his bunk to pull off his boots, and the hair on the back of his neck lifted. His gaze raked the pitch-dark room. Nothing stirred, yet finely honed instincts screamed a silent warning. Something was wrong. He stopped removing his boots. Instead, he made a show of yawning and stretching widely as he stood, half expecting an attack or a shot to come winging out of the dark.

Feigning exaggerated sleepiness, he opened his dresser drawer. His fingers closed comfortingly over the thirty-eight inside. Tugging the gun from its holster, he whirled, going into a defensive crouch.

Nothing moved.

A heavy silence hung over the room. Why was he so

certain he wasn't alone? Gun in hand, he moved cautiously
to the wall switch. Light flooded the room.

Empty.

He walked around to be sure. Something glinted on the
floor near his dresser. His eyes narrowed. Picking it up, he
turned it over in his hand. A small crystal earring winked
up at him.

Kendra.

He'd been subconsciously aware of her scent from the
moment he first sat down. That's what had put his senses
on alert. He fingered the bit of jewelry.

"Come on out, Kendra."

For a long tense moment, nothing happened. Rafe wondered if he'd been mistaken. There was a slight scuffle of
sound and a leg encased in a baggy pair of cranberry sweats
appeared from under his bunk. An arm followed, then a red-
faced slip of a female.

Kendra pushed her glasses against the bridge of her nose
defiantly, then brushed at some dust on her clothing.

Rafe gave her full marks for facing him. He stuck the gun
in his waistband and regarded her.

"Want to explain what you were doing in here?"

"No."

"No?"

"No."

She always managed to catch him off stride. Absurdly, he
wanted to smile. He curbed the impulse, reminding himself
that she was an unknown element in what would soon be a
dangerous situation.

"I'm afraid I'm going to have to insist."

"Go ahead."

"What?"

"Insist."

"Kendra, I'm not playing games. I could have shot you."

"You wouldn't shoot unless you were certain of your target."

She was right, but that only annoyed him further. He grabbed her by the shoulders and gave her a shake.

"This isn't a game! It's late, I'm tired, and I'm jumpy. Now what were you doing in here?"

Her eyes met his, wide and guileless. She didn't seem the least bit afraid of him. She should be. She was much smaller—almost fragile beneath his fingers.

He watched the rapid pulse beat against her slender throat. So she wasn't as unmoved as she'd have him believe.

Good.

"I didn't expect you back so early," she said calmly. Only that pulse gave lie to her composure. "I couldn't sleep and I knew the bunkhouse was empty tonight. I wanted a look around."

"Find anything interesting?" he drawled.

Her eyes widened a fraction and her pulse stepped up its fascinating rhythm. His own heart rate began accelerating.

"It's cleaner than I would have expected. You only have a small colony of dust bunnies under your bed."

"You could try the patience of a saint, you know that?"

"Then you should be safe enough."

A chuckle nearly broke free. He curbed it and stared into her pretty, wide eyes. Before he even realized he was going to do it, he removed the blocky glasses from her face. Startled into immobility, she gazed up at him, her face suddenly defenseless.

"Give me those back!"

"In a minute. You have pretty eyes."

Warily she blinked at him.

"It's a shame to hide such pretty eyes behind these ugly lenses," he said softly.

Her lips parted while her pulse beat an erratic tattoo against her skin. He lowered his head. He wanted to taste those lips, to feel her body pressed against his own and watch her respond in his arms.

She jerked back, snatching the glasses from his fingers.

"It would be a bigger shame if I started walking into walls," she announced primly, replacing the glasses and offering him a glare. But the slight tremor in her hands told him she wasn't as much in control as she wanted him to believe.

He leaned back against the dresser. He found he still wanted to kiss her! "Tell me what you were doing in here, Kendra," he coaxed.

"Looking around. I was curious."

She was also lying. Why?

"I don't figure you came to steal anything—"

"Of course I didn't!"

"—so that means you must have planned to go through my belongings."

Color deepened in her cheeks.

"Darlin', I don't have any secrets." He stepped back from the dresser and gestured with his hand. "You want to look around, be my guest."

"Give me my earring back!"

He'd forgotten about the bit of glass. He held it up, watching the colors reflect in the prism. "I sort of like it. Don't they say finders' keepers?"

"It belonged to my mother," she said so bleakly that he took a harder look at her. Something dark and infinitely sad crossed her features. Rafe wondered what that was all about. Hadn't Penny said her parents retired to Arizona? He held out the earring to her.

"Thank you." Her fingers closed over it. "I'll go back to the house now. I'm sorry I intruded here tonight. I didn't mean to cause any harm."

"Other than raising my blood pressure a little, you didn't cause any harm."

"Then, good night."

"Yes."

He was probably seven kinds of a fool to let her go so easily, but he followed her to the door and watched her walk back to the main house. She didn't run, but she didn't dawdle. Had she really expected to discover something in a bunkhouse that he often shared with half a dozen other men?

He thought for a minute, then moved back to the dresser and opened another drawer. Sure enough, Kendra's knife was gone. The little she-devil had actually had the nerve to come in here to steal back her knife!

A grin of admiration worked its way across his lips. Several emotions warred within him, not the least of which was the disturbing realization of how close he had come to kissing her. He was still slightly aroused by the thought.

Kendra wasn't his type at all. So why did he have to keep reminding himself of that fact?

She'd managed to slip past whoever was supposed to be watching her tonight. Maybe she wouldn't make such a bad "partner" after all. If only he could be sure what her secret agenda was. He didn't doubt for a minute that she had one.

As he took a quick shower and fell into bed, Rafe accepted that Kendra was unlike any other woman of his acquaintance. Thoughts of her had distracted him all evening, despite the fact that Janet was a wonderful companion— exciting, fun, tall and beautifully proportioned. Yet he'd refused her invitation to come inside when he dropped her at home because by then he'd been mentally planning his strategy for the morning's shopping trip. Kendra was playing havoc with his love life and she wasn't even trying.

Now that he thought about it, he realized he'd better revamp his earlier plans. He was going to need more than mere wits to get Kendra to cooperate with him tomorrow. The woman would no doubt argue over every suggestion he made.

Rafe smiled. He was looking forward to the challenge.

KENDRA WASN'T at the breakfast table, but Lydia was, sharing a cup of coffee with Rosa.

"*La señorita no comió,* no eat," Rosa announced in offended tones. "Only the juice and coffee."

"But she's up?" Rafe questioned.

"Of course I'm up. You said to be ready by eight-thirty. It's eight-fifteen. I'm ready."

Kendra challenged him from the doorway. Her newly styled hair framed her face making him long to pluck those ugly glasses away once more. She looked fresh and pretty and incredibly defenseless in a shapeless dark tunic and a pair of leggings that reminded him Kendra had nicely shaped legs under the baggy stuff she usually wore. He couldn't wait to see her in something flattering.

"Let's get going then."

"I love to shop," Lydia chirped. "Don't you, Kendra?"

"No."

It was going to be a long day.

Lydia suggested they take her new convertible and Kendra climbed in the back before Rafe could object. Lydia handed him the keys with a beaming smile. "You drive. You're so much better than I am. He's a very smooth driver," she told Kendra.

"I can imagine," Kendra said drolly.

Rafe caught her expression as he walked around the car and could almost hear her thoughts. A very long day, he decided. What on earth had possessed him to invite Lydia along? He should have known better.

Kendra was silent, while Lydia chatted happily. Kendra didn't seem to mind the breeze from the open top flinging her hair all over the place, but Rafe was thankful when they finally reached the mall and headed inside.

"I know the perfect store," Lydia announced. "They have a good selection of business attire. It's upstairs on the second level," she added as they wound their way past the small cart vendors in the middle of the mall. Rafe had told Lydia that Mitchell wanted his friend's daughter treated to an entire wardrobe for a new job she'd be starting next week.

"She also needs something appropriate for a formal office party this weekend," he reminded Lydia.

"I know the perfect outfit—if they still have it. And there is this darling pair of shoes…"

Rafe turned around on the escalator to throw Kendra a sympathetic look. A plump, middle-aged woman smiled inquiringly at him. Kendra wasn't behind her. She wasn't anywhere in sight at all.

"Where's Kendra?" he demanded of the woman.

"What?"

"Kendra!"

Rafe brushed past her heading down the up escalator.

"Well, really!"

"Kendra!"

Shoppers turned to stare. He heard Lydia call him, but he swept the milling people carefully, looking for the only face he wanted to see.

A sudden vision of the coiled snake about to strike made his gut clench. Kendra!

From somewhere nearby came the distorted sound of a woman's scream.

Chapter Six

Kendra had studied the back of Rafe's head on the drive into the city, resisting an impulse to touch his clean, wavy hair. Where it was getting too long, the ends had a tendency to curl that fascinated her. Inwardly she admitted that everything about the man was starting to fascinate her. That wasn't a good thing. It must mean she'd been spending too much time with her computers. She should get out more. Date some nice man.

One who didn't already have a harem.

It said a lot about Rafe that none of his women really seemed to mind being part of a group. But *she* would mind.

Last night Rafe had nearly caught her sitting on his bunk like some smitten schoolgirl. And she'd nearly kissed him! The memory haunted her dreams well into the night. Of course, it made a nice change from the normal nightmares.

She had to get her hormones under control. Rafe was a tool, nothing more. He wouldn't get within ten feet of her if he knew what she really planned to do. She fingered the hidden knife, glad to have it with her again, if only to annoy Rafe. Had he even discovered it was missing?

Lydia chatted all the way into the city. Once at the mall, they had quickly forged ahead, focused on their mission. Kendra strolled more slowly, not anxious for the battle she was sure would come. Her attention was caught by an array of crystals on a portable cart in the mall. As Lydia and Rafe headed for the escalator, she paused to look at the display.

The men came out of nowhere. Hands grabbed her arms in punishing grips as two dirty cowboys moved in on either side of her.

"Keep walking."

"Wha—"

"Don't make a scene or someone will get hurt."

She saw the gun partially concealed in the hand of the man on her right. Fear charged her system as they had shoved through a nearby fire exit door before she could think.

She forced herself to remain calm. Maybe Rafe was testing her. It would be just like him to want to see how much she had learned.

"Is this a joke?" she demanded.

"No, it's a forty-five," the skinny man on her right growled without humor. He shoved the gun against her skin. "And it will put a big hole in a small woman like you."

His expression was more annoyed than menacing, but if this was a test he was taking it seriously. A concrete hallway stretched before them, dimly lit. There was a door at the far end.

Fear churned her stomach as she remembered the snake. It didn't seem like a good idea to find out where that door would lead on the arms of these two grungy-looking cowboys.

Kendra had never actually expected to use the training Rafe had put her through, but now she let her body slump toward the ground. The sudden shift in weight caused both men to stumble and relax their grips. She brought her arms up and down again fast and hard like Rafe had shown her, breaking their hold. With a blood curdling scream to give her a psychological edge, Kendra twisted away. She used her new fingernails to rake the gunman's startled face.

He leaped back, blood welling from three long gouges right below his eyes. She brought her knee up with all the force she could muster. His scream was almost as loud as hers had been. The gun fell from his fingers, clattering against the concrete.

The other man grabbed her from behind. She stomped back on the arch of his foot, bringing her head back into his face. His hold broke, but undeterred, he reached for her again. She twisted her hip into him, letting his own momentum carry him over her hip and forward into the wall.

The first man had turned back in her direction. She screamed again even as her hand sought her knife.

His face was a snarling mask of rage—until he saw the knife. He hesitated, his expression incredulous as he stared at her. She crouched, holding the knife low and against her body. She wouldn't let him take it from her as easily as Rafe had done.

Part of her heard the door behind them crash open, but she kept her focus on the two men.

As the second man tried to retrieve the gun, she slashed at him, catching his hand. Someone yelled. Faced with reinforcements the two men fled toward the door at the end of the corridor, trailing drops of blood.

RAFE SPOTTED the emergency exit as a second scream rang out. He flung open the door and found Kendra crouched in a menacing fashion, facing down two men.

Rafe yelled. They turned toward him, startled, before running down the corridor. Rafe raced to Kendra's side.

"Are you okay?"

"Yes! Don't let them get away!"

Rafe sprinted after the pair.

The two had reached their illegally parked car by the time he got outside. Rafe yanked open the nearest door, but before he could get a grip on the passenger, the vehicle roared away. Rafe noted the tag number and the dented left fender before he turned back to Kendra.

Bent at the waist, for a minute he thought she was ill. Then she straightened and he saw the gun in one hand, something else in the other. The knife had already disappeared from view. The mall door opened and security belatedly charged inside. They immediately came to a halt at the sight of the gun.

"Holy sh…put the gun down, lady!"

"She's the victim," Rafe called to the man. "Her two attackers just took off in a blue pickup truck. Kendra, are you okay?"

"Fine." She sounded shaky. "The only casualty was my glasses." She held out the two pieces of broken frame. "I don't even remember them coming off."

Ignoring security, Rafe took the gun from her limp fingers and folded her trembling body against his chest.

"I'm shaking," she said wonderingly.

"Shock."

"But everything's all over."

He stroked her hair back from her face with fingers that shook as well. "Delayed reaction," he assured her.

"You didn't tell me about this part."

"I never expected you to need what I taught you."

"You want to put that gun down, mister?" one of the security people asked.

"No, I want to give it to you." He'd forgotten he even held it in his other hand. "Have you called the police yet?"

"Rafe! What's going on?" Lydia called out.

Good question.

"Lady, step back outside."

It took awhile to straighten out the scene and then the police arrived and they had to start all over again. Rafe didn't release Kendra until her shaking stopped. His never did. At least not where it didn't show. He'd nearly let a pair of thugs take her because he'd let his guard down completely. Mitchell would be justified in asking for his resignation after this incident.

Kendra not only weathered the crisis, but she stayed with her prepared story about the reason for their shopping expedition. Her recounting of the attack was sharp and precise. A man could do a lot worse than have a partner like Kendra Kincade.

The police treated the whole thing as an attempted abduction for the purpose of rape. Nobody argued. Kendra gave them a verbal description of the attackers that matched Rafe's, but she insisted she couldn't look at mug shots until she replaced her broken glasses.

"You have an appointment with the optician upstairs this afternoon," Rafe told her when the police finished with them. "They can make you another set of glasses in an hour. I'm afraid Janet didn't have an opening until one-thirty."

"Janet?" Kendra tilted her head to stare at him. "Your date-from-last-night Janet?"

"Uh, yeah."

"She's an optician."

"Is that a problem?"

Kendra rolled her eyes. Lydia interrupted. "Rafe, if her appointment isn't until then, what if we get something to eat first?"

"Kendra?"

"Only if we can go someplace where you aren't dating half the wait staff."

Oddly embarrassed, Rafe led them to the steak house. Now, more than ever, he wished Lydia wasn't along. He wanted to question Kendra privately. Lydia, however, was all excited and continued to bring the conversation back to what had happened.

"You were so lucky, Kendra. Wasn't she lucky, Rafe? There are perverts everywhere. Imagine thinking they could walk into a shopping mall and abduct someone without a thought. Good thing Rafe showed you how to defend yourself.''

Their eyes met and held. ''Yes, it was.''

''I would have been absolutely terrified. What did they say to you?''

''Lydia, I'd really rather not talk about it.''

''Oh, sure. I understand. I mean, I'm just so shocked. It's so hard to believe. I'll bet you'll be glad to get away from this part of Texas soon. When does your new job start?''

''Next week.'' She pushed aside her barely touched salad. ''I'm not very hungry.''

''I'm not surprised. That was enough to put anyone off their feed.'' Lydia nibbled daintily at her own salad.

Rafe was relieved when he could finally signal for the check. Lydia decided to shop in the department store around the corner while they waited for Kendra's eye appointment. ''After all, it takes an hour to get the glasses made once she finally gets her prescription.''

''Fine, Lydia.''

''Just be careful,'' Kendra cautioned.

''Don't worry. No one is going to grab me! I'd scream my head off.''

''I tried that. They weren't impressed.''

Lydia looked uncertain how to react to that statement. Inwardly, Rafe grinned. Kendra was something else.

''I'm sorry,'' he told her when they were alone.

''Lydia's just nervous.''

''I meant for not keeping a closer eye on you.''

''I'm not a child, Rafe.''

Her face was pretty without those glasses getting in the way. Pretty, yet vulnerable in a way that reached something inside him and twisted.

''No, you're definitely not a child.''

Her lips parted. A flare of new tension shimmered between them. He'd always been aware of her as a female, but he'd ignored those vibes, treating her like a kid sister.

"I'm glad you aren't my sister."

"What?"

Her eyes rounded, staring at him with a naiveté that was somehow sexy and innocent all at the same time. Desire went from a flicker to a flame. Caught off guard, his hand started to reach out for her and stopped.

Kendra averted her eyes. She wasn't being coy, she didn't know how to handle the chemistry that now flowed openly between them. And for the first time in his life, neither did he.

Kendra didn't know how to play the flirting game that he'd always enjoyed so much. She wasn't the sort of woman a man took to his bed for a night of casual fun and that put her off-limits. Definitely time to get his mind back on business.

"I should have been more alert for trouble after that snake."

Her gaze swung back to meet his, sweetly uncertain. "You think the two are connected?"

"Don't you? Hey, you aren't buying into the police theory that these two were opportunistic rapists, are you?"

She looked down at her feet. "It's not inconceivable."

"You know better. Someone is out to hurt or scare you, Kendra."

"Well they're doing a great job," she told him with more of her old sass. "I still feel weak and jittery."

He touched her then, rubbing her shoulder tenderly. Her light, fragrant scent tantalized his nose. "That's understandable."

"Maybe for you. I'm not used to being accosted. It doesn't make any sense. I don't have enemies, Rafe—not like this. In fact, when those men first grabbed me, I thought you were testing me."

"What?" His body tightened.

"You do have a reputation as a practical joker."

"I would never joke about a person's safety, Kendra."

"No," she agreed. "And they didn't look like they were playing."

He dropped his hand to his side and scowled thoughtfully.

"What?" she asked.

"I just realized they made no attempt to disguise their looks. Either they weren't worried about being recognized or…"

"Or they didn't plan on my being around to point a finger?"

"Delicately put, but yes."

Kendra shook her head. "I was scared, but…"

"But what?"

"I'm not sure. There was something strange about that whole thing. If they had wanted to hurt me, they could have. You should have seen their expression when I pulled out that knife."

"Yes, we need to have a talk about that knife."

"I'm serious, Rafe. They were shocked when I defended myself. Like they weren't expecting resistance."

Guilt chewed on him. He should have protected her. "You did a great job."

"I had a good teacher."

She looked him in the eye. He didn't deserve the trust he saw in that look. He'd let her down. They both knew it. Yet Kendra's expression held complete faith—and something else. He cursed himself for a fool, but his body responded to that look all the same.

"We need to figure out why this happened, Kendra," he said almost gruffly.

Her eyes clouded with a trace of disappointment that vanished so fast he might have imagined it.

"Go for it," she said leaning back in her chair. "I don't have a clue why anyone would come after me."

"A jealous ex-lover?"

"I had one lover in college. He wouldn't qualify as the jealous type. He barely qualified as a lover. I've never had what you could call an active social life, Rafe."

He felt like he'd been punched in the gut. She'd only had one lover? "How come?"

Kendra shifted and looked over his shoulder. "My work doesn't lend itself to social situations."

"That's a cop-out."

Her cheeks flushed but she didn't look away. "Call it what you like, but do remember, most people don't have the stamina for the amount of 'socializing' you do."

Ouch. He'd forgotten she had claws of her own. "Jealous?"

"Hardly. Amazed perhaps. I'd think keeping a harem would grow tiresome after awhile. How do you keep them all straight?"

The harem comment rankled, but he didn't let it show. Rafe leaned close to her face. "Practice," he whispered.

Her flush deepened, making him all the more aware of how pretty she was. Especially without those horrid glasses obscuring her features.

"You know, you ought to ask Janet about getting contact lenses," he told her. "Maybe even laser eye surgery. I'll bet Janet could recommend someone."

"Really."

He ignored the warning in her sugary sweet tone. "Talk with Janet about the possibility."

Kendra gripped the arms of her chair. "You should have considered the military when you were searching for a career. At least there if you gave an order someone might have to obey you."

"Ms. Kincade?" a voice interrupted. "If you'll come with me the doctor will see you now."

"Look at that," she told him, standing quickly. "Your women even have impeccable timing."

His ego took a direct hit.

"You said it yourself. I'm a good instructor," he rejoined.

Kendra didn't dignify that with so much as a look. Rafe watched her move out of sight before heading for a quiet spot to use his cell phone. Penny answered on the second ring.

"That was a quick shopping trip, or are you calling for reinforcements?"

"Kendra was attacked," Rafe said without preamble. He gave her the particulars including the license plate number of the car, something he'd held back from the police.

"Do you need backup?" Penny asked, all business as well.

"No. I think we're safe enough now. We'll go ahead and—"

"Hold on a minute, Rafe."

He heard Penny talking with someone in the background. Mitchell began speaking in his ear a few seconds later.

"She's okay?"

"Better than okay. She dropped both of them and was holding them at bay with a knife by the time I got there. I'm beginning to think you've got the wrong one of us on payroll."

"Lydia's brother called here a few minutes ago. He needs Lydia to return home and her cell phone's busy. I'm going to send Jake in to pick you up. Where should I have him meet you?"

"Outside the west mall entrance. With luck we can get what we need and be ready to go in two hours."

He hung up and started in search of Lydia. She found him first, her own cell phone in hand. "Rafe, I just spoke to my brother. You'd think he could manage without me for a few hours, but he insists I come home right away. Mrs. Barnesly is one of his regulars and—''

"That's okay, Lydia. I just spoke with Mitchell. He's sending Jake to pick us up.''

"Oh, but I thought—''

"You go ahead and take off. I'll explain to Kendra.''

"What about her clothing?''

"We'll muddle through. I'll check on you as soon as I get back.''

"Are you sure? Despite what my brother thinks, Mrs. Barnesly can wait, you know.''

"I'm sure he wouldn't have called if it wasn't urgent, Lydia.''

Lydia hesitated, then she nodded. She reached up and stroked his cheek. "You'll be careful?''

He took her hand and kissed the back of it, willing her to be gone. "I'll be fine. And I'll call you when we get back. Drive carefully, all right?''

"Yes, of course.'' Before he realized her intent, she pulled his face down and kissed him hard on the mouth. "I'll wait for your call.''

Rafe frowned. Lydia was acting strange. He turned and found Kendra watching with a bland expression.

"Trouble with the troops?''

"Lydia had to leave. Some sort of crisis with one of her brother's guests.''

"Too bad.''

He nearly smiled at her insincerity. "How did you make out?''

"They'll have my glasses ready in an hour.''

"You already picked out the frames?'' Disappointment warred with worry. He wished she'd gone for the contacts, and he worried over the sort of frames she might have picked.

"I like to see walls before I walk into them."

"Just how bad *is* your vision?"

"Not so bad I can't select a week's worth of outfits."

Rafe sighed. "Okay. Now don't worry about cost. Mitchell's footing the bill, remember? And he's sending Jake in to pick us up in two hours."

"Then we'd better get moving. I don't imagine he likes losing another one of his men during such a busy season on the ranch."

"About your clothing, Kendra."

"Yes?"

"I have a few ideas."

"I didn't doubt it for a second."

Rafe found himself smiling again as she started toward the nearest shop. This was going to be fun.

"WHAT'S THE matter with the blue outfit?"

The battle was not going as planned—and it was anything but fun.

"I prefer this one."

"But it's gray." Kendra was immune to his charm and she didn't take orders worth a damn. She vetoed most of his selections, ignoring the brighter colors in favor of black, navy and gray.

"You know your colors," she responded sweetly.

In this battle of wits he finally had to admit that he was badly outclassed. Kendra could give stubborn lessons. Maybe he'd needed Lydia after all.

"You're going to look like a librarian."

"Don't tell me you date one of them, too."

Rafe yanked her behind a rack of formal dresses, away from the prying eyes of the amused sales clerk. "Kendra—"

Her chin lifted. "I don't know a single librarian who could afford clothing this expensive, Rafe. These are stylish, professional outfits."

"We don't want professional. We want chic and sexy."

"I'm supposed to be your assistant, not your lover."

Rafe lifted a shimmery green dress from the rack beside him. "Rialto will expect you to be both."

"What?" Kendra's eyes narrowed. "Why?"

"He figures we're having an affair. Why else do you think he agreed to let me bring you along?"

"You led him to believe that!"

"It's the only logical assumption. Why else wouldn't I work with whoever he already has in place?"

"Because you're comfortable working with me?" she asked archly.

"Comfortable? The two of us? No one would buy that story for a minute."

She glared at him. "I can pretend effectively."

"Good. Then pretend we're lovers." He moved into her space. She flinched, but stood her ground.

"I will not."

"Chicken?"

"Oh! You make me so mad I could spit!"

"The feeling is becoming mutual. Try the green dress on."

"I am not wearing that bit of kelly-green nothing. I couldn't even wear a bra with it!"

"Exactly! Lose the bra, unfasten a few extra buttons, hike up the hemline. We're going for sexy here."

"*You're* going for sexy. *I'm* going for professional." Her eyes glittered with the spark of battle.

"Kendra do you have to fight me on every single point?"

"So it seems. I am not part of your harem."

"For which I am grateful."

The flash of hurt made him regret his hasty words.

"Okay, I surrender. Pick out whatever you want, but if you insist on the prim look, then we have to make Rialto believe that you are anything but prim once the clothing comes off. That means sexy underwear.''

Her face flamed. ''It does not! How is he going to know what I have on under my clothing, Rafe?''

''Because he's going to go through our stuff, Kendra. And if he doesn't believe that you and I are sleeping together, the whole thing will come apart in our faces.''

She hesitated and Rafe drove home his point.

''You tell me you've studied the man. You must have also studied the people who work for him.''

Her rosy cheeks deepened with further color.

''Kendra, his secretary was wearing a dress very similar to that red one over there when I went for the interview.''

Her gaze flew to the sexy red sheath. He'd wanted her to try it on earlier.

''And I promise you,'' Rafe went on, ''she wasn't wearing much of anything underneath it. Rialto surrounds himself with competent beauty. He'll expect no less from me—or from you. This isn't a game, Kendra, it's our lives.''

She tore her eyes from the dress, looked at the one he was holding and began shaking her head. ''I can't wear something like that.''

''Why not?'' But he knew the answer. Kendra might be a whiz on the computer, but she didn't have a clue about her ability to be an alluring woman. Worse, if he pushed her into clothing she wasn't comfortable with, she probably wouldn't have the confidence to carry the outfits off.

''Never mind. We don't have a lot of time. I'll compromise. You pick out the stuff on the outside and I'll pick what you wear underneath.''

Red suffused her features. ''No.''

''Excuse me.''

They both stared at the clerk who'd approached them.

''Can I help you find something specific?''

Kendra tore her gaze from his. ''No. I want to try on this

black dress.'' She lifted a demure black dress from the rack. ''It's simple, elegant, classy. Perfect for any occasion.''

Rafe nodded. ''Including a funeral.''

The clock was ticking away. He was going to have to sell Rialto on the idea that he found Kendra irresistible despite her prissy wardrobe. This was his own fault. He hadn't really expected to take her along. Despite all the time he'd spent with her, he hadn't prepared her for what was important. He should have spent time making her more comfortable in his company. Now she wasn't ready for her role.

He eyed the green dress and decided it was a shame she hadn't at least tried it on. He would have liked to see her in the bright bit of material.

While she was inside the dressing room, he headed for the lingerie department. She wouldn't appreciate the sexy bits of nylon and lace that he selected, but he hadn't been kidding about Rialto. There was no doubt in his mind that the man would have someone search their luggage to learn more about them. Kendra must convey the proper image. He took his selections to the counter and pulled out a credit card. While the clerk rang them up, his gaze landed on a lovely emerald silk gown and matching robe.

''Uh, hold it a minute. What size does that come in?''

''Oh, we should have it in all three sizes, small, medium and large. Isn't it gorgeous?''

''Yes.'' He held up a medium, eyed it critically and chose the small. ''Perfect.''

The young woman giggled and quickly added it to his purchases.

Kendra was waiting when he returned to the dress department. ''Where were you? I was going to show you the black dress.''

''Shopping.''

''Well, you'll be happy to know that I'm going to get that

blouse you liked and that print dress we agreed on in addition to the suits.''

''Okay.''

''I thought you'd be pleased.''

''I am. I'm just worried about the time,'' he lied.

''Oh.''

He reached for his wallet and she started shaking her head.

''I'll pay for them.''

''Kendra, this is part of the deal, remember?''

''I'm not comfortable with this deal.''

''Why not?''

''Because.''

He waited, but she didn't elaborate. ''Because why?''

''Just because.''

''Will that be all, sir?''

He resisted an impulse to add the green dress and nodded. ''You are a stubborn woman.''

''Thank you.''

''But I'm going to follow orders and pay the bill.'' And he handed the woman the credit card while Kendra glared at him. Finally her glance dropped to the bag at his feet.

''What did you buy?''

She pulled a pair of black nylon panties from the top of the bag he'd set at his feet. Other colored scraps of nylon and lace lay beneath it. The peignoir was on the bottom, thank heavens.

Kendra held up the sexy black briefs. ''They don't look like your size.''

The clerk goggled.

Rafe felt his cheeks heat. He took the panties from her fingers and shoved them back inside the bag. The clerk handed him a pen to sign the receipt, her expression openly curious.

''Behave yourself,'' he told Kendra.

"Sorry." She gazed at him innocently. "Did you remember to get yourself a matching bra?"

He ran a hand through his hair in exasperation. He took back his credit card, jammed it into his wallet and gathered up the two shopping bags.

"Grab the other bag and come on. We have to meet Jake."

"Do you think he'll like the black? Maybe you should have gone with virginal white."

"You're really asking for it, you know that?"

They turned away from the counter and Kendra reached back inside the smaller bag of intimate apparel and pulled out the panties again.

"You don't really expect me to wear these, do you?" she asked as they headed for the escalator.

Rafe came to a halt. "Kendra, you said it yourself. Who will know what you wear underneath your clothing except someone who goes through our suitcase? Don't fight me on this, okay? No one else will know." Except him. And standing there watching her holding that scrap of nylon he wanted very much to see what Kendra would look like wearing them and nothing else.

As if she could read his mind she stuffed the panties back in the bag.

"Fine, if it will make you happy—"

"It will," he assured her, unable to shake his mental image of her standing there in those black briefs. "And the answer is yes."

"What was the question?"

"I got you the matching bra."

She wouldn't meet his look. "Are we finished?"

"Shoes?"

"Spiked heels, I suppose?"

"That'd be great—if you can walk in them."

She thrust the other bag into his hands. "You can meet me in the shoe department."

Rafe watched the subtle sway of her backside as she strode away from him. Oh yeah, he really wanted to see her in those panties—but now he added a pair of spiked heels to the image.

Rafe hesitated, then he turned around and went back to the dress department. Kendra had three boxes of shoes on the counter by the time he got downstairs with yet another bag.

"I'll get that," he told her, reaching for his wallet.

"It's already taken care of," she announced.

"What did you buy?"

"Shoes fit for a librarian," she answered smugly. "Shall we go pick up my new glasses? We're going to be late to meet Jake if we don't hurry."

"Don't worry. He'll wait."

The optical center had her glasses waiting. Rafe was pleasantly surprised by Kendra's new frames. Small and lightweight, they reminded him of Penny's glasses. These fit Kendra's face far more attractively than the heavy black frames he was used to seeing her in. Too bad he couldn't have talked her into contacts.

They were walking to meet Jake when Rafe caught her wistful glance at the cart of lead glass crystal pieces. This was near where she'd been grabbed this morning. He would have agreed to stop, but she didn't ask. Cody, rather than Jake, waited for them near the entrance.

"You don't look like Jake to me," he greeted.

"That's what I like about you, Rafe, you're perceptive. Jake had to go to his cabin because the windows he ordered for the renovations he's doing are being delivered. Mitchell grabbed me instead. And I am eternally grateful to you. Mitchell's snapping at everyone over this roundup."

And everyone knew Mitchell tended to be especially hard

on Cody. Rafe figured it was because he was the youngest and the newest member of the Confidentials. Still there were times when Rafe really sympathized with the younger man.

"Looks like we may have more cattle missing," Cody continued. "Hey Kendra, I really like your new glasses."

"Thank you, *Cody.*"

Rafe got the message. He hadn't said anything to her about her choice. In fact, he hadn't complimented her on her new hairstyle either. No wonder she didn't respond to his charm. He hadn't displayed any where she was concerned.

The smile she offered Cody was genuine, lighting up her features. She'd never smiled like that for him.

"Here." Rafe thrust the packages at the younger man. "I need to get something else. I'll be right back. Stay with her," he ordered.

"Don't worry. I don't let *my* women get picked up by other guys."

Rafe bit back a curse. "Watch her!"

"Who put a burr under his saddle?" he heard Cody ask as he strode away.

"You mean he isn't always surly, bossy and a pain in the neck?" she called out mock sweetly.

"Well yeah, but most of his women don't seem to mind."

"*I'm* not one of his women."

"Want to be one of mine?"

Rafe resisted an urge to turn around and slug Cody. Instead he made his way back to the cart in the middle of the mall, cursing under his breath. Bits of glass shimmered, tossing rainbows beneath the high intensity lights of the display. A Pegasus caught his eye, but it was the delicate swan that his hand lifted carefully from its glass perch.

"I'll take this one."

Minutes later, he returned to the west entrance to find they hadn't waited inside for him. They'd gone out to the truck that Cody had pulled up to the door. The two of them sat inside laughing together.

A spear of jealousy lanced him. Kendra had never laughed like that with him either. In fact, he'd never heard her laugh out loud before. It was a compelling sound. One he wanted to hear again.

"All set?" Cody asked.

"Yeah." He climbed in back, annoyed that she was sitting up front and not beside him. He was coming unraveled, that was all there was to it. Rafael Alvarez had never had a jealous bone in his body.

Until now.

Ludicrous. He set his purchase on the floor and decided he wouldn't give her the swan after all. She might read more into the gift than he intended.

Or was he afraid that maybe she wouldn't read enough?

Chapter Seven

"I need to talk with you after dinner," Rafe told her, setting packages down on her bed. "Penny says we're eating early. Half an hour."

Kendra wondered what had put him in such a surly mood. He'd been quiet all the way back to the Smoking Barrel she realized. She hadn't really noticed because Cody had gone out of his way to be funny and talkative. But when Cody had offered to help carry everything inside, Rafe had come to life, practically snapping the other man's head off. Instead of getting angry, Cody had begun to chuckle as if he knew a secret.

Who could understand these people? They were all driving her crazy. Especially Rafe. When he looked at her with those sultry eyes she felt as if her insides were melting. This quivery, fluttery feeling was scary. She mustn't feel this way over Rafe.

"What do we need to talk about?"

"Come're."

The room seemed to shrink. She was much too aware of the big poster bed at his back. A broad back. A strong back. A vast, empty bed.

"Come here, Kendra." He said it softly this time.

Something went wrong with her lungs. She couldn't seem to draw a breath. His eyes shimmered with a look that was dangerous—forbidden—enticing. She took a hesitant step in his direction.

"It occurs to me that I've been negligent about the most important part of your training."

His low-pitched voice mesmerized her. The scent of danger was stronger now but it was overwhelmed by the scent of man—this man.

Excitement thrummed through her body in a heady wave. When she came to a stop directly in front of him she knew she was quivering. Could he see? Did he guess the reason?

"What part is that?"

Her voice sounded as breathless as she felt.

"Lift your head."

"Why?" Her lips were suddenly dry.

"Because I'm going to kiss you."

Her stomach flipped, then contracted. "Oh."

Ever so gently, he removed the glasses from her face, leaving her strangely naked before him. He set them on the dresser with slow, deliberate movements. When he turned back to her, Kendra forgot to breathe.

Slowly, he angled his head and lowered his face to hers. Her eyes fluttered closed while her heart tried to suffocate her with its frantic beating. She shouldn't permit this.

His lips touched hers lightly—feathering across their stiff, dry surface. The contact was electric and more than she could stand. With a tiny moan, she sagged pliantly against him, reaching for the support of his neck because she needed an anchor for the wild sensations rioting inside her.

"Open your lips, Kendra," he breathed.

Her free will melted right along with the rest of her. Knowing it was stupid she parted her lips to allow him entrance. The world spun dizzily. Time lost all meaning. She was lost as his mouth and tongue aroused sensations she had never experienced before. She kissed him back with all the pent-up longing her body clamored to release.

His tongue withdrew, pausing to trace her puffy lips. A mew of protest came from somewhere deep inside her as he lifted his head.

"Shh. Easy." He steadied her with his hands, pillowing her head against the hard wall of his chest. His scent enveloped her. One broad hand stroked her back with soothing sweeps of his fingers and palm.

Her nipples ached with stubborn need and a throbbing curl of desire continued to pulse inside her. She had never experienced such a high state of arousal—had never wanted anyone the way she wanted this man, right now, right here. But as she calmed, embarrassment scalded her face. She couldn't raise her eyes to look up at him.

"Hey, you okay?" He lifted her chin with his knuckle.

"Wh-why?"

"Ah-hem. Excuse me, am I interrupting?"

Kendra would have pulled away at the sound of Penny's voice, but Rafe held her securely. Kendra was thankful that her back was to the open bedroom door.

"I'll be with you in a minute," Rafe said dismissively without turning around. He searched her face as if he'd never seen her before. With the barest of touches, his knuckle stroked her cheek. Every coherent thought she'd ever had flew right out the window. The world winnowed down to just her and this man.

"Why did you kiss me?" She'd meant her voice to sound strong and accusing. Instead it came out whispery and uncertain. His lips lifted in a partial smile.

"Why did you kiss me back?" he asked gently.

Though it cost her, she refused to look away. "That isn't an answer."

"No," he agreed, "but I'm sort of pressed for time. I need to see what Mitchell wants."

She'd forgotten all about Penny!

"We'll talk after dinner."

He kissed the tip of her nose and stepped away before she could protest. No one stood in the doorway as he closed it behind him.

On rubbery legs, she stepped into the connecting bathroom and gripped the vanity for support. She stared at the face of a complete stranger in the mirror, unable to reconcile the flushed skin and throbbing lips with the features she was so familiar with. Her body tingled everywhere from the power of that kiss.

What had she done?

Oh, lord, she was very much afraid she knew exactly what she had done. And it was going to complicate everything.

The door connecting to Penny's room opened without warning.

"Oops. Sorry again," Penny apologized.

"That's okay. I'm done in here."

"Are you...all right?"

Kendra's chagrin deepened. How much had Penny seen?

"I'm fine," she lied.

"Rafe said you laid out your two attackers today. I'm impressed."

"Don't be. Fear is a hugely successful motivating factor. And Rafe is a good teacher," she tacked on. "The bathroom is all yours. I'll give you some privacy."

"Kendra?"

She paused, hand on the doorknob leading into her own room.

"He's not the marrying kind."

Kendra didn't pretend to misunderstand. "Don't worry." She managed a smile of sorts. "I'm not either."

Penny didn't appear convinced. Her expression offered sympathy and something more. "I don't want to see you get hurt."

Too late. But she kept the thought inside. She smiled back at Penny, welcoming this olive branch of friendship. It had been a long time since she'd had a friend she could talk with face-to-face. On the other hand, they did share a peculiar sort of kinship. Both of them had fallen under Rafe's sensual spell and were struggling to endure.

"Thank you, Penny. Don't worry. I'm a survivor."

"Some things are easier to survive than others. I'll see you at dinner."

Kendra closed the door thoughtfully. She liked Penny more and more. She was glad the feeling seemed to be mutual. She still had twenty minutes before she had to be downstairs and she needed something to hold her riotous thoughts at bay. She turned to the new clothing and began emptying bags.

Penny was right, Kendra thought, hanging up the first of the outfits. Falling in love with Rafe was the most foolish, stupid, disastrous thing she could do. Especially now when her goal was so close at hand. When this was all over, he would hate her for using him. They all would.

She hung the clothing automatically, chiding herself as she went. "If a person can fall in love this quickly, they can fall out again just as fast," she muttered. "It's nothing but pheromones. Heaven knows that man's got more than his share. No wonder he has a harem."

She reached for the next bag and realized it was the one Rafe had picked up after she left to go buy shoes. She hesitated, but curiosity got the better of her. Folded inside was the kelly-green dress he had pointed out on the rack earlier. The one she couldn't wear with a bra.

Her stomach cartwheeled while her heart began to pound insanely. She clutched the shimmery material, unable to withdraw her gaze. The dress was made for seduction. In fact, it practically screamed a sensual promise. She couldn't wear something like this. She *wouldn't* wear it.

But she wanted to.

Why had he bought it? A taunt, or because he genuinely wanted to see her in it? Did she dare try it on?

Before she could change her mind, she skimmed out of her sweats and started to slip into the dress. But no, with that neckline, she'd have to take off her bra. It seemed like a sinfully wicked thing to be doing in this house with the late afternoon sun filling the room, but Kendra unhooked her plain white cotton bra and dropped it on the bed. The dress slid over her head, settling against her body like a second skin.

"Oh!" Shock held her motionless as she stared at her reflection in the mirror over the dresser. She looked... different. If only she could see the entire image. The woman in the mirror certainly didn't resemble a computer nerd. With her still puffy lips and her hair tousled around her face, the image looked very much like a magazine ad for a sensual perfume or something.

There was an abrupt knock on the bathroom door, pulling her from her thoughts. Before she could move, the door opened and Penny stuck her head inside. "Bathroom's fr— Oh. You look... Wow!" And Penny appeared totally stunned.

"I didn't—"

"That dress is the sexiest thing I've ever seen. It's absolutely perfect on you. You'll knock them dead."

Kendra didn't know what to say. Penny's admiration was obviously genuine.

"What do you think I'd have to do to get Rafe to take *me* shopping sometime?"

"This isn't me," Kendra said quickly.

"Sure it is. And I'm impressed. Rafe's in the wrong line of work. He should be selling makeovers to women everywhere. He'd make a fortune. Oh. I'm sorry. I'm embarrassing you."

"No. Yes."

"Don't be embarrassed. You look fantastic. But you ought to try contacts. I like your new glasses but—"

"I did. I just didn't tell Rafe."

"You mean you got a pair of contacts?"

"Yes, I just don't want Rafe to know that."

"Mind if I ask why?"

"He was giving orders and—"

Penny laughed out loud. "Say no more. Men are a pain in the patootie."

"Especially Rafe."

"Has he seen you in this dress?"

"No!"

"Good. Spring it on him. I'd give anything to be a fly on the wall when he does see you in it. You're going to knock him over."

"Oh, I can't wear this in public."

"Why not?"

"Because…I…because I can't."

"Sure you can. Hold your head up, put your shoulders back and walk like you mean business. You'll have men panting in your wake."

"Good grief."

Penny grinned at her conspiratorially. "I'll see you downstairs. You've got about ten minutes. There's a full-length mirror in my room if you want to get the entire affect."

"No! I mean thanks. Maybe later."

Penny smiled a little wistfully. "I wonder if that dress comes in my size. I'd love to see Neil's expression if I went out with him looking like that."

Kendra nearly sagged with relief as Penny left the way she had entered. She pulled off the dress with haste, put it on a hanger and shoved it to the very back of the closet, away from all the other new outfits. She stared at the remaining bag feeling snake bit. The sexy black briefs were still on top and she glimpsed other bits of scanty nylon and lace beneath.

No way. She couldn't wear any underwear that he had selected for her. Not even pretty, silky things like these. Her fingers drifted over the garments hesitantly until she reached the bottom. What on earth?

Rafe had a thing for green, she decided as she pulled emerald satin from the bottom of the bag. Once again she found it hard to catch her breath. The gown and matching robe were made for sin. A woman would only wear something like this to bed for one purpose—to have a man remove it. Slowly.

While secretly delighted by Rafe's sensuous surprises, she was mildly alarmed by her reactions to the decadent items. If Rafe wanted to charge her emotions he'd succeeded beyond his wildest dreams.

She had to remind herself that he wasn't really coming on to her. This was all part of the show he wanted her to put on. She must keep that in mind at all times. It would serve Rafe right if she didn't even mention the gown, or the dress. Let him stew over her reaction to finding the two items. Would she, or wouldn't she wear them?

She stuffed the bit of sexy lingerie in the bottom dresser drawer and slammed it shut. Eyeing the bag, she decided she would deal with the rest later.

Much later.

Now if she could just put the memory of Rafe's kiss away as easily.

"KENDRA, I WONDER if you'd mind joining us in the library?" Mitchell asked as they finished dinner. Her gaze flew to Rafe first, before nodding nervously.

Maddie stood up. "I think that's my cue to help Rosa."

"It isn't necessary," Mitchell scolded.

"Of course it is."

"Dinner was wonderful," Rafe told her sincerely.

"That's for sure," Cody piped up. "Nobody does flaky rolls like you and Rosa. Maddie, I've been giving this a lot of thought and I think you should leave this dump and run off with me."

"You're too young," she said with a smile.

"I'll grow older."

"Not if you don't stop poaching on the boss's lady," Brady told him.

"Knock it off and let's get this meeting underway," Mitchell ordered. But he paused beside Maddie and laid a hand tenderly on her shoulder. Maddie smiled up at him with such devotion it was almost painful to see. Rafe shook his head. He still couldn't understand why Mitchell hadn't married the neighboring rancher a long time ago. Neither could Maddie. He knew it was the major source of irritation between the two of them.

Rafe fell into step behind Kendra and Penny.

"Someone got inside our computer system again yesterday," Penny said quietly as she led the way to the library.

Because he was watching her so closely, he saw the telltale start Kendra gave.

"We have safeguards but they don't seem to be enough. I'd like to pump you on ways to protect our computer system from outside tampering," Penny continued.

"I don't think you have to worry about yesterday, does she, Kendra?"

A sudden silence fell on the group as everyone looked from Rafe to Kendra. Something that might have been shame clouded her features, but Kendra didn't look away.

"That depends on how much of a threat you still think I am."

"You got inside? How?" Penny asked.

"I accessed your system from my laptop upstairs."

"Why?" Mitchell growled.

"Truthfully? I was looking for blueprints to the house."

"What for?" Jake asked.

Kendra shrugged apologetically. "I was curious about your hidden operation center. I assumed there must be one and I've noticed the basement area doesn't cover the entire width of the house. I wanted to see the plans to see if my hunch was right."

Mitchell looked from Kendra to Rafe. Rafe didn't even try to suppress his grin. "I told you she was smart."

Mitchell chomped down on his unlit cigar and harrumphed.

"Smart? Somehow that's not how I remember the conversation," Cody teased.

"He thought I was stupid?" Kendra asked archly.

"No," Brady said, "I think it was more on the lines of being a pain in the—"

Rafe took a step toward Brady who spread his hands and grinned.

"You wouldn't hit a married man, would you?"

"Yes."

"Save it for later," Mitchell commanded.

Rafe watched Kendra's reaction as Penny activated the opening for the bookcase, revealing the elevator hidden behind.

"Oh. How stupid. I never thought to check the width of the house from the outside to see if that matched."

Mitchell looked pained, but Rafe's admiration grew.

"Real secret agent stuff, huh, Kendra?" Cody asked.

Her eyes sparkled behind her new glasses. "Better than the movies. You'll be happy to know that your house plans aren't in your computer system so this isn't something an outsider can tap into."

"But you did get inside our system," Penny said.

"Afraid so."

"Can you fix it?" Mitchell demanded.

"You mean build you some better safeguards? Of course."

"You're hired," Penny said immediately.

The elevator doors parted and Rafe studied Kendra's reaction as she gazed around curiously.

"Welcome to the real headquarters of Texas Confidential," he said softly against her hair. She turned and looked up at him, her expression completely vulnerable.

His groin stirred to life. He'd been walking around mildly aroused ever since he'd kissed her. Right now he had an insatiable urge to tug those glasses from her face and kiss her again.

"Kendra, have a seat," Mitchell invited.

Cody immediately scooted forward to hold out a chair for her at the briefing table. Before Rafe could protest, he slid into the seat on her left, even though it wasn't where he usually sat. Rafe gave him a warning glare and took the chair on her right. Mitchell sat across from them while the others grabbed seats at random.

Mitchell settled his cane against his chair and looked at each of them in turn, coming to rest on Kendra. His silver lighter appeared between his fingers. "Rafe told us what happened today, but I want to hear it from you."

Kendra didn't hesitate. Once again Rafe was pleased by the concise way she described the attack and attackers.

"And you have no idea who they were or what they wanted?"

"None."

"I ran the plate number Rafe gave me," Penny piped up. "The plate belongs to a 1999 Toyota, not a pickup truck. The owner is a thirty-three-year-old secretary who happens to be married to a deputy sheriff. Imagine how he's going to feel to learn someone switched his plates without his knowledge."

"They probably stole the truck then, too," Brady said.

Jake frowned. "Where does that leave us?"

"Wondering if our operation has been compromised or if someone is out to get Kendra for personal reasons," Jake said immediately.

"As I've explained to Rafe, I don't have any enemies that I know of."

"You do now," he pointed out.

"That leaves us with the possibility that this mission is compromised." Mitchell stated.

"How?" Rafe demanded.

Mitchell made a process out of lighting his cigar. Once again, he looked at each of them in turn, resting on Kendra. "Would Rialto be keeping tabs on you?"

"Of course not. I doubt he even knows I exist. Why would he?"

"Because of your aunt and uncle? Isn't that why you want to work with us? Revenge for their deaths?"

Her cheeks paled, but she raised her chin and looked straight at him. "You left out my cousin."

"Do you want to tell us about it?" Mitchell asked.

"There's nothing to tell. It's all a matter of record which you must have seen. Rialto shot them to death, then rigged the furnace so the house would fill with gas until it exploded." She leaned forward intently. "He has to be stopped. Life means nothing to him. He has to pay! Whatever it takes, I'll do it. The man is a monster."

"So it's possible he knows of your connection to his former chauffeur," Mitchell pursued.

"It's a matter of public record, but why would he? My aunt, uncle and cousin didn't even share the same last name. And if he did know, I doubt he'd care. I'm less than nothing to him. We've had no dealings of any kind. I was just a kid when he killed them. I can't imagine that he keeps track of all the relatives of all his victims. That would be a full-time job," she added scornfully.

"But you recently examined his bank records," Rafe pointed out.

"The only people who know that are sitting right here in this room. I didn't tamper and I didn't leave any traces behind."

"Maybe yes, maybe no. I knew someone had been in our system," Penny pointed out.

"I wasn't taking precautions here. All along I intended to show you how vulnerable your system is. How do you think I knew so much about you and your plans to go after Rialto in the first place? Everything I needed to know is in your computer for anyone with the skill and knowledge to access."

"Could Rialto do what you did?"

"Sure, if he had the abilities, which he doesn't."

"But if he has someone on staff…" Jake began.

"If he has someone as good as me, and if he knows you exist, then yes, it's not difficult. All a hacker needs is time and perseverance."

"There are measures to keep that from happening," Rafe said.

"Sure, but they aren't foolproof. I deliberately tripped yours when I went in to show you how easy it is. You're a sitting duck for a skilled hacker."

"Which you are." Mitchell leaned back against his chair.

"Yes."

"Then perhaps we should scrub this mission."

"No!" Kendra jerked in her chair. "This is the best chance we've got!"

Rafe noticed the pronoun and relaxed. She had come to think of herself as part of the team.

"I can access anything on his computer," Kendra insisted. "Don't you realize what that means? Rafe and I will be inside his home overnight. His personal files will be ours, things like letters, notes, all sorts of stuff that could prove useful.''

''And if he knows you're coming?'' Mitchell asked mildly.

''I've seen his personnel records, remember? If he's got a genuine hacker on staff I'll be amazed. Imagine the trust that would require. Rialto's private files would be vulnerable to attack. He'd never knowingly trust anyone that far. I can almost guarantee he hasn't been in your system. Trust me.''

Mitchell puffed away on his cigar, but his eyes were watchful. ''It's Rafe who has to do that. If you're wrong, Rialto will kill you both.''

WHEN THE MEETING finally broke up, Brady and Jake headed home to their wives while Cody went to the kitchen to raid another slice of Rosa's pie. Rafe left Kendra showing Mitchell and Penny several things on the computer system. He smiled at Maddie and Rosa, snatched a cold soda from the refrigerator and walked outside to the front porch where he could relax and watch the night steal away the evening.

The meeting had gone well. Mitchell's concern was understandable but they were going to go ahead with the plan. Rafe hadn't wanted Kendra along initially, but after what had happened this past week, he had changed his mind. She would be an asset. His only problem would be keeping his hands off her.

He'd never expected her to kiss him back this afternoon, and certainly not with the untried passion she'd exhibited. The feel of her body and the taste of her were firmly embedded in his mind. Her untutored body had responded in a way that was exhilarating and new. She didn't practice any of the coy, flirtatiousness that he was used to. In fact, she didn't seem to have any artifices at all.

Cody stepped outside and gave a start. ''Geeze, you tryin' to give me a heart attack? I didn't see you sitting there.''

"Storm's comin' in over the mountains. You can see the lightning in the distance."

"Great. Just what we need. More rain. Jake is not going to be happy. This will slow down the construction on his cabin even further."

"Uh-huh."

"Have you seen the plans for that addition he's building? I'll have to stop calling it a cabin. It'll be a full-scale house once he's done."

"He needs to accommodate Elena and Abby," Rafe reminded Cody mildly. "Did you con Rosa and Maddie out of more pie?"

"Sure. Maddie even threw on some ice cream."

"Better watch it or you'll be too fat to sit a horse. And I wouldn't let Slim catch you flirting with Rosa if I were you." Rafe saw the flash of teeth as Cody grinned.

"I figured I was safe since he's standing watch tonight. Mitchell and Maddie went upstairs already. I don't think he's feeling good."

"You noticed that too, huh?"

"Hard to miss. He ought to see the doctor for a checkup."

"You want to tell him that?"

"Not me, pal. He growls at me enough as it is. I just don't understand why he doesn't marry her."

"Their business."

"I know, but it seems so stupid, you know?"

Rafe didn't bother agreeing.

"Rosa said she was going to lock up in a few minutes. I'm headin' over to the bunkhouse to watch some television. You coming?"

"Guess so."

The door slammed open sending both men whirling in alarm. Kendra came to an abrupt halt. Light from the hall streamed over her hair and shoulders giving her an other-worldly sort of look.

"You ring-tailed bastard," she cried. "You flea-ridden louse!"

"She must mean you," Cody said. "I think I'll head back to the bunkhouse."

Kendra ignored the interruption. "How dare you? I'm not leaving, do you understand? Get it through your dense, thick skull that I don't care what tactics you use. I *am* going with you or you aren't going either! I warned you I could ruin this, and I meant it."

"You want to calm down and tell me what you're yelling about?" Rafe asked softly.

She practically spit in anger. But it was the sheen of tears glistening in her eyes that got to him.

"You can slice every outfit I own, I don't care. I'll just replace them later, but I *am* going with you."

Something cold unfurled in his stomach.

"Someone cut your clothing?" Cody asked. Kendra didn't seem to hear the question.

"I didn't push it about the snake because you made sure no one got hurt. And I probably did more damage to your 'friends' today than the scare they gave me. But cutting up my clothing is pretty juvenile, don't you think, Alvarez? I noticed you didn't hack up the green dress. Pretty telling, wouldn't you say?"

She pushed past him when he went to reach for her and ran toward the corral.

"What's she talking about?" Cody asked.

"I don't know, but I intend to find out. Go with her."

Rafe reached for the back door, his stomach muscles churning bile as he raced up the stairs. He came to a halt in her doorway, surveying the wreckage spread before him.

Every suit, every dress they had purchased, lay strewn across the floor and the bed, viciously cut beyond repair.

Chapter Eight

"Whoa! What a mess."

Rafe tore his gaze from the heart-stopping scene of destruction and whirled on Cody. He flung the other man back against the wall, fist cocked at his side. "I told you to go with her! Whoever did this may still be here!"

Cody tore free and sprinted for the stairs without a sound. Penny flung open her door and stepped out. "What's all the commotion?"

Grimly, Rafe gestured her forward. "Have a look."

He stepped inside and walked over to the gaping closet. The few items of clothing Kendra had originally brought with her still hung from hangers. At the very back of the closet the green cocktail dress was barely visible behind a baggy sweatshirt. Whoever had done this had probably overlooked it.

Or they wanted Kendra to think exactly what she did think.

"Who did this?" Penny asked.

"Good question. I'll let Mitchell know."

"You don't think Kendra…?"

Rafe swore. "Of course not."

"Okay, I'll check with Rosa to see if she or Maddie heard or saw anything. Where is Kendra?"

"She ran toward the corral. I sent Cody after her. She thought I did it," he admitted bleakly.

Penny gaped. "You can't be serious."

Rafe shrugged and headed for Mitchell's room. He didn't want to admit how much Kendra's accusations had hurt. He tried to tell himself he could see why she made them, but that didn't take away the sting.

KENDRA SPURRED the horse on recklessly, chasing across the open fields. Tears dried on her cheeks or were whipped away by the wind. She'd been bitterly wounded by what she saw as Rafe's betrayal, but even as she finally slowed the large chestnut horse to a more sedate pace, she recognized the foolishness of her accusations.

If she'd paused to think, even for a minute instead of instantly reacting, she would have realized Rafe wouldn't have done something like that. Maybe he didn't want her along, but the snake and the attack at the mall and now tonight… Kendra shook her head. Not Rafe. He might have hired someone to test her new skills, but he wouldn't have done it in such a way that they had to file a police report. She had an enemy on the Smoking Barrel all right, but it wasn't Rafe.

She didn't want to believe it was Penny either, but Penny was the next obvious person. Penny had a crush on Rafe. Penny had seen Rafe kissing her. And Penny had been distant and cold when Kendra first arrived. In fact, this sudden turnaround was suspicious itself.

How could Penny view her as a rival for Rafe's affections? Of all people, Penny knew what was really going on. Besides, even Penny had said Rafe wasn't the marrying kind. That kiss he'd given Kendra had been for show—to get her to loosen up. Rafe wanted her to behave like a woman having an affair with him but he wasn't seriously interested in her.

Didn't Penny understand that?

Maybe not. Kendra and Rafe *had* been spending a great deal of time together. Perhaps Penny thought Rafe was carrying over the playacting into reality. Face it, in her dreams, hadn't Kendra briefly fantasized the same thing?

It would be so easy to fall for a man like Rafe. Kendra didn't blame his harem one bit. The man reeked of charm and self-confidence. He made a woman feel special just being near him. Kendra had to keep reminding herself that the warmth in his eyes, the thrilling way he touched her, was the same way he treated every woman he came in contact with. The knowledge was depressing.

Mentally, Kendra shrugged off thoughts of Rafe, and tried concentrating on other possibilities. There were no other possibilities. She had never had an enemy in her life—except Rialto. And Rialto didn't even know she existed. No, the trouble had started after she met Rafe. That meant it was connected to Texas Confidential, and that brought her right back to Rafe and Penny.

From the start, Penny had been polite, but cool. Sort of the way she treated Lydia, even though anyone could see Rafe wasn't serious about Lydia.

But did Lydia know that?

The new thought wouldn't go away. Lydia obviously didn't view Kendra as a rival, but it wouldn't take much of a stretch to envision the charming Lydia turning vicious. Only vicious enough to sneak into the house and hack up her clothing?

"Lydia has never once acted jealous around me," she muttered aloud. That still left Phoebe or Tammy or Janet or someone she had yet to meet.

"If I assume Rafe is the motivating factor here I've got too many possibilities to calculate."

But none of them had free access to the Smoking Barrel. *Only Penny.*

"I don't want it to be Penny."

She admired the other woman. In fact, she was starting to like all of the people connected with Texas Confidential.

Sitting in that meeting tonight, guilt had churned her stomach over the act of betrayal she planned to commit. They were professional, dedicated agents who would hate her when this was all over. To bad she couldn't have met them under different circumstances.

The horse came to a creek and hesitated. Kendra urged him forward, but he balked at stepping in what was no doubt ice-cold water from the runoff in the mountains. She let him have his head and he plodded beside the creek instead. He stopped to sniff a patch of ground when suddenly he pricked up his ears and turned his head alertly. Kendra twisted in the saddle.

A horse and rider were bearing down on them, coming at a good clip. Rafe? The bark of the rifle startled her as well as her horse.

He was shooting at her?

Kendra kicked her horse into a run. The other rider was still a good distance off, but he was closing fast. Her horse needed little urging, but the situation was dangerous. Loose rock and soil made the footing uncertain. If her horse stumbled...

Up ahead a stand of cedars broke the desolate landscape. If she reached them, maybe she could use them as a temporary shield. She tossed a look over her shoulder. Without moonlight overhead it was too dark to see much, and the rider was still too far away to make out any details.

The creek bed drifted down in a shallow ravine that unfortunately grew steeper and more narrow the farther into it she went. Belatedly, Kendra realized she'd made a poor choice. She should have sent the horse across the stream bed. Now she wouldn't be able to get him up and out of here without turning around.

"Whoa, boy. Easy." She brought the lathered animal to a halt and slid a hand down his neck. Saddle leather creaked as Kendra surveyed her surroundings. There was no longer any sign or sound of the other rider. She couldn't have lost him. There was no place else for her to go. So where was he?

Distant lightning illuminated the sky. The world took on an eerie cast. "Great, just what I need."

She realized she'd ridden a good distance from the main house. What if she'd ridden far enough to stumble into the rustlers she kept hearing so much about? Maybe he'd fired at her to scare her away.

"Well, it worked, I'm scared. But now what am I going to do?"

The bark of a nearby scrub pine suddenly splintered. The sound of the shot echoed as an afterthought down the ravine. The other rider hadn't given up. He'd crossed the stream and moved to a position of power above her! He could cut her off if she tried to double back, but going forward wasn't a good option. The arroyo plunged deeper and deeper. The sides were already impossibly steep. There was little cover beyond a few sparse trees. She couldn't stay here.

A second shot sounded. Lightning splintered the sky. Thunder rocked the ground. Her horse danced nervously, whinnying in protest. Another shot rang out. Without warning, her horse reared, squealing in pain. She struggled to bring him under control but a clap of thunder spooked him past any hope of that. Kendra was thrown in an undignified heap hard enough to jar the air from her lungs. The horse whirled and streaked away leaving her totally vulnerable to the gunman.

Kendra scrambled to her feet and began to run. She heard, more than saw the splinter of a nearby rock shear away as the rifle spoke again. Pulse-pounding fear drove her over a boulder. She crouched beside it as the first raindrop landed with a loud splat.

Kendra squirmed farther back against another rock. A cluster of mesquite sprawled beside her. That would hardly serve as adequate cover, but it was all she had.

Rain began to fall in earnest. She had to get out of here. Kendra began to scramble up the rocky side of the ravine. Thunder merged with the panic roaring in her ears. The gunman couldn't keep missing all night.

Unless that was his intent.

She wasn't prepared to take that chance. Rain blurred her vision. Kendra glimpsed the person in the next blast of lightning. The figure was on foot, too, moving down to get a better shot. Frantically, Kendra began to climb, trying to angle away from him.

Rain soaked her to the skin. Footing quickly became treacherous. Loud claps of thunder applauded the lightning, making her cringe. Shivering, she sought toeholds in the steep sides of her prison. She didn't bother looking for her stalker. She'd probably fall before he shot her.

Nothing in Rafe's training had covered this particular scenario. Scrub pine tore at her clothing as she plunged into their protection. Lightning and thunder clashed immediately overhead. Kendra cowered, more afraid of Mother Nature than the gunman. The lightning was like nothing she'd ever seen before. Each bolt left her momentarily blinded. And beneath the fury of the storm a new sound was building. The roaring, rushing sound of water.

"WHAT DO YOU MEAN she's gone?" Rafe grabbed Cody by the shirtfront.

"I screwed up, okay?"

"No it is not okay!" Rafe felt violent in a way he never had before. Still gripping Cody's shirt, his other hand fisted.

"Do you want to hear what happened or would you rather punch me out?"

Rafe shoved Cody backward, trying to get a grip on his fear and anger. The person who had done that to Kendra's belongings was dangerous.

"What happened?" Mitchell demanded, coming up behind them.

"Dusty threw a shoe," Cody explained. "Slim came back to get Chester. He saddled him, then stopped to use the bathroom. Kendra took Chester."

"Why didn't you stop her?" Rafe demanded.

Cody's eyes blazed. "She was on him and out of the corral before I could reach her. Slim's saddling Whicker. Now if you want to waste more time by taking a poke at me, go ahead."

Rafe curbed the primitive impulse to release his tension by taking a swing at the younger man. It wasn't Cody's fault, it was his own. Kendra was his responsibility. He should have gone after her as soon as she made the accusation and dragged her back inside with him.

"Slim says this storm could be a bad one," Cody called after him as he started to run for the barn. "He heard it on the radio."

Rafe didn't acknowledge the warning. Storm or no storm, he needed to get to Kendra before the person who savaged her room did the same thing to her. Rain would wipe out her path and Rafe wasn't an accomplished tracker to begin with.

"She headed straight into the storm," Slim told him as he entered the barn. "I'm saddling up so I'll be right behind you," he added.

Slim was a tracker.

"Thanks." Rafe swung up into the saddle. Whicker side-stepped nervously to one side. Rafe gentled him with practiced movements before sending him out into the night at a gallop.

While Kendra had a head start, if she gave Chester his head she would probably travel in a fairly straight line. She shouldn't be too difficult to find. She wasn't riding with a destination in mind. Convincing her that he had nothing to do with what had happened might be another story, but he'd worry about that after he found her.

The storm spread across the sky like a vengeful wraith. He winced as lightning lit the empty landscape. The added danger made riding a risky thing to be doing, but he had no choice. There weren't many places she could take cover. Part of him expected to meet Kendra any moment on her way back to the ranch. But as Whicker ate up the ground, further and further from the ranch, he began to worry.

By the time he finally spotted a horse moving toward him through the rain in a frenzied run, worry had given way to an anxiety that bordered on outright panic. Then he saw that the horse was riderless.

Ice-cold panic settled in his stomach. Rafe directed Whicker to intercept. Chester slowed as if grateful to see another living creature in this nightmare. Rafe reached for the dangling reins and brought the animal to a quivering stop.

His own heart threatened to stop as well when he ran his hand down the lathered neck and his fingers came away dark with blood. Chester squealed and pulled away. Rafe let him go. The animal wasn't seriously hurt and he was well trained. He'd continue his path back to the ranch and safety.

Rafe tried to push down his panic. Up ahead, Garvey Creek wound its way through a ravine before it ultimately dumped into Ash Pond. Had she crossed the stream? There was a very real danger of flash flooding. The wind-driven rain made visibility difficult, but the memory of Chester's wound spurred him forward.

At the creek he hesitated. In a terrifying display of lighting, he glimpsed another horse at the top of the ridge some
distance off. Even as he strained to see, someone mounted
the horse and turned the animal away at a dead run.

Rafe debated going after the rider, but swiftly moving
water began rising up around his horse's ankles. And despite
the storm, he heard the chilling sound of water rushing down
the shallow creek bed. Rafe urged Whicker up the rocky
slope ahead of the water that raced through the narrow chan-
nel. In what seemed like seconds, the stream spilled from
its banks.

At the top of the ridge, Rafe swung down from the saddle.
He couldn't have said what made him stop to peer over the
edge, but a movement several yards down on the wall caught
his attention. A lone figure clung there as the water swelled
higher and higher.

In his gut, he knew it was Kendra. Rafe grabbed the rope
from his saddle, knotting one end around a broken cedar and
wrapping part of it around his own body. Slim appeared
before he could descend.

"I'll anchor you," the older man shouted to be heard.

Rafe nodded and began to work his way down to Kendra.
He also yelled to her to be heard over the thunder from
above and below.

"Kendra! Don't move left!"

Obviously, she couldn't hear him. She continued to move
sideways away from him, slipping dangerously on the wet
rocks.

"Kendra! Stay where you are!"

If she fell into that raging water she wouldn't have a
chance.

Rafe began working his way down to her. The footing
was treacherous. Kendra had stopped moving, because she'd
run out of places to climb. The rock face was shear several
feet above her.

"Don't move!"

She heard him. Her upturned face told him of her terror and her exhaustion. Rafe renewed his efforts, slipping, sliding, bleeding from where he'd torn a nail. The water level was already dangerously close to where she waited.

"Grab my hand."

"You'll fall!"

"No, I won't. Come on. We don't have much time."

Her fingers were ice cold, but her grip was strong. Quickly he wrapped the extra length of rope around her quaking body, praying it would support both of them. Together, they began to climb. He felt the pull when she slipped. He reached back for her, nearly losing his own tentative grip on the exposed root of a tree.

"Come on, you can do this!"

Kendra never made a sound. Shivers wracked her body, but she let him guide her hands and began struggling all over again. They climbed with equal measures of desperation and panic as Slim took up the slack. The water had stopped rising, but it rushed beneath their feet with deadly force. Thunder and lightning still savaged the night. It had finally moved off so it was no longer directly overhead. The wind, however, picked up, driving needles of rain against their backs.

Slim tugged Rafe back up and over the lip. Together, they had to physically pull Kendra the last few feet. Her movements had become uncoordinated with cold and exhaustion. Her sodden sweat suit clung to her body as she lay in the dirt, totally spent.

"We have to go."

Her eyes remained firmly closed. He could hear her teeth chattering. His own shirt was plastered against his skin. He lifted her to put her in the saddle.

"I c-c-can d-do it."

Rafe didn't waste energy arguing with her. He slung her

up and onto the saddle. When he would have mounted as well and turned Whicker for home, Slim produced jackets and slickers.

"Penny figured you might need these."

Slim, Rafe realized for the first time was already dressed in a yellow slicker. "Penny's a genius," he said gratefully.

He mounted behind Kendra and drew the jacket on over her shivering form before pulling on his own. They were both already wet clear through, but it would help. He tugged her body back against his own, hoping their mutual body heat would offer some extra warmth.

"Okay?" he asked against her ear.

"Y-yes," she got past chattering teeth. "He s-shot m-m-my horse."

Rafe cursed. "Who?"

"I d-don't know."

"Just a flesh wound," Slim offered. "Chester's a right smart old fella. That horse is already back at the stable by now."

But someone had shot at her.

Anger offered Rafe some protection from the cold, though he'd begun feeling the effects as well. If he'd crossed the stream ahead of the flood, he could have caught the bastard.

And Kendra would have died.

"Th-th-ank you."

Rafe squeezed her gently in response. Kendra fell silent.

"Rustlers?" Slim asked as they turned the horses toward home.

"I don't know, but there isn't much point to going after the bastards now," Rafe told him.

Rafe urged Whicker toward the house. Penny and Maddie met them on the front porch. The women hustled Kendra inside the moment he swung her down from the saddle.

"I'll take Whicker," Slim offered.

Rafe nodded gratefully as Mitchell appeared on the front porch. "Thanks, Slim. I appreciate all your help tonight."

"Grab a shower and come back over to the house," Mitchell ordered Rafe.

Rafe hurried, glad to be out of his cold, wet clothing. The rain had tapered off by the time he returned to the main house. Rosa had coffee and hot chocolate waiting along with slices of pie and cookies on the table. She'd already gone back to bed, but Maddie rose and offered to serve him.

"Sit down, Maddie. I know where everything is. Where's Kendra?"

"Still upstairs. Penny went to check on her."

Rafe poured a mug of the steaming cocoa and walked over and sat down. Tersely, he described what he'd seen and done.

"She probably would have made it up without me or Slim," he ended gruffly.

"No, I wouldn't." Kendra walked forward wearing an old flannel robe of Penny's. Her eyes were fixed on him. "I owe you both my life."

Silently, Maddie poured her a mug of hot chocolate. She accepted with a wan smile. She took the chair directly across from him and began to recite what had happened.

Mitchell fingered his lighter, though surprisingly, there was no cigar in sight. "No idea who it was?"

"He was never close enough for me to see."

"You didn't recognize the horse?" Mitchell asked Rafe.

"I wasn't close enough either."

"So it could have been connected to what happened upstairs," Mitchell said thoughtfully.

"Or I rode too close to where the rustlers were operating," Kendra said softly without meeting Rafe's gaze.

Mitchell rocked back in his chair looking thoughtful. "Perhaps it might be best if you return home and—"

"No!"

Everyone looked at Rafe in surprise, including Kendra whose own voiced protest had been drowned out by his.

"If someone is stalking her, she's safer with us," he said.

"Not so far," Penny pointed out.

"That will change," Mitchell announced firmly. "Kendra, I don't want you going anywhere or doing anything without someone beside you."

"I pee alone," Kendra said.

Mitchell scowled, but she surprised chuckles and smiles out of the others. Rafe felt unaccountably proud of her.

Kendra focused her attention on him. Her skin was pale, but color had returned to her face. "I owe you an apology. I should have known from the start you had nothing to do with what happened upstairs. By the time I came to my senses the gunman was chasing me. I'm really sorry, Rafe." She turned to Mitchell. "And I apologize for causing so much trouble. Rafe could have been killed trying to rescue me. It was a stupid reaction on my part."

"Kendra—" Rafe tried to interrupt.

"Please. Hear me out. I don't believe these attacks on me are related to the Rialto investigation, but if you want me to go, I'll understand."

"You can hardly leave now," Penny said into the silence. "Rialto is expecting Rafe to bring his assistant."

"You could take my place."

"No." Rafe said forcefully. "Penny's good, but she doesn't know computers the way you do. You were right about that. We go in as planned."

He looked to Mitchell who nodded slowly.

"I'll go see to your bedroom," Rafe said.

Mitchell shook his head. "Cody, and I already took care of it."

"Did you get anything?" Rafe demanded.

"Nothing decisive," the older man stated. "Some hairs, a few prints. We bagged everything, took pictures, tested what we could. I'll have Cody run the evidence into town for a better analysis first thing tomorrow.''

"Thank you," Kendra said softly.

"Thanks aren't necessary," Mitchell said gruffly.

"Why don't you spend the rest of the night in my room?" Penny offered. "I've got some work to do tonight anyhow."

"I couldn't do that!"

"Excellent idea," Mitchell announced and pushed back his chair. "We'll need to keep your room closed until tomorrow, Kendra. Okay, people. It's late and we've got a long day ahead of us. I called Brady and Jake. They'll be here in the morning."

"But—"

"Do what they say, Kendra," Rafe advised.

"Don't worry, I won't go without a bed tonight," Penny promised.

Maddie slipped her arm in Mitchell's. He smiled with his eyes, but Rafe noted that he actually seemed to be leaning on his cane tonight. Frowning, Rafe watched them leave.

Kendra started to reach for the nearest cups and plates.

"Rosa will get those in the morning," Penny said.

"I'm not ready to go upstairs just yet."

Penny looked from Kendra to Rafe and nodded. "Okay. Good night. Holler if you need anything."

"You want to wash or dry?" he asked Kendra.

"You don't have to stay."

"Neither do you." He flipped her a towel and walked to the sink, filling it with hot, sudsy water.

They cleaned up the few dishes in a silence that was oddly comfortable.

"I don't really know how to thank you," she said softly, hanging the dish towel on a hook.

Rafe leaned back against the sink. Thinking about what could have happened tonight made him physically ill. "Come're."

Kendra stood in front of him.

"According to the code of the old West, heroes are supposed to get kissed by the damsels that they rescue."

Slowly, the hesitation left her expression, replaced by a gradual smile.

"Is that right?" She cocked her head to one side, pushed the glasses up further on the bridge of her nose and took another step closer.

"Absolutely."

"I thought western heroes only kissed their horses."

"Just the dumb ones."

Kendra laughed out loud. He really liked the sound of that.

"Well, I guess if it's the code…"

"Definitely."

"Then prepare to be kissed."

She pulled off her glasses and shoved them in a pocket. Then she stepped forward and deliberately slid her arms up his chest slowly, locking her hands around his neck. His heart picked up the pace.

"You'll have to bend your neck or your knees, cowboy, or else I'll need a stool."

His lips twitched. "You won't need a stool," he promised.

Rafe couldn't have said if she moved or he did, but their kiss robbed him of coherent thought. She tasted of cocoa, smelled of some indefinable fragrance, and kissed him with an innocent passion that made his head whirl.

When she parted her lips to taste him, her body pressed excitingly against his. That fast, he was hard and ready, spurred on by the reckless way her hands ran up and down his back in wild caresses. Before conscious thought could catch up with action, his hand slipped inside the robe and cupped the lush round curve of her breast through the thin material of the nightgown beneath.

"You aren't wearing a bra!"

Her smile was pure temptation. "I never wear them to bed."

His mouth covered hers while her nipple puckered against his hand in silent invitation. He deepened the kiss hungrily. Her fingers moved restlessly over the front of his jeans sending thermal shockwaves through his system. It took her soft moan of passion to jar him back to reality. He couldn't take her here in the kitchen where anyone could walk in on them. Yet his body said otherwise.

When had they switched positions? He didn't remember turning Kendra so it was her body being pressed against the bank of cupboards. He couldn't even remember insinuating his leg between hers, but it felt good. Better than good. He wanted her with a desire that threatened every ounce of his self-control.

"Kendra. We can't do this here."

"I know." And her mouth sought his once again.

Rafe groaned, straining against her. Letting her feel what she was doing to him.

They drew apart slowly. Her lips were swollen, her eyes slumberous with desire. Rafe drew in a ragged breath. Reluctantly, he released her. She stepped away without taking her eyes from him.

"Did that meet the code of the West?" she asked shakily.

"I think it set new standards."

"Good." She walked to the doorway. Her hips swayed with a tantalizing magic that held his gaze prisoner until she stopped and looked back over her shoulder.

"No wonder you have a harem."

She was gone before his brain reconnected.

"I do not have a harem," he called out after her. But damned if he wasn't going to need another shower tonight.

Chapter Nine

"What do you mean she's gone?" Rafe demanded. "Gone where? With who?"

"Hey, man, take it easy," Cody cautioned. The others sitting around the conference table stared at him with shocked expressions.

Rafe tried to control the rising anxiety in his stomach. He'd overslept and hurried to the house only to learn the others were already assembled in the command center. Everyone except Kendra.

"Where is she?"

"Sit down, Rafael," Mitchell commanded.

"Kendra's with Catherine, Abby and Maddie," Brady put in.

Penny laid a comforting hand on his arm. "They went shopping."

"Shopping? After what happened last night?"

"Abby is armed," Jake said mildly.

"And the women have no intention of letting her out of their sight," Brady added.

"Whose stupid idea was this?" Rafe demanded.

"Mine." Mitchell regarded him steadily. "Have a seat."

With every eye staring at him, Rafe had little choice, but he wasn't happy as he took his usual chair.

"It is my belief that she will be safe with the women.

They can go into dressing rooms and ladies' rooms with her. And they will be constantly alert for possible trouble. Abby and Maddie are both armed. Catherine is carrying a telephone. Slim drove them into town and he will wait for them. He is also armed. We are taking no chances.''

It seemed to Rafe that they were taking a major chance, but he didn't say so under the intensity of Mitchell's stare.

''If I didn't know better I'd think our resident playboy had finally met his match,'' Brady teased. ''The women of Texas will be devastated.''

Rafe glared, silently chafing under the need to get out and go after Kendra to be sure she was safe.

''Listen up. Rafe and Kendra leave tomorrow and we need to go over a few things that have come up. We lost three more head of cattle last night not far from where Kendra was attacked. I believe we can safely assume she rode too close to the rustlers and was shot at as a result.''

Rafe paid close attention.

Mitchell turned to Penny.

''There are rumors that Rialto is gearing up for something big,'' she said. ''Since the DEA intercepted their last shipment of drugs, Rialto has to move to another source quickly. One of our informants has turned up dead, another has disappeared.''

''We need information badly.'' Mitchell said. ''It's vital that Rafe and Kendra get inside and assimilate whatever they can as fast as they can.''

By the time the meeting broke up, Rafe was having second and third thoughts about taking Kendra in with him. The situation had become too dangerous. It would be better if he went in alone. But he'd have to convince her of that first.

Lydia arrived at the ranch house right after the meeting ended. Rafe subdued his annoyance. She was the last person he wanted to see right now.

"Hi!"

"What are you doing here, Lydia?"

"That's a friendly greeting. Hi, Mitchell, Penny. Actually, I came to see if Kendra wanted to go into town with me. It isn't the city, but our general store has some nice things."

"Kendra went into Pecos with Maddie and Abby and Catherine this morning," he told her.

"Oh. Well, we could try to meet up with them for a late lunch or something."

Mitchell stepped forward. "I'm afraid Rafe has work to do. Slim says we have some fence posts that need replacing. I told him you could use the exercise."

Rafe groaned out loud, but part of him was grateful to the older man for getting him out of what could have been an awkward moment. He liked Lydia, and he understood why she didn't want to be alone right now, but his job took precedence.

Lydia grinned good-naturedly. "Far be it for me to come between a man and his fence posts."

"Come between them, please," he teased halfheartedly.

"Thanks, but I do believe I hear my brother calling. I'll catch you later."

"Thanks anyhow, Lydia. I know Kendra will appreciate your offer."

"No problem. See you later."

Rafe waved her off and turned to find Mitchell and Penny still standing behind him.

"Isn't this the anniversary of her husband's death?" Mitchell asked.

"Yeah."

"Maybe I should have offered to go with her," Penny said.

Rafe shook his head. "She'll be okay."

"They never caught the guy who robbed and shot her husband did they?" Mitchell asked.

"No."

"Well, have fun digging holes," Penny said.

Rafe turned to Mitchell. "You were serious?"

"When have you ever known me to joke about work?"

"I was going to go—"

Mitchell shook his head. "The women don't need you. I do."

Penny smirked. Rafe sighed. "Post holes. I hate digging post holes."

But he spent the entire afternoon doing just that while he worried about Kendra.

"YOU'RE GOING to knock him over," Catherine told Kendra with a smile.

Abby nodded. "He'll never know what hit him."

Kendra knew her face was flushed. "This isn't about Rafe. You know that."

"Who said anything about Rafe?" Abby teased.

Maddie patted Kendra's hand and smiled. "If I was thirty years younger dear, I'd have matched you dress for dress."

"Who are you kidding?" Catherine demanded. "You're gorgeous and you know it. If only Mitchell wasn't so stubborn he'd open his eyes and make an honest woman of you."

"What is the problem, Maddie, or are we prying?" Abby asked.

Maddie smiled sadly. "You're prying, but I don't mind. I'm not sure why, but Mitchell isn't ready to get married. I intend to change his mind."

"Good for you!" Abby exclaimed. "If that black dress you bought doesn't get his blood pumping, nothing will."

Kendra sat quietly, listening to them talk. She'd been a loner most of her life, never feeling like she fit in. Yet these women accepted her as if she'd been their friend for years. They wouldn't let her hide in silence. They drew her in, demanding she be part of their camaraderie. And amazingly, she'd had fun today.

She'd let them convince her to buy the sort of outfits Rafe had wanted her to buy in the first place. The suits and dresses hugged her figure, the materials rich with vibrant colors. The skirts were shorter, the blouses more daring than she'd ever worn, but the others assured her she looked great. And the new styles did make her feel—different. Rafe would definitely notice.

It pained her to know that shortly she would take an action she'd waited most of her life to take. An action that would put these women and their gift of friendship irrevocably out of reach. Once she killed Rialto, nothing would ever be the same again.

They returned home as happily upbeat as they'd been when they left. Nothing had happened to jar the afternoon. Now she sat quietly at the crowded dinner table, conscious of Rafe across from her. He'd obviously just come from a shower and had never looked sexier. His hair was damp and combed neatly and he'd shaved. While the tiny nick on his jaw had stopped bleeding, she still had an insane urge to kiss that spot. When she caught his dark eyes on her, her stomach lurched with physical longing.

She glanced at the cupboard where he'd pinned her last night. She grew hot and damp just remembering the feel of his hands and the taste of his mouth. Their gazes collided. His heated expression said he knew exactly what she was thinking. Quickly, she looked down at her half-eaten dinner with no idea what food sat there.

Beside her, Brady suddenly pulled Catherine to her feet.

"I have an announcement to make. Since we're all gathered here together this seems like the perfect time to tell everyone," he began. "Catherine and I are going to have a baby."

The room erupted in happy congratulations. Catherine

hadn't said a word all day, a fact that Abby and Maddie were quick to point out. Elena, Jake and Abby's little girl, bounced up and down in excitement. Even Mitchell looked vastly pleased.

Kendra stared with a combination of joy and acute envy. She wondered if Catherine knew how lucky she was to have a husband like Brady and a child conceived in love. The knowledge hit her that if she went through with her plan, she would never know that particular joy herself.

Rafe's intent stare brought her out of her maudlin thoughts and she quickly voiced her own congratulations. The evening immediately turned into an impromptu celebration. Kendra had to work to stay away from Rafe, but she was aware of his eyes on her most of the evening as Rosa brought out pie and champagne. Avoiding Rafe in such a small crowd was serious work. Finally, in desperation, she retired early, feigning exhaustion.

Upstairs, she entered her bedroom cautiously and searched for any unexpected surprises. There were none, with the exception of all the packages dumped on her bed and the expensive new luggage Maddie had insisted Kendra purchase for her stay at Rialto's.

Kendra set about removing price tags and packing the new clothing. She even included the green dress Rafe had selected. In an impulsive moment, she'd splurged on a pair of strappy heels and some jewelry to go with the dress.

She also packed the underwear Rafe had purchased with mixed feelings, wondering how she'd dare to wear it. The emerald gown and robe made her hesitate. Before she let herself think about it, she stripped off her clothing and slipped the silk over her head. In the mirror, she studied her reflection. Rafe had been right again, the glasses had to go. She took out her new contact lenses and studied the results in Penny's full-length mirror.

Kendra Kincade was gone. At least the Kendra Kincade

she usually faced in the mirror. The image looking back at her belonged to a boldly sensual woman. A confident woman who could only be waiting for her lover.

Someone knocked on her bedroom door. It opened before she could reach the knob. Rafe's expression went from concern to stunned amazement. His eyes feasted, making her feel more like a woman than she ever had in her life.

"I thought everything was destroyed," he said.

"Only the clothing. I had the underwear in a drawer."

"I'm glad."

His obvious approval fanned the fire of her need. "So am I."

He came farther into the room, handing her a package.

"What's this?"

"Something I picked up when we went shopping the other day."

Her fingers weren't quite steady as she opened the small box. She gasped in delight as the light caught the small glass swan.

"Oh, Rafe. It's beautiful! Thank you!" She struggled against sudden tears. No man had ever given her a gift before.

Rafe looked pleased. The tenderness in his expression made her work all the harder at holding back her tears of pleasure.

"You're welcome. I thought you'd like it."

"I love it." She set it on the dresser where it sparkled with life.

"You were quiet at dinner."

"It was a long day."

She couldn't admit to her envy of Catherine and Abby and their families. Kendra hated to admit even to herself that she yearned for the same sort of love they had found. The sort her parents shared. The sort she secretly yearned to share with Rafe.

"I wondered if you were having second thoughts about tomorrow. It isn't too late to back out, you know."

But it was. It had been too late from the moment Rialto destroyed her life and her innocence. She touched the swan lightly, squared her shoulders and lifted her chin. "I won't change my mind." She couldn't.

"I don't want to see you hurt, Kendra."

His quiet words brought another lump to her throat. "Don't worry."

He touched her shoulder, his hand a brand on soul. For a moment, he stood there without moving.

"What are you doing, Rafe?"

"Going over all the reasons why I shouldn't kiss you."

"Oh."

"They aren't working. Maybe you'd better tell me to go."

Her blood raced. She couldn't seem to tear her eyes from his mouth. He had such a sexy mouth. The memory of what that mouth could do made her weak.

"I don't want you to go away, Rafe," she managed to whisper.

He tilted her chin and lowered his head. "I'm glad."

Their mouths fused hungrily. She melted against him as if it were the most natural thing in the world to do. The light scent of his aftershave seemed to enfold her in a cocoon of sensuality. How she wanted him.

His hand cupped her breast, touching the sensitive nipple. Her body vibrated in answer. She felt the press of his arousal through the thin material of her gown and she reveled in the knowledge that he wanted her as much as she wanted him. Rafe deepened the kiss. She was lost, welcoming his passion, running her hands over him, tracing the length of his arousal.

Rafe groaned. She felt heady with female triumph.

"I want to see all of you," he said thickly.

"Yes."

A door closed down the hall. Mitchell's door.

They moved apart, breathing heavily and frustrated beyond all reason. Rafe ran a hand raggedly through his hair. "I have to go."

"Yes."

"I don't want to leave."

"I know." She didn't want him to go, but despite what her body demanded, she couldn't make love to Rafe here in this room with Mitchell down the hall and Penny right next door.

"It isn't too late."

She knew he meant about changing her mind. "I'll be ready in the morning."

He dropped his hand to his side. She saw the slight tremor there. "At least we won't have any trouble convincing Rialto that you're more than my assistant."

The words struck her like a slap. "I told you I could handle the situation," she managed to say.

His expression reflected surprise. "I didn't mean that the way it came out. Never mind. Get some rest, Kendra. We have a long day ahead of us tomorrow."

"I know."

She could see Rafe wanted to say more, but he turned and left the room. Kendra sank down on the end of the bed and stared at the lovely crystal swan until her vision blurred. How could she have been so stupid? She'd fallen in love with Rafe.

She fisted the bedspread, refusing to cry. Kendra didn't want to be part of his harem. She didn't have meaningless affairs. She wasn't like Phoebe and Tammy and Lydia and Janet. She was more like Penny—yearning from afar.

With an oath, she stood up and pulled off the sexy nightgown. She was tempted to unpack the sexy outfits and fill the bag with her baggy sweats. But who would she be running from, Rafe, or herself? He'd been upfront from the start. She was a fool.

Closing her eyes, she hugged the gown to her chest. There had never been any possibility of a relationship between them. She'd always known that. She opened her eyes to gaze at the suitcase. A sexy red dress hung in the closet, waiting to be worn in the morning.

She couldn't have Rafe. But she could make sure she was one woman he never forgot. She folded the green nightgown carefully and added it to the suitcase.

Rafael Alvarez was in for the shock of his life come morning. She was going to knock him on his ear.

RAFE SAT AT the table ignoring the huge platter of food Rosa had set before him, sipping glumly on his coffee. It had finally dawned on him after tossing and turning for hours last night that for a reasonably sensitive male, he'd really blown things with Kendra. Funny, he generally had no problem communicating with women. But then, no other woman had affected him the way she did. He couldn't stop thinking about her, worrying about her, caring about her.

He owed her an apology for last night. She'd misunderstood and he'd bungled an explanation. But at least he'd done one thing right. She'd liked the crystal swan.

A low wolf whistle broke in on his thoughts. Every head turned toward the hall including his. Shock slammed into him as Kendra stepped fully into the kitchen. Dressed in a short, vibrant red dress and a pair of spiked heels that showed off an enticing amount of well-shaped leg, Kendra Kincade was enough to make any man whistle.

How had he ever thought her plain?

Cody was out of his seat and pulling out the chair next to him with a grand sweeping gesture.

Rafe wanted to slug his fellow agent.

''You look stunning this morning, Kendra,'' Brady said. ''Doesn't she, Rafe?''

''You're married,'' he snapped.

Brady grinned.

''Coffee?'' Jake asked her.

Rafe resisted an impulse to tell Jake what to do with the pot of coffee. It was bad enough that Cody was fawning all over her, but even Mitchell and Slim were watching her much too appreciatively for a couple of men their age. Jake and Brady had no business watching her at all. They were happily married.

''Nice dress,'' Penny said evenly. ''That color really suits you.''

''Thank you. Rafe picked it out.''

''You refused to buy it,'' he snapped.

Kendra smiled. ''I changed my mind. Don't you like it?''

Yes he liked it. Entirely too much. He wanted to rip it off her sexy body and finish what those kisses had begun last night. And he did not like the way the rest of his fellow agents were staring at her.

''Contact lenses?'' Jake asked.

''Yes. Rafe suggested them. They're more comfortable than I expected. Thank you, Rosa.''

''*No es nada,* señorita,'' she said setting down a full plate of food. ''You look *muy bonita.*''

''Thank you. Rafe wanted me to make a strong impression on Rialto today. So I'd fit in.''

Cody snorted but it was Brady who responded.

''I don't think you'll have any problems making an impression on him in that outfit, do you, Rafe?''

Rafe gnashed his teeth to keep from opening his mouth. He was afraid of what he might say. Why the devil was he feeling this rush of wild emotions? Kendra had done exactly as he'd asked. More than he'd asked. He should be pleased. How had he never realized how beautiful Kendra was?

"Cat got your tongue?" Penny whispered to him.

Rafe set his coffee cup down with a clatter.

"You'll do more than fit in, Kendra," Cody was saying. "You're going to knock them all on their respective butts."

"Why, thank you, Cody. Would you pass me the butter, please?"

Three hands reached for the butter dish. Rafe kicked back his chair and stood so abruptly it nearly fell over. "I'll be outside. When you finish turning on these panting puppies, let me know."

Every eye in the room was on him, but the only ones he really saw were the startlingly hazel ones across the table from him. "Is something wrong?" Kendra asked.

He strode for the door feeling like a complete fool.

"Don't worry," he heard Cody say, "He's always grumpy first thing in the morning."

"Yes, I'd noticed that."

By the time he'd collected his suitcase and put it in the trunk of the expensive sedan currently registered in his name, Rafe had calmed down, feeling more of a fool than ever.

But if he'd expected Kendra to hurry after his outburst inside, he was sadly mistaken. Ten minutes passed and then it was Mitchell who came outside, not Kendra.

"All set?"

"Just waiting for our computer genius." He tried not to flinch under Mitchell's scrutiny.

"You gonna be able to handle this, Rafe?"

"Of course."

"You did a good job with the makeover."

Too good. "Yeah."

"There isn't room for any personal involvement right now. Not until the job is done."

"I'm not personally involved."

Mitchell gave him a look that cut through his calm facade.

"You can lie to me all you want, son, but don't make the mistake of lying to yourself. That could get you killed. I've got more than half a mind to call this whole thing off right now."

"What are you talking about?" Alarm swelled in his chest. "We've come a long way to reach this point. You can't call it off now."

"Care to make book on that?"

"Why?"

"Look what almost happened with Jake and Brady. They let their emotions dominate and came much too close to getting themselves killed. There isn't room for romance in a scenario like this one."

"Hey, wait a minute. This situation is nothing like theirs. I'm in lust with the woman, not in love."

"Don't worry, Mitchell," Kendra said from behind him. "I'll see that he keeps his lust under control and his mind on the job at hand."

His heart plunged to his toes as he whirled to find Kendra descending the front porch with a travel case in one hand, her computer case in the other. Slim trailed behind carrying two expensive looking matching bags.

"I didn't mean—"

"I know exactly what you meant," she said coolly. "Don't worry that I harbor any silly feminine emotions just because you nearly made love to me last night. This is business."

He couldn't remember another woman making him blush, but he could feel the rush of heat in his cheeks. Kendra remained cool and aloft, looking as desirable and as unattainable as some movie star from a bygone era.

"We have a job to do, Alvarez," Kendra continued. "Beneath this wardrobe and makeup is the same little computer nerd you wanted out of your life the night you mistook me for a rustler. Nothing's changed except the packaging—so get over it. We go in as planned and when this is all over, your life goes right back to normal.'' She handed Slim her travel case. ''Thank you, Slim. I'll keep the computer up front with me. Is there room in the trunk for everything else?''

''Yes, ma'am.''

''Nice car. Yours?'' she asked Mitchell.

''Currently it's registered to Rafe. Part of the window dressing for the job.''

She eyed the expensive luxury car appreciatively. ''Nice dressing. Leather seats?''

Mitchell smiled faintly. ''Of course. There's a built-in telephone, a computerized mapping program, a tracking device—''

''If it shoots machine guns out the back or has an ejection system I'm going to know I'm in a James Bond dream.''

Slim chortled.

''Nothing that elaborate, I'm afraid.''

''Good. For a minute there I was worried.''

''The car is a tool, much like your makeover and Rafe's custom-tailored wardrobe. Rialto must believe the setting or he'll kill both of you out of hand.'' Mitchell studied the two of them with pleated brows. ''My instinct is telling me to pull the plug.''

''No,'' Rafe protested.

Kendra shook her head. ''Please don't. I'd hate to think I went through all this,'' she waved a hand dismissively at her body, ''for nothing.''

''Hardly for nothing, if you'll pardon me saying so, ma'am,'' Slim piped up.

Kendra patted his hand. ''Thanks.''

Rafe knew Mitchell was waiting for his response. The entire mission hinged on his next words.

''Frankly, I think I outdid myself,'' he told Mitchell, striving for his usual cocky tone as he tried to eye Kendra objectively. "Now that the shock is wearing off I realize she'll not only fit the image, she has got the guts to pull it off."

"We can do this," Kendra hurriedly agreed. "Rafe's insatiable lust won't get in the way."

"Insatiable lust?"

"Should I have said sex-starved behavior?"

Rafe growled. "I ought to turn you over my knee."

"Are you into that as well?"

Slim laughed out loud. Even Mitchell couldn't prevent a chuckle. Rafe knew he'd been bested. He bowed in defeat and turned to Mitchell. "I'll check in after we get there and scope out the situation."

"You're certain?"

"Positive."

"Kendra?"

She nodded tightly. "I have no intention of blowing this opportunity."

Something in her tone set off a mental warning. Rafe tried to read below the surface of her comment, wondering what she was really thinking.

"All right then, be careful and good luck."

Slim held the door open for Kendra who slid inside the low vehicle revealing a long length of stocking-clad leg. Rafe tore his eyes from the view and walked around to his own side of the car. As he slipped behind the steering wheel, the enticingly light fragrance of her perfume tantalized his nose. He started the car and immediately opened his window all the way. With a jaunty salute, he headed the car toward the main road.

"We're never going to make it, you know," he said conversationally. "I'm going to have to throttle you long before we reach Rialto's."

"Fine. Concentrate on that thought while you drive. I plan to read a book."

"What book?"

"Ever hear of the book, *Men Are From Mars?* Well this is the plan to send them back."

"Very funny."

"I thought so. It's that or *War and Peace.* In German," she added with a brief smile.

Rafe knew he was missing some point, but he decided not to pursue the topic.

"I apologize."

"For what?"

"I acted like an idiot this morning."

"Don't apologize. I think I'm flattered. I've never had a man act jealous of me before."

"What makes you think it was an act?"

Her lips parted. He felt her staring at him, but he kept his eyes on the road.

"There's been chemistry between us since the night I knocked you off that horse, Kendra. I'm usually a bit more polished in my approach, but make no doubt about it. I wanted you last night and I want you now. My insatiable lust, you know."

"Oh. That."

"Uh-huh. And that sexy red dress is simply fuel for the fire."

She was silent for so long, he thought she wasn't going to respond.

"Do I get a say here?"

"The final say is always yours," he promised. "But tonight we'll probably be sharing a bed if not each other. You need to be ready for that."

The silence was longer this time.

"So do you, Alvarez."

Chapter Ten

"Mr. Rialto conveys his deepest regrets. He's been delayed in town this morning, but the staff has been instructed to see to every need you might have."

Kendra took an involuntary step closer to Rafe as Marcus Slade's wintry gray eyes made her all too aware that the red dress was short, tight, and designed for just this sort of attention. She knew Slade was Rialto's right-hand man. She just hadn't expected to dislike him so strongly.

"And it will be my personal pleasure to help in any way that I can," Slade leered.

Rafe suddenly loomed larger, almost ferally intimidating as he stepped in front of her.

"We'll settle for being shown to our room. It was a long drive."

The clipped words were calm enough, but the challenge was unmistakable. Marcus smiled coldly. "Of course. Right this way."

Following the men through the two-story, hacienda-style house, Kendra barely had the presence of mind to study the layout. All her senses were urging her to turn tail and go in the opposite direction. Her apprehension mounted with every step.

The house sprawled elegantly amid lushly appointed grounds. She was edgily reminded of a movie set where everything was fake. The decor and the colors were too rich, too bright, too phony. The house formed a U-shape around a center courtyard that sported an enormous, kidney-shaped pool. Even the water sparkled like a special effect.

Kendra realized she was in danger of hysterics if she didn't get a grip, so she tried to focus on things that might be of importance later. The bedrooms had sliding glass doors that opened onto a balcony that ran the length of the house overlooking the pool.

The bedroom Marcus Slade ushered them inside was midway down an impressively long hallway with a series of closed doors in the left wing of the building. Hard to think of a place like this as a house. It reminded her of a fancy hotel.

"Uh, how many bedrooms are there?" she ventured.

"Four in this wing," Slade told her with a greasy smile.

Were there four more on the other side? The furnishings were ornate, but about what you'd expect from a good hotel, she decided. A queen-sized bed, dresser, end tables, two chairs and a table. They'd carried the Spanish-style motif down to the deep red flocking on the wallpaper of one wall.

"The pool is heated," Marcus Slade was saying, "Feel free to take advantage. If you forgot to pack a suit, we have some very nice bikinis available in the cabana downstairs." He was definitely leering. "Help yourself. If you're hungry—"

"It's a little cool for swimming, even in a heated pool, and we stopped and had a late lunch," Rafe interrupted. "We'll get settled and have a look around."

His words were clear dismissal. Marcus Slade lost his smile and replaced it with a hard look. "Of course. I'll see you at the party tonight then."

Kendra shivered as his gaze traveled to her. Rafe narrowed his eyes in clear warning. Tension hummed in the air like a secret observer. Marcus Slade inclined his head at her and stepped from the room, closing the door softly behind him.

Kendra drew in a breath. "Should you have been so antagonistic?" she asked, relieved that the other man was gone and knowing that Rafe had just made a formidable enemy.

"No. I should have broken his nose."

Secretly warmed by this, she watched Rafe stalk to his suitcase and retrieve a boxy device. He began to prowl the room. Kendra has seen this done on television once. Rafe was checking for listening devices.

Her tension had mounted with each mile until now it had escalated to mild panic. Flashbacks to the past ate away at her self-confidence. What was she doing here?

What if she'd been wrong? What if the string of recent events had been because of her past? What if Rialto did know who and where she was? What if Rafe had just walked into a trap because of her?

The device in Rafe's hands emitted a scratchy tone. Rafe paused at the ornate headboard. He produced a pocket knife and dug at the dark wood until he removed something imbedded there. Kendra watched, wide-eyed as he held up a tiny round transmitter. Her mouth opened, but she couldn't think of a thing to say. She watched him remove another device from the mirror and a third one from the drape near the window.

"You okay?" Rafe asked.

"Great," she responded thinly. "You?"

"Annoyed. I assume these were placed here to test my abilities." He eyed the walls, finally pulling a chair over to the flocked wallpaper in the far corner of the room. Climbing up on the chair, he began to dig at the paper in the corner right below the ornate cornice. In seconds, he revealed the lens of a camera.

Kendra gasped. "That's carrying a test a bit far, don't you think?"

"Yeah. I do."

Rafe cut the device free, damaging the paper. He climbed down with the lens in hand. "I didn't expect someone like Rialto to play such childish pranks, did you?"

He was speaking for the benefit of the microphones. She took a deep breath and tried to act like his assistant instead of some shocked innocent.

"At least he could have been more creative," she said.

Rafe flashed her a pleased smile. "I'm going across the hall to sweep the bathroom. Go ahead and unpack."

"All right."

She tried to sound blasé instead of shocked anew by the thought of cameras and bugs inside the bathroom.

This wasn't how she'd expected things to go. In the first place, she'd been braced to meet Rialto as soon as they arrived. That he wasn't even at the estate when they arrived was somehow disconcerting.

Her nerves jangled as she opened her suitcase and did as Rafe had suggested. She was annoyed at the way her hands had a small quiver she couldn't quite control.

Rafe returned with two more devices. He dumped everything unceremoniously into a metal tin bandage box he must have taken from the bathroom. Then he shook the cup hard. "Hopefully, I just gave someone a headache."

"Are we clear now?"

"Relatively speaking. I'll unpack and then we'll go exploring."

"What are you going to do with those?"

Rafe opened his bag and set the tin inside and the suitcase on the floor in the closet. Then he began to unpack. "I plan to dump them in our host's hand this evening."

"Is that wise?"

"We'll find out. You handled it well."

Kendra managed a smile. "I didn't mind the bugs, but the camera—"

"Tell him so. We aren't taking guff from anyone. Remember that. Rialto doesn't employ timid people. And if Slade gets out of line, let me know immediately."

"I can handle Marcus Slade." But secretly, she wasn't so sure and she hoped it wouldn't come to that. The man reminded her of Stephen Rialto without the urbane mask.

"Maybe so, but tell me," he ordered. "I'd like an opportunity to teach him some manners."

Kendra studied Rafe as he hung up a dark tuxedo jacket. The almost primitive savagery of his expression surprised her.

"We don't have much time to explore before we have to get ready for tonight's party," he continued more calmly.

"Then we'd better make the most of what time we do have."

Rafe smiled, reducing some of the chill that had settled over her. She'd never had a man defend her honor before. It gave her a weird feeling.

He finished and held out his arm. Together they stepped onto the balcony and began to stroll its length, unabashedly looking inside rooms wherever the open drapes allowed.

"Do you think all these rooms have cameras and bugs?"

"Probably."

"That's sick."

Rafe didn't comment. Workmen were setting up a makeshift bar on the deck, partially beneath the balcony. Men in white uniforms circulated about the handful of guests who were already making use of the water despite the chilly temperatures.

"Hardy souls," she commented.

Rafe's lips twitched. "Don't you swim?"

"Not in early May."

They started down the steps on the far side of the house. "I'm betting this right wing houses Rialto's suite," Rafe said, nodding toward the closed drapes.

"Why?"

"He'd set himself apart from the majority of his guests, so he'd put us on the opposite side of the house. Let's head inside before we have to make small talk with any of the other guests."

Kendra followed Rafe's lead which avoided the small cluster of men in business suits standing nearby. She felt heads turn in her direction. This sort of masculine attention was new to her, but secretly she admitted it was stimulating. Especially when she realized Rafe had noticed.

While staff moved about the enormous dining area setting out trays of food, Rafe quietly pointed out camera locations in the halls. There were no guards posted anywhere that she could see.

"Listening devices?" she asked.

"Not likely, but it's always possible."

"How are we—?" she hesitated to ask how they were going to find, let alone access Rialto's private office with cameras everywhere, in case Rafe was wrong about the halls being bugged.

"Going to relax?" he finished for her. Obviously, he was taking no chances either. "We aren't. Ah. The library."

The library was down the hall off the vast living room. Large and formally decorated, the room was lined with books she'd bet no one had ever opened.

"Want to bet that's his office?" Rafe nodded toward a closed door that was nearly invisible since it blended against the dark paneling.

"Think so?"

Rafe reached out and turned the handle. "Locked."

He led her back to the hall and tried the next door. Also locked. Without missing a beat, he tried the door across from it. It refused to yield either, but the next door he tried on the pool side of the house, opened to reveal a sitting room done in a distinctly masculine style.

"Told you this was probably his private wing," Rafe said.

"Help you find something?" A large man asked from behind them.

Kendra started. Unperturbed by the man's size and gruff demeanor, Rafe shook his head. "Nope, just looking."

"This area is off-limits to the guests," the guard said.

"Oh? Marcus didn't say anything about that," Rafe said. "We were just looking around."

"The private wing is off-limits," the man repeated more belligerently.

"Okay. I'm Rafael Alvarez."

The guard looked momentarily disconcerted, but he didn't take Rafe's extended hand.

"Why don't you and the lady go back and join the other guests." It wasn't a request.

"I need to go upstairs and get ready anyhow," Kendra announced. Rafe might be comfortable pushing the big man, but she wasn't. The beefy guard wore a thinly concealed gun beneath his white suit coat. No one was going to believe this guy was part of the wait staff.

"We'll ask Mr. Rialto to show us the rest of the house later," Rafe told Kendra conversationally.

"Follow me," the security man ordered.

Kendra didn't breathe easily until they were back in the privacy of their assigned bedroom a few minutes later. She was a little disconcerted when Rafe took out the box again and once more swept the room.

"We've only been gone a few minutes," she protested.

"That's all it would take, but we're clear. I'll leave you to get ready."

"Where are you going?"

"I want another look at the private wing."

She tried to swallow and couldn't. "Are you crazy? That goon will beat you to a pulp."

Rafe grinned impudently. "I should be offended that you

have so little faith, but I think I'm more touched to find out you care.''

''Don't you dare laugh at me.''

''Wouldn't dream of it.'' But his eyes sparkled.

''Oh, for crying out…. Wait. I'll come with you.''

His smile disappeared. ''I'd rather you wouldn't. I want to check something and it will be safer if I go alone.''

''But—''

He lifted her chin. Before she could move, his lips settled over hers in the briefest of kisses. ''I'll be right back.''

''But—''

''Get ready.'' He stepped out into the hall, closing the door before she could muster another protest.

''Fine. Get yourself beaten to a pulp. See if I care.'' But she did care. Entirely too much. She touched a finger lightly to her lips where he'd kissed her and for some inexplicable reason, wanted to cry.

''Baby,'' she muttered, drawing herself up. If Rafe wanted to risk the whole plan by being a hotdog, there wasn't a thing she could do to stop him. It was his neck. She only hoped he wouldn't stretch it too far. She'd hate to have to explain to Mitchell Forbes how he got it chopped off.

With time to kill, Kendra opted for a bath rather than a shower. First she found herself checking the opulent bathroom carefully for any sign of a camera that Rafe might have missed. Then she ran the water. The lightly scented oil didn't have its usual soothing effect. Her tension wasn't about to be so easily mollified. Her stomach felt like it housed a nest of crows. Tomorrow this would be all over.

And Rafe would hate her.

Kendra closed her eyes, wishing things could be different. Visions of her family's bloody bodies served to remind her that her actions were fully justified. The law couldn't touch Stephen Rialto. Police and government agencies like Rafe's had been trying for years. But Kendra could touch him. She could exact the justice that no one else could.

She took her time applying the exotic makeup and doing her hair on top of her head the way Phoebe had shown her. The transformation startled her anew. She no longer resembled Kendra Kincade.

"Not bad, for a computer nerd and an amateur." Too bad she hadn't learned these girl skills when she was younger. But would that really have changed anything after what Rialto had done?

She headed across the hall to the bedroom. Hot, loud, foot-stamping music drifted up from downstairs. Voices were raised in greeting. The party was obviously underway.

Kendra expected to find Rafe waiting for her, but he wasn't. He'd been back to the room and left again because the clothing he'd worn earlier was folded neatly on the chair near the bed. His boots sat below.

He'd dressed and gone downstairs without her.

She couldn't pretend she wasn't disappointed as she dropped her robe and pulled the green dress from the closet. On the other hand, she would have been self-conscious getting dressed in the same room with Rafe.

Kendra stepped into the green satin panties and matching garter belt. Gartering was a frustrating process. She told herself the results would be worth the work. Finished, she smoothed the shiny material of the dress down over her hips, enjoying the feel of it against her bare skin.

And the plunging neckline revealed a great deal of bare skin. She knew she looked good. The strappy high heels were the perfect touch, even if her feet were bound to protest before the evening ended.

She was putting on her last earring when the bedroom door opened without warning.

Rafe stopped midstep. His gaze swept her, heating in instant approval. "Very, very nice."

Kendra basked under that masculine appraisal. Her cheeks warmed with pleasure as she took in the perfect fit of his tuxedo. Rafe was breathtakingly handsome.

"You clean up pretty good yourself, cowboy." And she was pleased that her voice came out sounding perfectly normal despite her pounding heart.

His gaze followed the deep V of the crossed bodice and he came toward her slowly. "I'm glad."

So was she.

"What are you wearing underneath?"

Her heart raced. "Bath oil, for the most part."

Desire quickened in his expression. Her pulse thundered in her ears, but she held up the palm of her hand when he would have closed the remaining distance. "If you kiss me, you'll smear my makeup," she said shakily.

He grinned, a slow, heart-stopping sort of grin. "I'm willing to take that chance." His voice was low, husky, sending sensual tremors all through her.

"But I'm not," she lied. "We have a job to do." And as hard as it was to push him away, Kendra knew it would be impossible to go through with her plans if she let him make love to her now.

But her body clamored in protest. She would have liked nothing more than to let Rafe strip the green dress from her body.

"The party will still be going strong in another hour," he coaxed.

His finger reached out to trace a path along the V of her dress. Kendra quivered. It took all her willpower to stand still beneath his touch and his gaze. She wanted to melt against him with every fiber of her being.

"Anticipation builds character," she said shakily.

"I don't think my anticipation needs any buildup."

A glance showed her that Rafe was every bit as aroused as she was. Oddly enough, it was that knowledge that calmed her racing senses. Never in all her life had she felt more like a woman. "I think we'd better join the party," she said softly.

Rafe stepped back, banking the heat that still showed in his gaze. "Spoilsport. You know I'll have to beat the men away with a club, don't you?"

"Just use that glare you perfected on Marcus Slade." As soon as the words left her mouth, she conjured up an image of the man that made her shiver.

"Nervous?"

"A little," she admitted.

"Me too."

"Ha."

"Hey, I'm always nervous before a job."

"I can't imagine you being nervous about anything."

He regarded her seriously. "You'd be surprised what makes me nervous, Kendra."

"I thought you were the iron man."

"Sorry to disillusion you, but I'm known as the chameleon of the group. My specialty is fitting into whatever role the situation calls for."

"Like James Bond?"

"On a smaller scale."

"Oh, I think you'd definitely give him a run for his money."

His grin was disturbingly endearing. She had no trouble seeing Rafe as James Bond.

His expression turned serious. "Are you really worried about tonight, Kendra?"

"Of course I am." Scared spitless would be closer to the truth, but she wasn't about to tell him that. "I'd be a fool not to worry, wouldn't I?"

"Yes. But I'll be nearby at all times," he promised.

"I know."

He stepped to one side and crooked his arm. Kendra slid her hand inside.

"Ready?"

"As I'll ever be."

"Then let's get this over with. Remember one thing," he said as they started down the hall. "All night long I'm going to be peeling that dress from your body in my mind. So if you want something to really worry about, think about what's going to happen when we have to share that bed later on."

KENDRA TURNED heads with every step. Her green dress stood out in the crowd of black and white. She carried herself with the effortless grace of a woman, sure of herself and her power. He couldn't believe this was the same woman he'd spent a week coaching.

They descended the staircase and were promptly surrounded by a noisy throng. In minutes he caught sight of Stephen Rialto heading in their direction. The man looked at least twenty years younger than his chronological age. Suave and polished, he approached them with a look of masculine appreciation that immediately raised Rafe's hackles. Kendra came to a complete stop. She'd seen him as well.

"Rafael! So glad you could make it this evening. I'm terribly sorry that I wasn't here to greet you when you and your beautiful assistant arrived."

He turned the full focus of his attention on Kendra.

"Allow me to introduce myself—"

"No introduction is necessary," she interrupted. "Your picture has made the business section more than once, Mr. Rialto. I would recognize you anywhere."

Her words were smooth and low with just the right inflection, but Rafe could practically feel the tension vibrating under the surface. Rialto, however, seemed unaware. He reached for her hand, raising it to his lips. Rafe had the strongest urge to pull her hand away, but Kendra's attention fixated on the large ruby and gold ring he wore.

"Ah, you like my ring?"

"It's quite...distinctive," she said quietly.

"A family heirloom. It belonged to my father and his father before him. I haven't taken it off since he passed away some twenty years ago."

Rafe rested a hand on her shoulder, diverting the man's gaze from the length of creamy skin revealed by Kendra's dress. "You have quite a place here," he told the other man.

"Thank you. I trust you've found everything to your satisfaction."

"Not entirely," Rafe told him. "You have a small problem."

Rialto's eyes narrowed.

Rafe reached inside his jacket pocket for the bandage box. Before the bodyguard who was watching the scene closely could react, Rafe turned over Rialto's hand and poured the contents into his palm.

"Bugs," he said succinctly.

The bodyguard suddenly loomed at his side, but Rafe didn't even glance at the man. He'd already noted that it was the same beefy guard who had stopped them earlier when they were looking around in the private wing.

Rialto barely glanced at the devices in his hand before handing them to the man and waving him off.

"I'll have a word with my staff."

"Do that. We wouldn't want to bore anyone with our home movies."

Rialto turned to Kendra. "I apologize for the misunderstanding."

"No problem," she said lightly. "I assume we passed the test?"

"Not one of my devising, I assure you. My staff tends to be a bit zealous in their efforts to protect me."

"Yes, I noticed," Rafe agreed. "Your guard jumped us when we were having a look around earlier. Something about your wing being off-limits."

"Yes, I confess with this many people about, I keep that area of the house off-limits. You understand."

"Absolutely. There was no harm done."

"And none meant, I'm sure."

"Loyalty is always a good thing," Rafe added.

"Yes. Still, I'll have a word with Mr. Slade later about the unfortunate problem you discovered. Right now, let me introduce you to a few people you'll need to know before you start work on Monday."

Rialto guided them to a large group nearby. Minutes later, he excused himself to greet some new arrivals. Rafe made it a point to study faces and remember names. This sort of social scene was one he was familiar with, and generally good at. For a woman who'd been living in a world of computers for most of her life, he was pleased to see Kendra blended into the social patter easily as well.

Waiters circulated around the room with food and drinks, and while Kendra accepted a glass of wine, Rafe noticed she never once drank from it. Nor did she eat any of the offered canapés. Smart woman. He'd meant to warn her about that very thing, but somehow, he'd forgotten. He didn't expect anyone to drug them. On the other hand, the bugs and the camera bothered him more than he'd wanted Kendra to know. Neither boded well.

Rafe had spent the time Kendra was getting ready scouting outside the building as well as inside. He'd managed to reach the fuse box and paid particular attention to the carefully marked wiring. He now knew for certain that the door in the library led into Rialto's office. He was also fairly certain that the room was locked, but didn't have its own alarm system.

As they moved from group to group and room to room,

he and Kendra were eventually separated. He was careful to keep her in sight, even while he kept track of Rialto and the men he'd identified as security staff. It was easy to keep track of Kendra. Not only did the green dress stand out in the crowd, but his gaze was constantly drawn to the way the shifting material clung briefly to the curve of her hip, or thigh as she moved.

She had him in a state of semiarousal without doing a darn thing. It was ludicrous, but he had to resist the urge to swoop her into his arms and carry her back up those stairs.

The party had spilled outdoors as well as into most of the open rooms downstairs. Rafe continued to speak with people while trying not to stare at Kendra.

Several men clustered around her. Rafe shuttled aside his irritation until he saw a tall, smooth-looking type begin to rub her shoulder. Kendra attempted to pull back, but the man went with her movement. Rafe began threading his way through the crush of people in Kendra's direction.

"Come on, little lady, Stephen's got a real nice garden out back, away from all this noise. Why don't you let me show you around? You're exceptionally beautiful you know," the man was saying.

"No, thank you," Kendra said politely. Rafe saw her skin quiver as the man boldly ran his hand down her bare arm.

Rafe removed the hand. "Kendra doesn't like being touched," he growled.

The man whirled in surprise, his sullen expression grew angry. "Find your own woman, pal."

"I already did, *pal*. And you had your hand on her arm."

"Is that right? Well why don't we let the lady decide."

"She already did. Kendra is my wife."

Chapter Eleven

Rafe caught Marcus Slade watching the scene as he led Kendra away.

"Why on earth did you tell him that?" Kendra objected. "I could have handled him."

"Yeah? Looked to me like he was the one doing all the handling."

Kendra scowled. "He didn't mean anything. He was drunk."

"He wasn't that drunk, Kendra. Or maybe you liked his attention," the last was said for the benefit of Marcus Slade who was following them discreetly.

She shuddered delicately. "No, but what if that wife comment gets back to Rialto?"

"What if it does? He should be pleased to learn he has a husband and wife security team working for him."

Kendra frowned. She didn't realize Slade had moved up to stand almost directly behind her, but she was sharp enough not to give the game away until she knew what was going on.

"If I didn't know better, *husband,* I'd think you were jealous."

Rafe knew any answer he gave could lead to a careless comment or a misinterpretation, so he did what he'd been wanting to do ever since he saw her in that green dress. He pulled her into his arms and sought the warmth of her mouth.

Kendra stiffened in shock, but as their lips touched it was like a switch had been ignited. She yielded, clinging sweetly—responding as if she'd always done so.

He'd only meant to stop the conversation, but his body had other ideas. It was scary how easily kissing her over-whelmed his common sense. Fortunately, Kendra finally had the presence of mind to draw back. Her eyes were luminous as she gazed up at him.

"Rafe?"

"Yeah, I know. We have an audience." A darting glance showed Slade, among others, watching them with a wide smirk. "Come on."

"Wha—? Where—? Rafe!"

He led her without hesitation to the fringes of the party-goers. "This way."

Amazingly, only one couple was inside the library. They stepped out, deep in their own private conversation as he tugged Kendra inside. Immediately, he turned and locked the door.

"What are you doing?"

"Assuring privacy."

"Have you taken complete leave of your senses?"

"Quite possibly."

Where she was concerned, the answer was a definite yes. She was like a strong wine, leaving him heady and a bit confused. This was no time to be thinking how badly he wanted her beneath him, but he couldn't stop the exciting image. He locked the patio door and pulled the drapes shut.

"You've been teasing me all night and you know it."

"What?"

"I want you right here. Right now."

Kendra gaped, her eyes wide pools of shock. "Pretend," he whispered against her hair.

Rafe felt the tension drain from her body. When she smiled at him it was with a siren's smile that whipped through him like an electric current. Though he knew she was only doing what he'd told her, his libido jump-started. He did want her. Here, now, immediately.

"You'd better turn off the light so no one tries to come in," she said in a sultry voice.

"That was my plan," he agreed readily. "I killed the surveillance cameras on this side of the building earlier," he whispered.

"But won't Rialto—?"

"Guess? Hopefully not. It should look like a malfunction."

He withdrew a pocket flash, motioning to Kendra as he made a noise like he was kissing her.

"It's a good thing you're a silent lover," he said for the microphone's benefit as he lighted the way to Rialto's private office.

"I can be as noisy as you want, lover," she promised. Her words vibrated right down his spinal column. He fumbled getting the lock pick out of his jacket pocket.

"Later," he managed to say out loud. If he sounded breathless, so much the better. "Undo my zipper."

"Only if you undo mine."

His body readied at her tempting words, even as his mind told it to stand down. He went to work with the lock pick. In seconds, despite his unsteady hand, he had the door open.

"Fifteen-twenty minutes tops," he whispered. "Zip disk," he told her, placing it in her hand. "See what you can do with the computer while I make appropriate noises for the microphone."

"Ah, Rafe," she moaned loudly with a breathy sound that stirred his groin. She took the pocket flash and headed for Rialto's computer. In seconds the big monitor began to glow softly. Rafe stood near the open doorway and started making appropriate sound effects.

His original plan had been entirely different, but the opportunity their little scene had created had been too good to pass up. Marcus Slade and anyone who had witnessed that exchange in the other room would find it highly believable that they'd snuck off to have a quickie in the middle of the party. There was just one problem.

Rafe really did want her. And not just a quickie either. This time his groan came straight from his imagination.

STEPHEN RIALTO had less protection on his machine than Penny had on the one belonging to the Confidentials, Kendra discovered. The biggest problem consisted of the sheer number of files to choose from. Without more time, she couldn't possibly go through them all. Besides, Kendra found it hard to concentrate with Rafe making subtle, stirring sounds in the doorway of the other room. Her mouth still tasted him and her nipples were still tight. He'd been putting on a show for the listening devices, but her body had a whole different take on the situation. She wanted him. And she knew it wasn't entirely one-sided.

She forced that thought aside and tried hard to concentrate on what she was doing. She copied any file that seemed to contain the sort of information that would help the Confidentials.

"That's it, baby," Rafe said. "Come on. Come for me."

While her body immediately reacted to his sexy tone, her brain knew his words were meant to warn her that time was running out. Naturally, that was when she found the hidden files. Her eyes skimmed the first document. It took all her restraint not to call out to Rafe in her excitement. They had just hit pay dirt. She copied the files, nodding as Rafe motioned to her to hurry.

Reluctantly, she shut the machine down, no longer listening to Rafe's noises. If she'd had more time....

Before she could pull the disk from the drive, she heard a key in the door that led to the hall. There was no time to dash across the room. No time to search for a hiding place. Kendra did the only thing available to her. She slipped under Rialto's desk, even as Rafe shut the library door.

Light flooded the room. Rialto's desk was big and wide and open, offering little concealment. As soon as the person came far enough into the room, they would see her huddled beneath the expensive dark walnut.

Her heart pounded in terror. She tried desperately to think up some excuse to explain her presence under Rialto's private desk. Nothing came to mind. In fact, fear had choked every coherent thought from her terrified brain.

The loud thump against the library door nearly sent her into cardiac arrest. Rafe's voice carried clearly.

"Geeze, baby, take it easy or someone will hear...I'm not Superman, you know... God, you're insatiable... Come're." He bumped against the door again.

The light winked out. She heard the door lock click. Kendra sprang from hiding, grabbed the diskette from the machine and raced across the room. She stepped inside the library as someone tried the doorknob in the hall. Rafe nearly tore her dress, unzipping the back and pulling it down to reveal most of one breast. He didn't seem to notice as he dropped to his knees, lifting her skirt.

Before she could think, his head was buried beneath the material that he'd rucked high on her legs. Shock held her motionless. She could feel his warm breath against her panties.

Kendra barely had enough presence of mind to let out a shocked moan as the door opened and the lights came on all around them. Rafe raised up quickly. A white-clad figure stepped into the room. Kendra had a quick view of Rafe's lips looking suspiciously wet before he stood and turned as if to block her from the intruder's view. The man did know how to stage a scene.

"What do you think you're doing?" Rafe demanded.

Kendra turned quickly away, aware that she didn't have to pretend embarrassment. Her cheeks were suffused with heat while her breathing came in shallow pants. Pins had already fallen from her hair due to her dive under the desk, and with one breast nearly exposed, she no doubt conveyed the image Rafe wanted.

She set about straightening her clothing, unable to meet the security man's expression. Not surprisingly, she was shaking all over. Rafe would be pleased. It would add to the farce. She barely heard their conversation as Rafe challenged the guard. The man openly sneered as he explained that the room needed to be left open for all the guests to use.

Kendra glanced over her shoulder in time to see Rafe's muscles bunch. For a second, she thought Rafe was going to hit the security man—the same guard who'd stopped them from exploring earlier.

The tension was diffused by the arrival of a group of party guests who wandered into the room, chatting as they came.

"Come on, Kendra," Rafe said, taking her hand. Instead of crossing past the smug guard, he opened the door onto the patio. His fingers surreptitiously removed the disk she held against her skirt. Without seeming to, he took the disk and pocketed it so deftly she barely realized what he'd done.

"What if that guard tries the connecting door?" she whispered.

"Then we'll have a problem. I suspect he'll be too titillated to bother."

Rafe glanced back inside and nodded in satisfaction more to himself than to her. "He's gone and I'm pretty sure he didn't check the door. That was close."

"Too close!" Her heart still pounded from the near miss.

"Nice garter belt," he said innocently.

Her cheeks flamed again, but she managed to rally. "You would know."

"Ah. I thought it looked familiar. I have good taste."

"But appalling manners."

"I'll do better later. Promise."

"You're incorrigible."

"Thank you."

"Are you enjoying yourselves?" Rialto asked, walking up to them.

"It's a lovely party," Kendra managed, astounded at how cool her voice sounded despite the adrenaline flooding her body. Her emotions were definitely on overload. For a moment she felt so giddy she thought she would pass out.

"Good. Good. I don't think I've had an opportunity to tell you what a lovely addition you will make to our staff, Ms. Kincade."

She knew if Rialto touched her she'd surely be ill right here in front of everyone. Hatred churned her stomach.

"Rafe assures me that he can't function without you as his assistant."

"We've been partners for some time," she told him, fighting to maintain control.

"No need to be modest, Kendra," Rafe interrupted. "You're damn good at what you do."

She knew he was referring to the diskette now in his pocket. "Thank you," she acknowledged with a sudden surge of spunk. "Modesty is an overrated virtue." She *was* good. And they'd pulled this coup off right under the bastard's nose.

Stephen Rialto laughed, oblivious to any undercurrent. "I like a woman who knows her value. We will have to get to know each other much better."

Not even if elephants sprouted wings and nested in tree tops.

The very idea of getting to know a creature like Rialto had her desperately swallowing the bile that threatened to spill into her throat. She mustered a cool smile. "Don't worry, I plan to show you exactly what I'm worth," she promised.

She'd had so many doubts. Until this moment she hadn't been sure she could go through with her plan, but her hatred of this man was complete.

She raised her eyes and found Rialto coldly assessing her. An icy stab of fear suddenly stole her confidence. For a second she was certain he knew who she was and why she was here. Then his expression changed and he turned to respond to a comment from the couple who joined them.

Her gaze flitted around the room, landing on Marcus Slade. His cold eyes looked through her. She tried not to shiver as he issued a frigid smile and turned away. She battled a rising sense of panic.

Somehow, she continued her pose, throwing herself into the role of politely professional guest. She smiled and joined in the myriad conversations swirling around her. All the while she was aware of Rafe beside her. His concern tangible, there was nothing she could do or say to reassure him.

Things were not right. They would never be right again. Rialto was the shadow man—the man who had haunted her dreams for twenty-one years—the man she had come here to kill.

She hoped she contained her shudder, but the memory of that snowy afternoon abruptly blotted out the noise of the party, eliminating every one and every thing.

She had ducked behind a chair so he wouldn't see her. Fear had made her chest feel all hard and tight—like now. *Her stomach had hurt because she knew he would kill her. But he had never looked toward her hiding place. Instead, he had looked down at the woman on the hall floor and fired his gun again.*

She'd wanted to scream. She wanted to scream now. *She had wanted to hurt that horrible shadow man with every fiber of her eight-year-old body.* Now she intended to kill this shadow man no matter what the consequences to her thirty-one-year-old self.

"Kendra, are you okay?" Rafe asked.

Slowly she became aware that they'd been left standing by themselves. She was holding a glass of champagne with no memory of picking it up. Kendra drank it down like medicine, ignoring the way the bubbles ticked the back of her throat making her want to cough.

"Fine."

He squeezed her hand. Her fingers were ice-cold.

"Can you hold it together just a little longer?" he asked.

"Of course." As long as it took. She'd waited years for this night, she was not going to go to pieces yet.

Rafe didn't look convinced, but he nodded as he took the glass from her hand and set it on a table. "I need to go back in the library and relock that door. Do you want to head to the room?"

"Alone?" She thought of Marcus Slade. "No. I'll wait for you. I'm fine. Don't worry."

Despite the concern so plainly etched on his features, he nodded and disappeared. The party was starting to thin, she observed. Rialto and Slade were near the front door saying good-night to a cluster of people. There were still many party-goers milling around, but the men in white now outnumbered the guests who were left. The evening had taken on a surreal glow.

"Come on."

Kendra jumped as Rafe returned and took her arm.

"Time for bed." He pulled her against his side. She allowed herself to lean into his solid frame. Her brain felt disconnected as he led her to the outside steps and the second-floor balcony.

"Did you fix it?" she asked for something to say. She didn't really care if he had relocked the door or not. This night would soon be over. Everything would soon be over.

"It's locked," he said, ducking his head and barely moving his lips. For the camera, she realized. She'd forgotten about the cameras.

Her crime would be recorded for posterity tonight. Too bad the only record of Rialto's atrocity was etched where only she could see it. But he would pay and the nightmares would finally cease.

As soon as they entered the room, Rafe left her side. She was appalled to realize that she missed the comfort of his touch. That was dangerous.

After turning on the light, he studied the room before retrieving his bug scanner and sweeping for newly placed bugs. Kendra headed across the hall to use the bathroom. She didn't want to know if Rialto had rebugged their room. She simply wanted to wash her face and fall into bed until it was time to do what had to be done.

Rafe studied her when she returned to the room. She knew he glimpsed the hopeless fear pressing against her chest like a heavy weight.

"What's wrong?"

"Just tired."

"If you're upset because of what I did downstairs—"

"Don't be silly. That was quick thinking on your part. It certainly kept us out of immediate trouble."

Rafe studied her.

"I'm fine."

Finally, he nodded. "Get undressed while I use the bathroom."

"Wait! I almost forgot. You need to see the jackpot." She could do this much for him at least. Perhaps the information would still help nab Calerdone.

''Calderone is coming into the country next week along with a shipment of drugs. He plans to meet with Rialto.''

''What?''

''It's on the disk. Everything you need.''

''Let me see!''

She pulled out the portable computer, glad to be able to do something besides think. She set up the machine and opened the file for his perusal.

Rafe grinned. ''You did it! This is huge!''

''*We* did it.''

''We certainly did! Partner.''

She managed a wan smile. Guilt threatened to choke her.

''Get ready for bed,'' he said kindly, no doubt taking her expression for exhaustion. ''I'll be back in a few minutes.'' He packed up the computer, carefully storing the diskette.

As soon as he left, she stripped off the green dress and the sexy garter belt and hose and donned the sexy green nightgown he'd selected. Exhausted, she slipped beneath the covers. Another time, she might have worried about sharing the large bed with Rafe. Tonight all she could think about was the end of her nightmare.

It wasn't too late to change her mind. She told herself she didn't have to go through with her plan.

But killing Stephen Rialto was the only way to put her mind to rest once and for all. She closed her eyes.

As time passed, she knew she was drifting into a state that was more asleep than awake. She ordered herself to stop remembering. Her mind refused to listen. Even though she knew she dreamed, the nightmare returned in full with devastating force.

SHE TASTED THE dry-edged fear that left its metallic flavor lingering in her mouth. Yet again, she tried to call a warning to the young girl slowly counting to twenty out of sight beyond the kitchen.

From inside the bottom of the linen closet she watched helplessly as the pretty blond woman stepped away from the stove and answered the brisk knock on the front door.

"Why, hello. We—weren't expecting you."

The shadow man entered, big and burly in his heavy winter coat, snowflakes melting against the dark material. Only now he had a face. The face of evil.

There was a popping sound. The woman crumpled to the floor without another word. At the kitchen table, her husband started to rise from his seat. "What the—?"

Two more popping sounds came. His outflung hand struck a glass of cola, spilling the sticky contents across the tabletop. Once more, the liquid began to drip, drip, drip against the clean tile floor.

In her head, she screamed a warning to the young girl who stopped counting and suddenly entered the kitchen from the dining room, innocently unaware.

Pop. Pop.

She fell like a broken rag doll. The shadow man stepped over her body and into the dining room.

In the closet, she drew herself into a tiny tight ball and closed her eyes. He would see her if she made a single sound. Suddenly, he bounded up the stairs, pausing to check each of the three bedrooms before moving straight for her hiding place.

She held her breath in terror as the closet door groaned all the way open. He rummaged on one of the upper shelves. She lifted her eyelids, hardly daring to breathe. A blanket fell to the floor in front of her.

She waited in an agony of fear for him to bend and pick it up. A towel landed on top of the blanket. He left them both. He pulled off his glove for a moment. The gun hand disappeared from her line of sight. His left hand fell to his side as he stood there silently.

The blood red stone sparkled in the ring he wore. As it had sparkled tonight.

Now she heard him moving in the basement. She told herself not to move, but silently, like a movie played over and over, she uncurled her body and crept down the stairs. When she paused in the hall she jumped as the woman's eyes fluttered open.

"Next door," she whispered. "Get Mr. Lee. Hurry! Run!"

The shadow man started up the steps from the basement level.

She ran into the living room, ducking behind a chair so he wouldn't see her. Fear made her chest feel all hard and tight. Her stomach hurt because she knew he would shoot her if he caught her. But he never looked toward her hiding place. Instead, he looked down at the woman on the hall floor and fired his gun again.

She wanted to scream. She wanted to hurt that horrible man with every fiber of her being. She was consumed with hate for the man who wore Stephen Rialto's cold face. She hated him and his shiny red ring and his big ugly gun.

He strode into the kitchen. Then he was gone, out the front door. She rose on legs that trembled violently.

The pungent scent of natural gas filled the house.

She turned to the sliding glass door in the dining room and struggled with the bar lock until she got it open. The smell was stronger. It made her feel sick.

Rafe stood outside, silhouetted against an empty sky. He watched her with a troubled expression. Somehow, he became Mr. Lee, the symbol of safety. She wanted to tell him how much she loved him, but the words jammed in her throat.

She stepped outside, closing the door behind her in case Rialto came after her.

It had started to snow again. Big fat white flakes that

*made her shiver. She wished she had her coat—and her
boots. The snow was deep. Rafe beckoned to her, telling her
to hurry. She started running across the pristine expanse of
white.*

And the world exploded at her back.

KENDRA WOKE with a gasp. The room was dark, but she
realized she was no longer alone on the bed. At some point
Rafe had climbed beneath the covers. It felt late, but the
bedside clock indicated only two hours had passed. She
waited, listening to the rise and fall of his breathing. She
knew what she had to do to stop the nightmare once and for
all.

Slowly, she folded back the covers and slipped from the
bed.

As silently as she could, she headed around to Rafe's side
of the bed. Her fingers found his holster on the nightstand.
Carefully, she slipped it from the sheath, the heavy metal
cold in her fingers. Rafe's breathing didn't change even
when she checked the clip.

Reluctantly, she left the room through the balcony door.
There was no turning back. This was where the big risk
came. If someone monitored the cameras twenty-four hours
a day, they would see her and probably stop her. She didn't
want to hurt anyone else. Only Rialto.

Barefoot, she walked along the concrete balcony, past
rooms containing other sleeping guests. She held the gun
out of sight in the folds of the green gown.

From below came a woman's high-pitched giggle. Kendra
hesitated. There was a splash, drawing her gaze to the pool.
A naked, lush woman climbed from the water. The brunette
threw back her long wet mane of hair and laughed again.
An equally naked, aroused Stephen Rialto heaved himself
onto the deck beside her. From the water rose yet another,
perfectly sculpted naked woman.

Kendra closed her eyes. She choked back a gag. She didn't want to see any more. But she had no choice.

Rialto and the blonde embraced. The brunette joined them. Kendra thought she would vomit. Abruptly, the brunette turned and ran to the diving board. Rialto and the blonde watched her make a perfect dive into the water.

Kendra shivered. The woman surfaced and laughed. The blonde scampered over to the diving board for a turn. Her dive was less perfect, raising a splash. Both women laughed and called to Rialto.

Kendra reached the bottom step. The makeshift bar was still in place. There were no white-clad men in attendance and the glasses and bottles had been cleared away, leaving the two women and Rialto to frolic beneath the cold moon.

Kendra shivered.

Rialto started toward the diving board. Kendra slunk to the table while his focus was on the two women. She would never have a better opportunity. When he moved onto the diving board, he'd be perfectly silhouetted.

She took a position behind the white-covered table.

The distance wasn't much further than the gun range Rafe had taught her on.

She wouldn't miss.

Rialto would die.

He posed on the diving board, laughing at the two women. Her finger rested on the trigger. All she had to do was squeeze gently.

Rialto called out something ribald. He posed, his arms outflung.

And she couldn't do it.

She couldn't make her finger apply the final bit of pressure needed to consign him to hell where he belonged.

Rialto entered the water in a clean dive, slicing the water perfectly. Kendra wanted to sob.

Instead, the light came on at her back. There was a snick

of sound as someone opened a patio door. Any moment, the person would see her. She ducked beneath the white tablecloth.

"Miguel?" Rialto called out. "What do you think you're doing?"

"*Lo siento.* I did not realize you were out here, señor. I came for the cloth. For the laundry, señor."

If he took the tablecloth, Kendra would be exposed.

"Never mind that tonight. Go to bed," Rialto ordered. "You can do it *mañana.*"

One of the women giggled. Kendra prayed Miguel would obey.

"*Sí, señor. Buenos tardes.*"

Kendra hovered, afraid to move. She ignored the new sounds coming from the pool and waited. Finally, she lifted the back of the cloth to peer out.

Miguel had left a light on in the living room. A light that spilled across the path she needed to cross to get back to her room. Something shifted in the darkness of the living room. She thought Miguel must have stayed behind to watch, but she realized the watcher was Marcus Slade.

She was trapped.

Chapter Twelve

Something pulled him from sleep. For a moment, Rafe didn't know what had wakened him, but his fingers automatically reached for the gun on the nightstand. He jerked to a sitting position when he encountered the empty holster.

The bed beside him was also empty.

Kendra was gone and had taken his gun!

His earlier misgivings about her motives rushed to fill his head. He sprang from the bed, groping for his pants. Then he remembered that he'd been trying to impress her. He'd hung his tuxedo neatly in the closet.

Rafe fumbled in the dark for pants and a shirt while two possibilities beat at his brain. She'd either gone to warn Rialto or to kill him. He was very much afraid it was the latter.

She didn't stand a chance. With the cameras not working in the far wing, Rialto's security would be extra alert for possible trouble. After all, they had a house filled with guests. No way were they going to let one roam free. The party had barely concluded. He'd listened to the sounds of its death throes before falling asleep half an hour ago.

He should have paid more attention to his instincts. He'd known something was wrong tonight. Why hadn't he demanded answers from her?

Because when she'd fallen into a dead sleep, he'd thought his only trouble would be sharing a bed without waking her to make love. What a fool he'd been. He shoved his feet into a pair of shoes.

Once he stepped out of the room, security would have him on tape—just as they must have her on tape. Looking around, he realized she hadn't even taken time to get dressed. And that gave him an idea.

Boldly, he walked onto the balcony. She was nowhere in sight. Noises issued from the pool area. Rialto and two playmates were unwinding in the water. The patio light suddenly flashed on. He caught a wisp of green disappearing beneath the makeshift bar.

Rafe hurried back through the room and out into the hall. His plan hinged on Kendra's ability to take a cue and run with it. Of course that assumed he could get to her before she did whatever it was she'd come here to do.

He saw the man called Miguel pass beneath him as he descended the main staircase. The patio light was still on outside while in the dark living room near the sliding glass door, a figure stood watching the scene silently. Had the watcher seen Kendra?

The figure whirled as he made his presence known.

"Slade," he said coolly.

"Alvarez. Did you need something?"

"Yes. I seem to have a small problem."

The man's hand hovered near his jacket and the gun that was no doubt carefully concealed beneath it.

"Maybe I can help?"

"I hope so. I'm looking for Kendra."

The man stilled. "You misplaced her?"

"Not exactly. She won't appreciate me telling you this, but she has a problem. We haven't had an incident in a long time, but she's been known to sleepwalk."

"Really." Skepticism filled his voice.

"Yeah, I know, it sounds unbelievable, but I've actually

seen her go out to the kitchen, make a sandwich, put on a pot of coffee, and have no idea she's doing any of it."

"You're right. It is unbelievable," he said, his voice thick with scorn. "And I assure you, she is not in the kitchen making a sandwich or anything else."

Rafe pasted an annoyed look on his face. "I didn't think she was. She could be anywhere. Look, I shared your disbelief the first couple of times it happened, but her doctor assures me it's a legitimate phenomenon. Mostly it happens when she's stressed."

"And she's stressed now?"

Rafe shrugged. "She isn't in the bedroom and she was sound asleep when I went to bed a short time ago. It sounded like someone was in the pool so I thought I'd go out and ask—"

"No!"

Marcus reached for the outside light switch and turned it off. He stood as if to block Rafe's view with his back to the pool area.

"Mr. Rialto and some friends are taking a late-night swim. Ms. Kincade is not with them. Did you check the bathroom across the hall from your bedroom?"

"The door was open as I went by."

Slade nodded. "I'll check with security. We'll find her. Please return to your room."

"Maybe I'd better go with you." If Kendra really did plan to kill Rialto tonight, Rafe had just given her the perfect opportunity.

"The house staff can handle the situation," Slade argued.

Rafe doubted that. He half expected to hear a gunshot at any moment. "Don't let them wake her, okay? She'll eventually wake on her own and be very confused."

Heck, he was the one who was confused. What was Kendra doing out there?

"I'll see to it personally," Slade promised.

Rafe saw the movement outside. He was pretty sure Kendra had seized the moment and fled back up the stairs.

It made no sense, but Rafe was too relieved to question his luck. He allowed himself to be guided to the main staircase. As he re-entered the bedroom, he flicked on the switch. Kendra blinked in the sudden light standing uncertainly beside his nightstand.

"Where were you?" she demanded.

"Don't you think that should be my question? But before you answer, let me tell you how this is going to play when Slade arrives."

Her body jerked at the name. "He saw me?"

"Fortunately, no. But the camera did and he just went to review the tapes. The camera will show you going down to the pool, but you were probably out of range at the table, unless you went around to the other side."

"I didn't. You knew?"

"I saw enough." He swallowed the bitter taste of anger. There'd be time for that later. Much later. "I told Slade you had an occasional problem with sleepwalking."

"You're joking."

"No, and you'd better be quite convincing. I suspect we have very little time—"

There was a knock on the door. The handle turned and Slade entered without waiting for an invitation. Rafe spun around, wondering if this was the end of everything.

"Ah, Ms. Kincade. I see you returned safe and sound."

Rafe moved protectively to her side, aware of how revealing the green nightgown was as it clung to the outline of her body. Kendra came to the same conclusion because she reached for the matching robe and drew it on without answering.

"Mr. Alvarez says you suffer from a sleepwalking disorder."

She rounded on Rafe, her face a mask of indignation. "You had no right to tell him about that!"

"What was I supposed to do, let security shoot you?" He didn't have to fake his annoyance. He drew on the anger that simmered inside him.

"I—" she looked from one man to another then walked over and sat down on the arm chair. "It's embarrassing. It hasn't happened in almost a year."

"So you *were* sleepwalking?" Slade asked skeptically.

"I must have been." She studied the hands clasped in her lap. "All of a sudden I was down by the pool and…"

Kendra should have been an actress. If Rafe hadn't known better, he would have bought the performance completely . And that made him wonder how much else had been an act.

"Mr. Rialto was in the pool. He—wasn't alone. I didn't know what to do. I was horribly embarrassed." She lifted her head and looked defiantly at Marcus Slade. "I didn't want him to think I was spying on him. To be honest, I didn't give security a thought. I was confused and horrified so I ducked behind the table and waited until the light went off outside the living room. Then I came back up here. I'm terribly sorry if I've caused a problem."

Slade's expression gave away none of his thoughts. "Is this apt to reoccur tonight?"

"No," they said in unison.

"It never has before," Kendra amended. She stood and squared her shoulders. "If there are any repercussions to this, the fault is mine, not Rafe's."

"Never mind that," Rafe said gruffly.

"No." She looked at him with troubled eyes. "I don't want you to lose your job because of me."

He could almost taste her sincerity. "Don't worry about it."

Slade shifted. "We'll see what Mr. Rialto has to say in

the morning. It would be best if you would remain in your room until then, however.''

"Of course," she agreed. "Good night."

"Good night."

Rafe locked the door behind him. When he turned he saw that Kendra had replaced his gun in its holster. Good. Slade wouldn't have missed a detail like that. Hopefully, it lent even more credence to their tale.

"Let's get some sleep," he said gruffly. "We'll talk in the morning."

Kendra nodded. Without a word she removed the dressing gown and slid under the covers. He pulled off his own clothing and slid in beside her.

"I'm sorry. I blew it. And maybe ruined your chances as well." Grief filled her voice. "I had him in my sights. I couldn't miss. And I couldn't pull the trigger. Years of scheming and dreaming and planning—all for nothing."

Rafe rolled toward her across the width of the bed. With the back of his knuckle, he wiped moisture from her cheek.

"You were going to kill him?"

"Yes."

"Because of your aunt and uncle?"

"They weren't." More tears fell and she wiped at them angrily.

"Weren't what?"

"My aunt and uncle."

And he guessed in that second what she was about to say next. It was the only thing that made any sense.

"They were my parents. I'm not Kendra Kincade. I'm Ginny Ford.

"Kendra was staying for dinner that night. My aunt and uncle were supposed to come over later to play pinochle with my parents. They often played cards together. Kendra and I were playing hide-and-go-seek. It was her turn to be it. If it had been my turn, I would have been the one to die."

Pain swelled his heart for the grief that filled her voice. He didn't doubt her words or her emotions. She couldn't be faking this.

"You don't have to tell me any more." But she didn't seem to hear him. It was as if a dam had burst inside her. The pain she'd been holding back all these years tumbled forth with the telling.

"Rialto knocked on the front door and my mother answered. He shot her right there in the hall." She shuddered.

Rafe cursed silently and pulled her into his arms.

"Daddy was sitting at the kitchen table."

"You saw the whole thing?"

"I was hiding in the closet at the top of the hall with the door cracked. We had a big open house. From there I could see everything." Tears clogged her throat but she went on grimly. "I wanted to yell to Kendra to run, but I was afraid. I should have warned her!"

"Shh. Hush." He stroked her back but her tears flowed all the faster as the nightmare tumbled past her lips.

"He shot Kendra when she came into the kitchen. There was so much blood."

"There was nothing you could have done."

"Don't you understand? I hid there like a coward while he killed my whole family!"

Sobs tore at her chest. A lump had risen in his own throat at her anguish.

"I couldn't even go for help when Mommy told me to."

"God," he said prayerfully, stroking her hair. "Your mother was still alive?"

She nodded blindly. "He shot her again when he came up from the basement." She pushed past her sobs. "I thought he'd find me then, but he never did."

"You actually saw him?"

Kendra nodded slowly. "His face, his ring. The same one he was wearing tonight." She shuddered.

He remembered how she'd stared at that ring with such grim fascination. "I'm sorry, Kendra."

Rafe held her while she cried brokenly. He wished he knew how to offer her some measure of comfort, but no amount of words would change the past. Obviously, she felt she'd failed her family, both that day so long ago and tonight when she'd sought her own form of restitution for them.

Rafe continued to hold her while the pain of her failure caused the tears to fall until she had no strength left to cry. All the while he held her, stroking her back or her hair and hurting for her.

"You couldn't pull the trigger because that would have made you no better than he is, Kendra," Rafe whispered against her hair when her sobs faded to hiccuppy snuffles. "Your parents wouldn't have wanted that for you, any more than they would have wanted you to die along with them that day."

His finger gently pressed her lips when she would have protested.

"You know I'm right. You can lie to me, but not to yourself. We're going to nail him, Kendra. Think how much more satisfying it will be to know that arrogant bastard is rotting in some prison. If you'd shot him, he wouldn't have suffered at all. This way, he'll live in fear of his fate. The information you got tonight will put him in a perfect hell because he'll have to fear more than the authorities. Once we have Rialto in custody, Calderone will want to stop any possibility that Rialto might talk. He'll be between the proverbial rock and a hard place. Calderone will go after him whether he talks or not. Rialto will never be able to rest after we nail him."

Rafe stroked her hair gently. She nestled closer and he hoped his words were getting to her, making sense.

"I'm counting on you to get even more evidence when we report for work this week," he continued. "We know

Rialto is using his legitimate company to launder drug money. You're the only one who can help us prove it.''

She sighed in response, nestling more firmly in his arms. Her hand rested against his chest. It was as if the steady thump of his heart beneath her palm, added a measure of reassurance.

Gradually, she calmed. Rafe held her long after her breathing deepened and her body relaxed. His mind churned over the things she'd told him. Why hadn't she named the killer to the police? Did the authorities know that Kendra and Ginny had switched places? Had it been the aunt and uncle's doing, or had it been suggested by law enforcement officials to protect her? Not that it really mattered either way, but he suspected life must have been very difficult for the small family. He wondered if anyone had sought professional help for the little girl Kendra had been.

Ginny. Not Kendra.

He gave a mental shake of his head. He'd never be able to think of her as Ginny. She was Kendra. She'd been Kendra most of her life. He could only imagine how difficult that must have been. No doubt her survivor guilt had been reinforced by her aunt and uncle, however unintentionally. They were bound to feel hurt that their child had died in her place. It must have been a cold, lonely life for the little girl she had been. No wonder she had sought refuge in the impersonal world of computers. Rafe stroked her hair tenderly.

Her lashes lifted.

''Go back to sleep.''

''I wasn't sleeping, I was thinking.''

He tried for levity. ''Sounds dangerous.''

''You aren't angry.'' He heard the surprise in her voice.

''No. I wish you'd told me all this before, but—''

''If I'd told you before, you wouldn't have let me come,'' she interrupted.

"True enough." He kissed the top of her hair. "Go to sleep, Kendra."

"I don't think I can sleep right now. Would—would you make love to me instead?"

All coherent thoughts flew right out of him mind. She'd caught him completely off guard.

"I know it's probably asking a lot, but—"

"Shh. It's not asking a lot, only I don't think this is a good time."

"Why not? No cameras, no hidden microphones. Seems like a perfect time to me." Her hand slid disturbingly over his bare chest. "Or don't you want me any more?"

His body was already responding to that question. "Oh, I want you, but this has been an emotionally charged night for you."

"And you don't want to take advantage?"

"No, I don't." He sensed her skepticism. "How can you think I don't want you? All you have to do is lower that hand to learn the truth."

She was vulnerable right now. He would not take advantage.

Fingers that had been toying with his chest hair stopped. She stared into his eyes. Very deliberately, her fingers slid lower. She leaned into him, her breasts pushing against his skin provocatively. Before he could draw back, she began placing soft kisses against his shoulder sending shivers of pleasure along his nerve endings.

"Kendra, I don't think—"

"Good. Don't think, just feel," she murmured. "You don't have to do a thing. *I'll* make love to *you*."

Her lips sought his mouth, even as her hand closed over the sensitive portion of his anatomy that would prove his ability to make love with her. Rafe tried not to groan at that erotic contact. Her mouth became hotly sweet and demanding as she kissed him. Her hand was also demanding—and getting an instant response.

Rafe gave up his noble effort to resist when she nibbled on his jaw, then ducked her head so her mouth closed over one of his nipples.

He'd be noble later.

With a groan of desire, he rolled her beneath him. His lips sought the sensitive skin of her neck beneath her ear lobe, eliciting a squirm of pleasure. Pulling aside the thin straps of her gown, he slid his hand beneath the material to cup her breast. The firm round flesh was a perfect fit. He teased the nipple to a rigid point before closing his mouth over the other breast right through the satiny material of her gown.

Kendra cried out in shocked pleasure. He quickly muffled the sound with his mouth. She trembled beneath him in anticipation as their tongues dueled silently. All the while her hand continued stroking him to fever pitch.

He wouldn't last long if she continued her sweet ministrations, but apparently Kendra didn't want to slow the frantic pace. She wouldn't release him as she kissed her way across his chest. The silky material of her gown added an element of sensuality as it slithered between them, rubbing enticingly.

They were climbing to a flash point despite his attempts to slow things down. No woman had ever excited him like this. Rafe grabbed a handful of material, drawing it up her leg until he felt the incredible smooth skin of her thigh. The illusive scent of her, combined with the heady taste of her mouth and skin, drove him past the point of coherent thought. Rafe knew he was lost. Only his determination to bring her as much pleasure as possible kept him from sliding between her feverishly moving legs right then and there.

His hand brushed the apex of her thighs. She shivered as he explored her. Their mouths clung in sweet passion.

"Please," she breathed against his mouth.

Her breathy whisper left him trembling. He'd always enjoyed loving and being loved by women, but tonight was different—important. He couldn't help the child she had been, but he could show the woman she was now what it was like to be loved.

Rafe barely had the presence of mind to pull away before he claimed her. She whimpered impatiently as he reached for his wallet, fumbling for the silver foil packet he carried inside.

"Hurry," she pleaded.

"You've got me so worked up I can barely get this thing open." He bent to kiss her before tearing the package apart.

"Let me put it on."

Excitement laced her expression. She leaned forward, tugging at his briefs. Rafe practically exploded when her hair brushed his erection. Her hands were so soft. They moved with such slow, tender care.

He was no novice to making love with a woman, yet he found himself inexplicably struggling to maintain control. It was as if this was his very first time all over again. He wanted to plunge inside of her in the most primitive way. This had never happened before, yet he felt a need to possess her completely—to brand her as his in every way possible.

She was driving him out of his mind.

He forced a mental grip on his control. He *would* bring her the same feverish pleasure she was creating in him—or die trying. She gasped in surprise when he moved over her again, but kept moving down her body until he positioned himself between her thighs.

"Rafe!"

Satisfaction rippled through him when she gripped his head at the first stroke of his tongue. Her sounds of pleasure mingled with the writhing of her body. The combination spurred him on until he felt her body tightening beneath him.

He moved up quickly, sheathing himself in her remarkably tight warmth.

Kendra gasped and stilled, her eyes luminous in the darkness of the room.

"Are you all right?" he whispered in concern, afraid to move.

"Oh. Yes." Breathlessly, she placed a butterfly kiss along his jaw.

He held his desire in check a moment longer, afraid to cause her pain. "It's been a long time for you, hasn't it?"

"A very long time, but please don't stop."

Rafe strangled on a half-laugh. "I'm afraid I couldn't even if I wanted to. You feel...incredible!"

She contracted around him. Rafe lost the thread of his control and he began to move. Her body immediately responded to the gentle thrusts. Soon, the age old rhythm captured both of them, catapulting them closer and closer to the brink of something wonderful.

"Rafe!"

His mouth swallowed the sound of her startled pleasure, and he watched, momentarily caught by the rapture of her pleasure before her tiny convulsions pushed him past the point of watching anything at all.

For a long time, they simply lay there, too sated to move. Finally, he withdrew and rolled over, snuggling her against his chest.

Kendra sighed contentedly as she lay her head in the crook of his shoulder.

"I love you," she breathed as her lashes fluttered closed.

For a very long time he lay there, unable and unwilling to move. Finally he roused to draw the covers up and over their damp skin. But he didn't release her as those three, half-heard words tumbled around in his head.

Many women had said them in the height of passion. Why

did it leave him feeling so frantically wild that she had
joined those ranks?

Because she didn't mean them?

Or because she did?

Chapter Thirteen

Rafe was still worrying that thought a week later as he watched her sitting at her desk so confidently, staring at the computer screen with total absorption.

Kendra fit the role as his assistant as if she'd been performing the job all her life. Even Stephen Rialto had commented on how delighted he was by her initiative and expertise. In fact, the man had gone out of his way to stop by her office several times to tell her what a good job she was doing.

Rafe should have been pleased. Instead, it rankled. He told himself it was not jealousy. He was simply concerned because Kendra was his responsibility.

And his lover.

The truth was, he didn't like Rialto or any of his people getting close to Kendra. Rafe's integration into the organization was not going as smoothly as it should. He'd always been able to blend into any given situation, but for the first time, it wasn't happening. At least, not with the same mastery he'd always had before.

Rafe couldn't put his finger on any one thing, but he'd begun to feel uneasy. Though Rialto had brushed aside the incident of Kendra's sleepwalking, Rafe wasn't making the sort of progress he should be making by now.

Except with Kendra. Since that incredible night, they'd

remained lovers and Rafe had discovered that he liked everything about her. She had a quick mind and a keen wit and she wasn't afraid to voice her own opinions. She didn't preen, she didn't use artifice and she held back nothing of herself, in bed or out.

And it continued to chew at him that she was a passionate, generous partner, but she'd never again spoken those sleepy words to him. Rafe wanted to hear them again. More, he was finding it increasingly important to know if she had meant them, or if they had simply been spoken carelessly in a moment of satisfaction.

His own feelings were confusing him. He had never been possessive before, yet he was coming to hate the sexy dresses and slinky suits she wore so effortlessly. And all because he hated the way other men noticed her.

He had to admit Kendra handled her admirers with calm, friendly banter—much like the way he and Penny had always interacted. There was no reason for any of this to bother him, but it did. And that was disconcerting.

Rafe didn't have much time to brood over their relationship. Though Kendra was seldom far from his thoughts, Rialto had kept both of them busy without really thrusting them into the setup at Rialto Industries. Kendra fretted that she was never alone long enough to do a decent search of the main computer files. Rafe was beginning to suspect it was intentional.

While the small Texas oil firm did brisk business, many of the details Rafe was asked to attend to seemed outside the scope of a security expert. He had the feeling Rialto was deliberately keeping him occupied with unimportant details. He didn't mind being tested, but this felt different. He was being deliberately kept out of the real loop.

Both of them worried that her actions had jeopardized the mission.

Mitchell had let Rafe know the trap was laid. The agents

were working closely with the DEA and the FBI. Kendra's brief searches had turned up several things of interest to the authorities despite her complaint that she couldn't make a proper search.

"Ready to call it a night?" Rafe asked.

Kendra looked up and nodded. "Just let me shut down the computer."

Rafe watched her move briskly about her office, all the while trying not to admire the fit of her suit, especially across her rounded derriere as she bent over a file drawer.

This was the woman who'd objected to going without a bra?

She wore her sexy new clothing with an ease that seemed second nature now. And an ease that stirred him every time he looked her way.

They headed outside to the car together as usual. They had rented a small furnished apartment in town near Rialto's office, though they spent very little time there, working long hours, trying to find time alone to search through the computers at work.

"I still think you should call in sick tomorrow," Rafe told her quietly as they headed for the apartment.

"Rafe, we've argued about this all weekend. You know we have to keep everything as normal as possible on the surface. If I suddenly call in sick the day Calderone is due to arrive I might alert Rialto that something isn't right."

"I know, but this assignment he just gave me bothers me. Sending me out to a site alone over such picky details isn't realistic. This isn't a job for his chief of security and he knows it."

"Are you sure he isn't sending you because he wants you to see the operation firsthand for some reason? Or do you think it's possible that he wants to know you are occupied while he meets with Calderone?"

"It's that last part that worries me. Unless he suspects

something, why would he care? I've got a bad feeling about this operation.''

''You think he knows who we are?''

''I don't see how he could, but I don't like it. If you're at the office, you're vulnerable if something goes wrong.''

''I appreciate you worrying over me, but I think I can handle whatever comes along.''

Rafe ran a knuckle across her cheek. He watched her eyes grow wide with answering awareness. All it ever took was a touch or a look from either of them. It was as if they were tuned to each other.

She set aside the glass of diet cola she'd been drinking and looked at him. ''Do you really think we have a problem?''

Oh, he definitely had a problem all right. For the first time in his career, he was having trouble keeping his mind on the job and his hands off the focus of his thoughts.

''Maybe. I don't like the fact that he's sending me out to the site alone.''

He told himself not to touch her again, but his gaze kept dropping to the deep V of what should have been a prim little red suit. The fit was anything but prim as it hugged Kendra's curves.

''Look at it this way, Rafe.'' Kendra said as she stepped into the elevator. ''Having an official reason to be out of the office makes it easier for you to join Mitchell and the others without anyone being the wiser.''

Rafe had his keys in his hand as they reached the door to their apartment. ''I need to be at the office to cover for you in case something does go wrong,'' Kendra continued. ''What if Rialto needs to get in touch with you before he goes to meet with Calderone?''

''I know.''

They stepped inside and he closed the door. Her breath hitched as his fingers reached out to toy with the V of her jacket. He stopped just short of the shiny brass button that kept it from being indecent.

Slowly he slipped the bit of metal through its narrow hole, revealing the top edge of her bra. The lace rested, bright red to match her suit, against the creamy slope of her round, firm breast.

"Rafe!" she admonished, sounding breathless. "You aren't paying attention."

"Sorry. Is this better?" And he kissed the exposed skin, delighting in the way she shivered delicately.

"Rafe!" But her fingers were reaching for the buttons on his shirt, even as she protested.

"No? I'm sorry," he lied as he parted the jacket and reached for the front clasp to free her breasts from the provocative restraint. "Red turns me on."

"So does every other color I wear."

"Then I guess it must be you." He parted the bra and bent to taste the nipple rising to meet his lips.

"Oh!" It came out a gasp of pleasure. "Shouldn't we go into the bedroom?"

"Too far," he told her, settling her back against the lumpy white couch. "Much too far."

RAFE FORCED his mind from their evening of passion as he waited in his assigned position inside the warehouse. He glanced at his watch and frowned. Calderone was late. More than that, the warehouse was far too quiet. Rialto hadn't yet put in an appearance. In fact, none of his people were anywhere to be seen. The sense of wrongness grew.

As the minutes ticked by, his anxiety over Kendra increased. Even if the truck was late, Rialto should have been here.

Unless he knew this was a trap.

Rafe slipped out of position, instincts screaming. He went to where Mitchell and a DEA agent were concealed. The rest of the Texas Confidential team were in various positions around the warehouse along with DEA and FBI agents working the case. Mitchell frowned at Rafe's approach.

"Something's wrong," Rafe said.

"I agree."

"I'm going to call Kendra." He pulled out his cell phone and dialed the office.

"Good afternoon, Rialto Industries, Barbara speaking."

Foreboding settled in his stomach like an acid weight. "This is Alvarez, where's Kendra?"

"Oh, hi. Kendra isn't here. Mr. Rialto needed her this afternoon. Can I help?"

Rafe willed his voice to remain calm and steady while every atom of him urged immediate action. "Barbara, I need to speak to Kendra for a quick minute. Can you patch me through to Rialto's office?"

"Oh, she isn't there," Barbara assured him blithely. "I saw them leave the building with Mr. Slade several hours ago."

Panic sent a buzzing sound to fill his ear. "Okay, thanks, Barbara."

"Is there anything I can do?" she asked hastily.

"No, not a thing." There was nothing anyone could do now. Including him.

Rafe closed the phone. "Rialto has Kendra," he said bleakly.

Mitchell cursed. "Where would he take her?"

"I'm going to guess his ranch. Send me some backup."

"Wait! It's got to be a trap."

"Yeah, I know."

Rafe ran for his car. Why hadn't he listened to his instincts? If anything happened to Kendra it would be all his fault.

KENDRA DIDN'T know what had been put in her coffee, but her mouth was dry with a bitter aftertaste. A pounding headache ate away at her ability to concentrate. It took her a moment before she recognized the office at Rialto's house. She had no memory of being brought here.

She choked back the incipient panic as she realized her hands were tightly bound behind her back. Her feet were tied as well. She was slumped on the guest chair, facing Rialto's desk. He was downloading files from his computer and stuffing disks and papers into a large briefcase.

He glanced in her direction and her heart froze right along with her breathing.

"So, you're finally awake."

Kendra lifted her chin and forced herself to return his stare. She would not cower before this evil man.

"Cat got your tongue? No matter, Ms. Kincade or whoever you really are."

"Ginny. Ginny Ford."

Rialto shrugged. As hard as it was to believe, the name obviously meant nothing to him.

"Whatever. Texas Confidential can run your obituary under any name they choose. By now Alvarez must realize Calderone isn't going to show. I expect he's on his way here to rescue you. Chivalry is nothing if not predictable."

His smile filled her with dread.

"Unfortunately for both of you, the attempted rescue will be a wasted effort." He turned the monitor so she could see what was on the screen. Numbers flashed, counting down. "A bit theatrical perhaps, but I've rigged this house to explode. If Alvarez hurries, you might have enough seconds for a touching farewell."

"Some things never change, huh? You still get off on blowing up houses," she managed to sneer.

Startled anger distorted his features, but there was also a

hint of puzzlement. Before he could respond, Marcus Slade entered the room through the sliding glass door leading to the pool.

"Helicopter will be here in five minutes," Slade said, ignoring her completely. "We're cutting it close."

"Calm yourself, Marcus. We have plenty of time. I'd hoped Mr. Alvarez would show before we left. I would have enjoyed putting a bullet in him." His cold eyes mocked Kendra. "I do so love a happy ending. No matter. Make a last sweep of the grounds. Be sure everyone else is gone."

Slade scowled and strode back outside. Rialto closed his briefcase. "I'll leave you with the computer screen for company. You can watch the remaining minutes of your life blink away." He lifted a gun from the desk.

Kendra tore her eyes from the screen and found her voice. "Aren't going to shoot me in cold blood the way you did my parents?" she baited.

"Your parents?" Rialto frowned. He came around the desk holding the gun and studied her intently. "Well, well, well. My old chauffeur was named Ford, and now that I think about it, he had a daughter named Ginny. But she's dead. I checked the corpse myself."

Kendra glared at him with all the hatred churning inside her. "You should really learn to pay closer attention to details. You shot my cousin Kendra by mistake. I was hiding upstairs in the linen closet."

Evil peered from his eyes. "How very clever of you. Too bad you didn't stay hidden. Like father like daughter, hmm? He once poked his nose in my business, too. Instead of staying with the car like a responsible chauffeur, he wandered into a garden where I was hosting a very private meeting one afternoon. An underling thought he could hold out for a bigger slice of the action. Instead, I removed him from the action permanently and your father saw first-hand what happens to people who try to cross me. I saw his expression and I knew it was only a matter of time before he felt it was his 'duty' to report the man's demise."

"So my whole family had to die?"

"I'm afraid so. Your 'whole' family must die."

He pointed the gun at her chest. Someone entered the room at his back.

RAFE THOUGHT his heart would stop when he saw Rialto take aim at Kendra. "Move away from the chair, Rialto."

Kendra twisted in shocked relief. Rafe kept his gun pointed at Stephen Rialto. Only training and discipline kept him from squeezing the trigger.

"Ah, Mr. Alvarez. So you did decide to join us."

"Rafe! Watch out!"

Rialto spun and fired. Something hot seared a path through Rafe's chest. The breath sailed from his lungs, buckling his legs. He held his own fire for fear of hitting Kendra.

Rialto had no such constraints. He took more careful aim, obviously intent on finishing the job. Kendra launched herself out of the chair crashing into him. The gun discharged harmlessly into the floor next to Rafe.

"Why you little—"

"Mr. Rialto!" Marcus Slade appeared in the doorway, his gun drawn as well. He kicked Rafe's gun hand and his weapon went sliding beneath the chair. "The helicopter's here. Let's go!"

Rialto lowered his gun and picked up his briefcase. They were going to get away! Rafe tried to reach for his backup weapon, but his coordination was off. Rialto kicked him in the side of the head. Pain exploded. Dimly, he heard Rialto address Kendra while Rafe struggled to stay conscious.

"I'm sure your parents will be happy to see you again, little girl."

"Go to hell!"

"You can wait for me there."

He heard them leave. He had to move, but steeped in cold, he couldn't make his body obey.

"Rafe!"

Waiting darkness enticed him.

"Rafe!"

In a detached way, he was aware of Kendra, but it took him a few minutes to focus. She was squirming along the carpet in an effort to reach his side. Too bad she'd had to watch him get shot, he thought. This was her nightmare all over again.

"Rafe, don't be dead. Please don't be dead. Rafe!"

He lifted his head.

"...not...dead." It was hard to draw a breath.

He coughed and spittle ran from his mouth. The coppery taste of blood filled his mouth. "Must have bit...my lip."

"Oh, my God, Rafe, he shot you!"

"Yeah. I missed."

"Never mind that. We've got to get out of here!"

"Help's...coming." He thought of Mitchell. The older man wouldn't be pleased by his showing here today, though Rafe had managed to stop a car full of Rialto's employees on his way in. They were cuffed along the side of the road, but the delay had nearly cost Kendra her life.

"We'll have to wait...for Mitchell."

"We can't wait. The house is rigged to explode!"

Rafe shut his eyes.

"Don't you dare pass out on me. We have to get out of here right now! Do you hear me?"

It took an effort, but he brought her back into focus. "...not deaf." He coughed again and wondered if the bullet had hit a lung. Something warm and wet and sticky was spreading across his chest. "Where's...your knife?"

"On my thigh."

"Good."

Rafe lifted himself slowly. Blood spread alarmingly across his white shirt. Surprisingly, there was no pain, just this strange cold. Shock. Once it wore off, he knew he'd be in a whole lot of pain. He ran his hand up her torn hose until he reached the sheath.

"Another time…I'd enjoy this," he said thickly.

"Don't tease, Rafe. You have to save your strength."

He worked the knife free and set to work on the cord that bound her wrists. His hands were clumsy. He hoped Kendra couldn't tell how much the effort cost him. Not only was he bleeding badly, but there was a wheezy sound whenever he drew a breath. His chest had started to hurt. He hoped his fellow agents were almost here. Rialto mustn't be allowed to get away. They had him on real charges now. Shooting a government agent was going to buy him some hard time for sure.

Kendra grimaced as her wrists came free of the ropes. Rafe sank back, letting her take the knife from his weak fingers. She sawed at the cord binding her legs.

"Rafe! We have to go!"

All he wanted to do was try and draw air into his lungs.

"Mitchell…will get him…when he drives away."

"He isn't driving. He's got a helicopter."

That roused him. He remembered Slade's comment about the helicopter. Rafe tried to concentrate on Kendra. If Rialto made it to the helicopter they would lose him for good. Rafe couldn't let that happen. It was his job to stop Rialto. "Where?"

"I don't know. He and Slade ran out back."

Rafe reached for his gun and struggled to stand. Kendra helped him up. For a moment, he allowed himself to lean heavily on her as the room spun and then steadied. "How much…time do we have?"

Kendra looked toward the computer screen.

"Four minutes! Come on!"

They wouldn't make it far enough away. There wasn't enough time. Rafe had to struggle for each breath, fighting the blackness that tried to drag him down. Doggedly, he stumbled along at her side as they hurried into the pool area.

Beyond the pool was a garden. Beyond that, the distant thump, thump, thump of a helicopter was loud. Rafe forced his legs to run. The blades were kicking up a swirl of dust. Rialto and Slade had just reached the impromptu landing pad. Rafe raised the gun he'd retrieved from the floor and fired.

He knew the distance was too great for accuracy. Marcus Slade climbed inside and raised his head. Before Rafe could fire again, Slade turned, gun in hand. He looked at Rafe, then he fired point-blank at Stephen Rialto.

Rialto crumpled to the ground. Rafe had always wondered if Slade was Calderone's man. Now he knew. Like he'd told Kendra—Calderone wanted no witnesses to testify against him.

The beefy guard who'd accosted Kendra and him climbed out of the helicopter and reached for Rialto's briefcase. He climbed back in and the helicopter began to lift.

Rafe had to stop them. Calderone must want the information in that briefcase. That was reason enough to keep it from going anywhere. Rafe raised his gun and took careful aim. He fired at the slowly rising machine until the clip was empty.

Without warning, the helicopter exploded. One of his shots had struck something vital after all. Rafe turned and grabbed Kendra. He pushed her into the deep end of the pool, going in with her as debris rained down on them.

When he surfaced, she was right beside him. He grabbed a lungful of air and her shoulders and plunged them under the surface again as the house exploded all around them.

Kendra's nightmare had come full circle.

Chapter Fourteen

"What do you mean she's going home?" Rafe struggled to sit up in the hospital bed, his heart beating wildly. "Kendra was here. I didn't dream her."

Cody laid a hand on his shoulder. "No, you didn't dream her. She barely left your side until the doctor promised you were out of danger. Today she announced she's going home."

"You mean to her home? Why?"

Troubled, Mitchell stared at him. "She said her job here was over."

"That's not the reason. She's running scared." He may be hurt, but there was nothing wrong with Rafe's memory or his hearing. He remembered everything clearly, until they loaded him in the ambulance.

The mingled smell of burning and chlorine had clogged his nose. It had been an effort to stay alert in the water, but he'd known there could be more of Rialto's people still around. Though he'd lost his gun somewhere, he still had his backup piece strapped to his ankle. At least he'd thought he did. It required too much effort to check for it just then.

He vividly remembered clinging to the side of the pool with Kendra half supporting his weight in water filled with debris.

"Don't you dare die on me, Rafael," she'd demanded.

He'd staved off the blackness by thinking how sexy she looked with her silky blue dress plastered against that sexy little body.

"Never mind my body," she'd told him, so he must have spoken his thoughts aloud. It had been getting harder and harder to stay focused. "I hear cars. Help's coming."

He'd wanted to brush a strand of wet hair from her cheek but his hand wouldn't cooperate. "...love you."

"Shh. You're going to be okay."

She'd cried. Fat tears that mingled with the water droplets. They'd reminded him of the way she'd cried the night she'd told him of the past. He'd tried to tell her things were going to be okay this time, but it required too much energy. Daylight faded in and out despite the fire dancing all around them.

Rafe refused to slip into unconsciousness, determined to keep her safe. The cars she'd heard might be part of Rialto's people instead of his fellow agents. He should go and see.

And he would.

In a minute.

"Rafe! Wake up! Don't you dare die! Do you understand me? Don't you dare!"

He'd managed a smile. She was always scolding him. A good sign that she still cared even if she'd never said the words since that one time. "Marry...me?"

"What? Oh, God. Help! Over here! In the pool!"

"Marry...me."

"Yes. Of course. Just hang on. Hang on, Rafe. Brady! Cody! Somebody! We're over here!"

Rafe let the memories fade away. The rest weren't nearly as pleasant. Now he looked at Cody as he tried to settle more comfortably against the pillow. "Who would have thought she'd run scared?"

"What are you talking about?"

"Big brave Kendra. You know, she's perfectly capable of

facing down rattlesnakes, flash floods, attackers and even the man who killed her family, yet she's scared of commitment. Who'd have thunk it?''

''Rafe, old buddy, you're starting to scare me. What are you talking about?''

Rafe knew he could overcome Kendra's fears. He wasn't known for his charm for nothing. ''How soon can I get out of here?''

Cody rubbed his jaw. ''Beats me. You do realize you nearly died. Not only did you lose a lot of blood, but that bullet collapsed your lung and did some other damage in there. You're one lucky son-of-a—''

''I know. I'm getting married.''

Cody straightened up. ''What did you say?''

''Where's Penny?''

''You're going to marry Penny?''

Rafe nearly laughed out loud, but his chest protested.

''Nope. I'm going to marry Kendra, but it looks like I'll need Penny's help.''

KENDRA STARED AT PENNY. ''What do you mean he's taken a turn for the worst? I just left the hospital. The doctor assured me he was doing fine.''

Penny turned and walked to the window of the bedroom Kendra had used since she arrived at the Smoking Barrel. ''He's asking for you,'' she said softly. ''You should go to him, Kendra. If a man loved me the way Rafe loves you—''

''Rafe doesn't love me.'' If only he did! ''Besides, you've got Neil.''

''I don't particularly want Neil. The fact is, I'm getting more than a little disenchanted with Neil. Rafe on the other hand—''

''Has got his harem and he likes it that way.'' Which was precisely why she was packing up her stuff and heading home. Rafe only thought he loved her. He'd soon forget his declaration once he saw how the other women were rallying around him.

Penny turned back, her eyes completely serious behind her chic glasses. "Not any more."

"Are you telling me that Lydia and Janet and the others aren't still camped outside his door waiting to visit Rafe?"

Penny looked down guiltily. "Uh—"

"I can't be part of a herd, Penny."

"You aren't. He's a cowboy, Kendra. He culled you from that herd."

"Penny—"

"All I can say is that I've known Rafael Alvarez a lot longer than you have. Believe me when I tell you, that man loves you."

Penny's voice held a wistfulness that made Kendra feel a pang of sympathy for the other woman. And also a thrill of hope.

Kendra stared at the bed filled with bright, slinky clothing waiting to be packed. She realized she didn't want to go back to her silent, empty house. The Smoking Barrel felt more like home than the place where she'd spent most of her youth. And the isolation of cyberspace no longer beckoned the way it once had. She liked being part of Texas Confidential.

She touched the glass swan Rafe had given her. Could Penny be right? Was she making a mistake? One she'd regret for the rest of her life?

"Marry…me?" he'd asked. What if he'd really meant it?

"I'm a fool."

"You are if you leave now," Penny agreed.

Kendra reached for the green dress waiting to be packed. Penny's eyes gleamed with approval.

"Is he really worse?" Kendra asked.

A smile brightened Penny's features. "That's what he told me to tell you."

"You're a good friend, Penny."

"Hey, I'm a sucker for a happy ending," she agreed.

RAFE FELT the familiar stirring of anticipation as he replaced the telephone. Penny had been successful. Kendra was on her way.

"That woman is going to be trouble," Mitchell said entering the private hospital room.

"Kendra?"

"Lydia Skerritt."

Rafe frowned. Lydia had left right after the telephone rang a few moments ago. Surprisingly, the blonde had become upset when Rafe told her his plans, explaining why he couldn't see her anymore.

Rafe frowned, momentarily distracted as Mitchell sat down heavily. Perspiration dotted the older man's forehead despite the fact that it wasn't warm inside the air-conditioned hospital.

"So she'll come?" Cody asked Rafe, coming in behind Mitchell with Brady and Jake on his heels.

"On her way," Rafe said, knowing his relief was obvious.

Cody shook his head. "How the mighty have fallen. Smitten by love's arrow at the peak of your youth. It's a tragedy."

"Your turn will come," Rafe promised.

"Hey, Mitchell, Rafe's making threats again."

Mitchell rubbed his chest and grimaced.

Rafe frowned, seriously alarmed. The older man's color wasn't good. He looked ill. "Mitchell? You okay?"

"Heartburn." He brushed aside Rafe's concern impatiently, but shadows deepened his eyes.

"Again?" Brady asked.

"Never mind—" The grimace turned into an expression of acute pain. Mitchell suddenly clutched his chest, struggling to breathe. Abruptly, he pitched forward. Only Cody's quick intervention saved him from toppling out of his chair.

"Mitchell!"

"I'll get a doctor." Jake whirled for the door.

"Is he breathing?" Brady demanded.

"Yeah, but it isn't good," Cody said grimly.

Rafe struggled out of bed. Mitchell was having a heart attack. In minutes, his room swarmed in organized chaos.

"AT LEAST he picked a good place for it," Jake said as he watched the doctor walk away.

Brady nodded. "It could have been a disaster if this had happened at the ranch. You doin' okay, Rafe?"

Rafe nodded as the men prepared to leave the Intensive Care Cardiac Unit. Rafe had threatened to pull out his IV tube until they let him join the others waiting for news of Mitchell's condition. Fortunately, the news had come quickly. Mitchell had suffered a relatively minor heart attack. They would keep him for awhile, monitoring him to be certain, but things looked pretty positive at the moment.

Cody had elected to wait there for Maddie who was on her way in. They hadn't been able to reach Penny to tell her the situation.

Rafe pinched the bridge of his nose, feeling more exhausted than he could ever remember. Visions of Mitchell being loaded onto the gurney were hard to shake. He hadn't realized how much he'd come to love the crusty old man he respected so deeply. The fact of the matter was, he'd give his life for any of the people connected with the Smoking Barrel ranch. The ranch was his home, and somewhere along the way, his fellow agents and the people connected with the ranch had become his family.

He wished Kendra would hurry and get here.

KENDRA turned away from the nurse's station and headed in the direction the woman had indicated. Penny had insisted on waiting downstairs. She claimed she saw Maddie pulling into the parking lot. Kendra knew Penny was just trying to allow Rafe and Kendra some private time and she appreciated that.

Stepping out of the elevator on Rafe's floor, Kendra was surprised to come face-to-face with Lydia Skerrit. There was no welcoming smile on the woman's pretty features this time.

"Bitch!"

Kendra gaped at her even as the elevator doors whooshed closed at her back. The hall stretched in either direction, oddly deserted at the moment.

"The rattlesnake, the clothing... You were too stupid to get the message," Lydia went on with surprising viciousness. "Maybe if those dumb cowhands hadn't screwed up, you would have run home to your computers and stayed there before it was too late. How unfortunate that flash flood didn't get you."

Stunned, Kendra gaped at the perfectly groomed woman with the maliciously evil eyes. "Are you saying you were behind the attacks on me?" Her stomach plunged hollowly. "But, why?"

"Why do you think? Rafe belongs to me."

Astonishingly, a revolver appeared in her hand. Lydia narrowed the gap between them.

"We're going to take a little ride you and I."

Kendra suddenly spotted Rafe and Brady and Jake coming slowly down the far end of the hall. If she didn't do something quick, Kendra knew all hell was going to break loose. She would not risk Rafe being shot a second time.

"You know something, Lydia, I'm getting real tired of people pointing guns at me."

Lydia made the mistake of getting close enough. Kendra brought her heavy purse up in a hard, short arc that smashed against Lydia's gun arm. The weapon discharged harmlessly, but noisily. Kendra spun, grabbing Lydia's arm even as she used the other woman's own momentum to trip her onto the institutional style carpeting. The gun skittered away, banging off the elevator.

Lydia screamed in rage. Her face was distorted by fury as she sprang to her feet. Brady jumped between them, taking the initial brunt of Lydia's next attack while Jake appeared, wrapping his arms around her writhing body. He pinned Lydia against his chest.

Rafe stooped painfully to retrieve the dropped weapon. The doors behind Kendra slid open and Penny and Maddie stepped from the elevator and came to an abrupt halt at the scene.

"It's over, Lydia," Rafe said, tiredly.

"Let me go! You can't do this!" Lydia screamed at Jake. She turned her crazed face toward Rafe. "You belong to me!"

"No," he said calmly.

Spittle dotted her chin. "But I got rid of my husband for you!"

Rafe handed Penny the weapon. Kendra stepped to his side and he reached out and drew her close.

"You killed your husband?" Brady demanded.

Lydia stopped struggling. The coldly calculating change in her expression was a scary thing to witness. "Let go of me!" she told Jake imperiously.

"Here comes hospital security," Maddie said.

Faced with the newcomers, Lydia's expression turned sullen and angry. She refused to say another word as security, then uniformed policemen joined the crowd that had gathered to watch the scene unfold. As the officers patted her down, a wicked looking knife blade appeared.

"Want to bet it matches some of the damaged clothing?" Penny asked no one in particular.

Rafe nuzzled Kendra's ear as Lydia was led away.

"Talk about black widow spiders," Jake muttered.

"I don't even remember meeting her when she was married," Rafe said.

"It's that lethal charm of yours," Brady told him.

"We found fingerprints and some dyed blonde hairs along with some fibers in the room after Kendra's clothing was destroyed, but we had nothing to compare them with," Penny said. "I meant to get a set of Lydia's prints and with one thing and another, I forgot."

"Don't worry about it," Rafe said, his hand unconsciously rubbing at his bandage.

Kendra raised her face to look at him. "Should you even be out of bed? Of course not. We need to have a little talk. What possessed you to charge over here when you saw she had a gun? Stupid heroics will get you killed one of these days."

Rafe frowned. "Stupid heroics?"

Brady and Jake exchanged grins while Kendra shared a speaking glance with Penny and shook her head. "Men! You were right. I'm going to have to take that job Mitchell offered me."

"Good," Penny said fervently.

"What job?" Rafe demanded.

"She's going to be our resident computer expert," Penny said.

"Well, somebody has to ride herd on Rafe to keep him out of trouble," Kendra said pointedly. "He shouldn't be out of bed yet! And where's his IV?"

Rafe relaxed. His lips twitched at her scolding tone. He realized he didn't mind being berated at all with that sort of love shining in her eyes. He nudged her chin higher.

"I like the sound of that."

Her eyes widened and a breathless quality entered her voice. "I meant you should be in bed *resting!*"

"Oh, we'll get to that part."

For a moment her lips pursed, then a gleam of mischief

appeared in her eyes. "Uh-huh. I'll have you begging for mercy inside an hour," she promised.

"Let's try for two."

Pink surged up her cheeks, but a pulse leaped to life in her throat.

"Promises, promises," she said softly, ignoring their audience.

Despite the exhaustion tugging at him, Rafe grinned, as the sensual pull between them strengthened. "We'll see about that."

"I don't know about anybody else around here, but I'm startin' to feel like a voyeur," Jake announced.

"I know what you mean," Penny agreed. "First Brady, then you, now Rafe. I wish Mitchell would send me on an assignment."

"Don't you people have cows to herd or something?" Rafe asked.

"I think that's a hint that they want to be alone," Penny said. "I just love a happy ending."

Rafe ignored his friends, touching Kendra's soft cheek gently as he gazed into her eyes. "Are we going to have a happy ending?" he asked softly, trying not to let his anxiety show.

"That depends. What are you going to do about your harem?"

"How about I leave them for Cody? You're enough of a harem for me."

"Are you sure, Rafe?"

"Positive."

He ran his hand down her bare arm, rewarded by a quiver of anticipation. His gaze came to rest on the gauzy material of her green dress. He could see the outline of her nipples as they tightened.

"What are you wearing under this dress?"

"Talcum powder."

Rafe drew in a surprised breath.

"And thong panties," she added.

He took her hand and led her toward his private room. "Come on—*partner*. We don't need or want an audience as we start our next adventure."

* * * * *

Don't miss the exciting conclusion of
TEXAS CONFIDENTIAL
coming next month

*Cody Gannon is the youngest of
the Texas Confidential agents;
but he's about to become the man
he's always wanted to be—
if he lives through it!*

Turn the page for a sneak preview of
THE OUTSIDER'S REDEMPTION
by Joanna Wayne.

Prologue

Cody Gannon's boots clicked against the hospital's polished tile floors as he hurried toward Mitchell Forbes's room. The old warhorse was recovering and already raising cane with the doctors to let him go back to the Smoking Barrel. Not that anyone was surprised. A mere heart attack could never keep a man like Mitchell down.

Still, Cody had been scared to death when Mitchell had doubled over with chest pains. The depth of his emotion had surprised him, especially since he was convinced he wasn't quite the man Mitchell had hoped for when he'd hired him on to work with Texas Confidential. The other three guys on the undercover team did no wrong. Cody seldom did anything right, at least in the critical eyes of Mitchell Forbes.

But the cantankerous old rancher lawman had recruited Cody himself, offered him a position based strictly on his one brush with fame and heroism. He'd said he had faith in Cody's ability to handle the job in spite of his trouble-plagued past.

So Cody was living at the Smoking Barrel, had been for two years. The rest of the Texas Confidential agents weren't all that impressed that he'd foiled a bank robbery attempt and saved a young girl in the process. They knew it was more instinct than bravery that had spurred him into action, but they'd welcomed him all the same and taught him what they could about working for the most exciting covert operation in the whole state of Texas.

No doubt about it, he owed Mitchell Forbes a lot for giving him the chance to be part of Texas Confidential and to finally make something of himself. He was going to make sure Mitchell knew that, and he was going to work twice as hard in the future to make the man proud of him. He picked up his pace, anxious to see for himself that Mitchell was doing as well as the others had reported.

He heard a female voice as he approached the room and recognized it at once. Maddie Wells, a neighboring rancher. He wasn't close enough to eavesdrop, but he could tell from her tone she was in one of her lecturing modes. Probably reading Mitchell the riot act about smoking his cigars. She was the only one who could jump him about his bad habits and get away with it. One day Mitchell was going to slow down a tad, and Maddie would snare him.

The door to Mitchell's room was open just a crack. He started to barge in but thought better of it. It was always a good idea to knock when a man was entertaining a woman, even if it was in a hospital room. He touched his knuckles to the door.

"Cody deserves to know the truth, Mitchell."

He hesitated, not sure he wanted to know any truth that brought that kind of seriousness to Maddie's tone. And if he was about to be canned, he sure didn't want to hear that.

"Give it up, Maddie."

Mitchell's voice was scratchy and Cody could picture him in the bed, his muscles tight, his face drawn into stubborn lines. He waited silently, torn, knowing he couldn't turn away until he knew what Maddie was talking about. After all, this did concern him.

"Suppose you had died when you had that heart attack," Maddie said, her voice far softer than usual. "You would have gone to your grave without Cody's ever knowing the truth.''

''That's the way I intend for it to be.''

Cody's muscles tightened. He'd had his share of ugly secrets in his life, but he'd thought they ended when he'd buried Frank Gannon.

''Are you telling me that you have no intention of talking to Cody about this?''

''That's exactly what I'm saying. My biggest mistake was in ever telling you.''

''No, your biggest mistake, Mitchell Forbes, was in walking away from your own flesh and blood in the first place. Cody Gannon is your son, and he deserves to know it.''

Cody backed away from the door, but the words still echoed in his mind, growing louder and louder until he wanted to scream at them to stop. He ducked into the stairwell and fell against the wall. He felt as if someone had slammed him in the gut with a two-by-four.

Maddie was wrong. He wasn't Mitchell Forbes's son. His father was Frank Gannon. He had the scars to prove it.

He took the steps two at a time, rounding one level and flying down the next. Scenes from his past reared up in his mind, dark, ugly images that filled him with a dread so real he could taste it. Could taste the blood. Taste the fear.

But as quickly as they'd come, they were replaced by new images. Mitchell Forbes and his mother. He'd gotten her pregnant and walked away. Left her to marry Frank Gannon. Left her to die in her misery.

Cody reached the first floor and pushed out the door and into the stifling Texas heat. But it was not the sweltering heat that crawled over his skin and sucked away his breath. It was a bitterness so strong it destroyed his ability to reason.

All he knew was that if he never saw Mitchell Forbes again, it would still be eons too soon for him.

Chapter One

Cody Gannon picked up the glass and downed the bourbon. He seldom touched hard liquor, but tonight was special. A hard ball of emptiness had settled in the spot where his heart should have resided, and he needed the burn in his throat and the pain-numbing sting of the drink as it plunged into the pit of his stomach.

Cody Gannon. Illegitimate son. The words tore at his insides like crushed glass. Or shrapnel.

"Mitchell Forbes." He said the name out loud, rolled it over his tongue, spit it past the disgusting lump that had settled in his throat.

A week ago, the man had been his hero. But that was before Cody had found out the truth about Mitchell. That's why Cody's gear was in his pickup truck. All he owned. Amazingly little. Jeans, shirts, boots, a couple of jackets, his guns and a saddle. Even his horse belonged to Mitchell and the Confidentials.

He had no idea where he was headed, wasn't even sure what town he'd stopped in. He didn't much care anymore, as long as it was far away from the Smoking Barrel.

Regret balled in his gut. He tried to force it away, but he hadn't drunk nearly enough to make it subside. Being a part of Texas Confidential had been more than a job. It had been his life. The first real commitment he'd ever made to anything. The best friends he'd ever had.

Now Cody had no choice but to walk away. Calderone and his band of murderous drug dealers would still be stopped, but Cody wouldn't be in on the operation that brought them down.

"Thank you, Mitchell Forbes." He downed the rest of the bourbon and pushed the glass away as a bearded man who smelled like he was two days past needing a bath slid onto the bar stool next to him.

"Buy me a drink, mister?"

"I'd sooner buy you a bar of soap."

"Then save your money."

"Suit yourself." Cody stood and turned away from the drunk, ready to move to another stool or one of the tables in the back of the smoky saloon.

"You better save your money anyway. You'll probably need it now that you've walked off your job." The stranger leaned over the bar, his hands spread out flat on the marred wood.

Cody stopped and stared at him. His hair was gray, thin and wiry, and his skin was bronzed and weathered from hours spent in the sun. "What makes you think I lost my job?" he asked, studying the man's facial expression as he waited for an answer.

"I don't think. I know." The man fingered the brim of a soiled western hat. "Tell me, is Penny still as bossy as ever?"

"I don't know any Penny," he lied.

"Sure you do. No one works at the Smoking Barrel without knowing Penny Archer."

So that was it. The dirty drunk had probably worked for a while on one of the ranches near the Smoking Barrel, though he didn't look familiar. It was no secret Cody worked for Mitchell Forbes. It was what he and other Texas Confidential agents really did for Mitchell Forbes that was kept under wraps.

Still, the man made Cody nervous, and he might as well move on. He reached for his wallet and pulled out a few bills, enough to pay his tab and purchase one drink for the aging cowboy.

"You're not leaving, are you?" The man reached over and wrapped his fingers around Cody's left wrist. "I thought we'd get to be buddies."

"Think again."

"But we have so much to talk about. Mutual friends. A mutual enemy."

Cody smoothed the bills he'd tossed on the table, instantly aware of the change to the man's voice. He was no longer slurring his words, and his voice had lost all traces of frailty.

He stared into the man's eyes, and experienced a vague sense of déjà vu. "What enemy would that be?"

"I was thinking Tomaso Calderone, but I guess if you're not a Texas Confidential anymore, you wouldn't be interested."

Cody swallowed hard. The man definitely had his attention now. No one outside of the powers in charge were supposed to know about Texas Confidential. The agents' ability to do their job depended on people believing that they were just everyday cowboys running a ranch. So did staying alive. He lowered his voice to a mere whisper. "Who are you?"

The man met his gaze. "Don't you recognize me, Cody?"

The voice was no longer disguised. It was smooth. Easy. Almost familiar. He squinted, taking in the wrinkles in the man's face, his stringy beard, his wispy gray hair. The voice and the appearance didn't match. He only knew one man who could come up with a disguise that good, and this couldn't be him.

"I don't have any idea who you are or what you want from me."

"I'm Daniel Austin."

"Daniel Austin is dead."

"No. I'm too tough to die, though I wished for it a time or two." His lips curled into a half smile. "I was captured by Rialto's men, kept prisoner for months. Finally, I escaped, but by then, I knew enough about Calderone and how he worked that I was able to infiltrate his organization. I've worked my way all the way to the top. Calderone and me— we're like that." He indicated how close with two fingers on his right hand.

Cody shook his head. "No, Daniel is dead."

"Because that's what Mitchell Forbes told you? Believe me, that doesn't make it true."

Suspicion reared up in Cody. He was supposed to be walking away from his life as a Texas Confidential agent, not being drawn into some secret conspiracy. But this man obviously knew all about them. And if he really was Daniel Austin… "Why would Mitchell be told you were dead if you're not?"

"You know the head honchos. They don't trust anyone."

"They trust Mitchell Forbes."

"Don't be so sure."

Cody tried to digest that last bit of information, but it boggled his mind. No one had ever infiltrated Calderone's circle. And if someone did, and Calderone found out, that man's body would be found in tiny pieces. Still, if anyone could do it, it would be Daniel Austin.

"So, if you're so close to Calderone, what in the hell are you doing here?"

"My job. But I can't do it alone."

"Then you need to talk to Rafe or one of the others. I'm out." Damn, here he was giving away information. The man was blowing his mind. He knew too much, but he couldn't be Daniel Austin. Or could he?

"Listen, Cody. I know what you're thinking, but you're

wrong. I didn't just happen into this bar tonight. I followed you here. I need you. But before I give you the assignment, I have to be certain you're not going to go running back to Mitchell Forbes.''

"Why's that?"

Daniel, or at least the man claiming to be Daniel, stared straight ahead, his back still hunched, his head still low, as if he really were an elderly man. He didn't face Cody when he talked, but when he paused, his Adam's apple rode up and down like it was bobbing in a pail of water.

"As you know, someone has been leaking secrets to Calderone. We think it might be Mitchell himself.''

A curl of smoke from the cigarette of a man a few stools down wafted into Cody's face. His eyes burned, but not nearly as severely as the acid that pooled in his stomach. There was a leak somewhere. That part was true. But, Mitchell?

Even as angry as Cody was with the man, he'd never imagined Mitchell capable of deceit where Texas Confidential was concerned. Not when stopping Calderone seemed to be the cause that fueled his incredible drive.

But this would be just like the department. The same minds that had dreamed up Texas Confidential would like nothing better than having Daniel Austin, their master of disguises, working so far undercover that even Calderone himself would take the man into his confidence.

"What is it you need me to do?" he asked, still suspicious, but warming to the idea of getting in on the action of bringing Calderone down. Especially when it meant he'd outdo Mitchell Forbes.

"I need you to go to the airport and pick up a woman named Sarah Rand. She'll be flying into San Antonio and arriving at five o'clock tomorrow afternoon. After you pick her up, I'll contact you and tell you where I'll meet the two of you."

"And who is this Sarah Rand?"

"She's a secretary for the DPS. Works for Elmore Cochran."

Cody recognized the name though he'd never met the man. He'd just been promoted and was now the final authority over anything involving the Confidentials.

Dan leaned in closer, his voice lowered to a barely audible whisper. "Evidence indicates that Miss Rand may have been selling secrets to Calderone, and that's what she thinks she's doing now. I've offered her one million dollars to deliver some secret files for me. If she delivers, it will prove her guilt."

Cody parted his lips as a low whistle escaped. "I don't see how this would prove anything except that she can be bribed for a million dollars. Selling you top secret info now doesn't mean she's done it before. Not to mention that there are laws against entrapment."

"You let me and the department worry about that end of it. All I need from you is a simple yes or no."

There was nothing simple about the answer Cody was about to give. If this man was Daniel Austin, then a yes would put Cody into the thick of things. He could be a major player in the action that brought the mighty Tomaso Calderone to his knees. And how sweet it would be to let Mitchell Forbes see that he was his own man.

But if this wasn't Daniel Austin, then he could be walking into a trap. He'd have to watch his back every minute. Nothing new there.

"I'll go with the yes."

Daniel nodded and his eyes warmed, though his lips stayed drawn in the same thin line.

"So after I pick up Miss Sarah Rand, where do I deliver her?" Cody asked.

"I'll let you know that at the time."

"How do I reach you?"

"You don't. I'll reach you. You just pick up the woman and get her into your truck. I'll make the connection at that point."

"I don't have a cellular phone anymore. The one I had belonged to Texas Confidential and I turned it in when I left. All I have is a beeper."

"Then I guess that will have to do."

Cody scribbled his pager number down on a napkin and handed it to Daniel though he had the sneaking suspicion the man already knew it. "How will I recognize this woman?"

"She's young—in her twenties. Her hair's a reddish blond and she wears it straight and just long enough to cover her ears. She'll be wearing a hot-pink suit." Daniel stood up. "Oh yeah," he added. "She'll be carrying a canvas tote that says 'So Many Cowboys, So Little Time.' You can't miss her."

With that, Daniel Austin slid off his stool and staggered to the door, doing a flawless performance as an elderly drunk. His baggy pants rode his thin hips, and the back of his gray hair zigzagged in and out of his shirt collar. One of the younger cowboys moved out of his way in deference to the man's apparent age and condition.

Cody waited a few minutes and then left the bar and walked back to his pickup truck. A few minutes ago, he'd been wallowing in his bad luck. But now the old juices were starting to flow. He was back in the saddle again.

THE SECRET IS OUT!

HARLEQUIN®

INTRIGUE®

presents

**By day these agents are cowboys;
by night they are specialized
government operatives.
Men bound by love, loyalty and the law—
they've vowed to keep their missions
and identities confidential....**

Harlequin Intrigue

HARLEQUIN®

Makes any time special ™

Visit us at www.eHarlequin.com

HITC

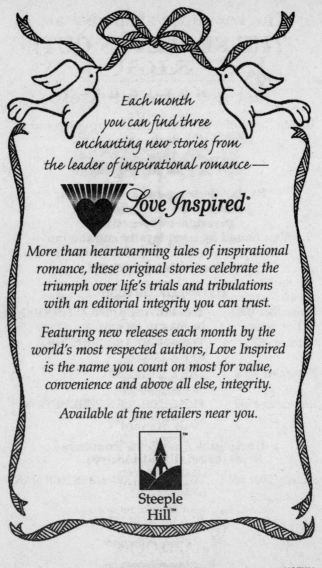

Each month
you can find three
enchanting new stories from
the leader of inspirational romance—

Love Inspired

More than heartwarming tales of inspirational
romance, these original stories celebrate the
triumph over life's trials and tribulations
with an editorial integrity you can trust.

Featuring new releases each month by the
world's most respected authors, Love Inspired
is the name you count on most for value,
convenience and above all else, integrity.

Available at fine retailers near you.

Steeple
Hill™

Visit us at www.steeplehill.com   LIGEN00

The romantic suspense at

HARLEQUIN®
INTRIGUE

just got more intense!

On the precipice between imminent danger and
smoldering desire, they are

When your back is against the wall
and nothing makes sense, only one man
is strong enough to pull you from the brink—
and into his loving arms!
Look for all the books in this riveting new
promotion:

WOMAN MOST WANTED (#599)
by **Harper Allen**
On sale January 2001

PRIVATE VOWS (#603)
by **Sally Steward**
On sale February 2001

NIGHTTIME GUARDIAN (#607)
by **Amanda Stevens**
On sale March 2001

Available at your favorite retail outlet.

HARLEQUIN®
Makes any time special ™

Visit us at www.eHarlequin.com   HIOTE

**Sometimes a little bundle of joy
can cause a whole lot of trouble...**

Judy Christenberry
Cathy Gillen Thacker

THE
BABY
GAME

2 Complete Novels

at the LOW PRICE of $4.99 U.S./$5.99 CAN.!

When wealthy Caroline Adkins woke up at the hospital, she felt like going right back to bed. First she learned she was suffering from amnesia—then she discovered she was pregnant, too! And to make matters worse, three men turned up claiming paternity!

Marrying Abby Kildaire after a whirlwind weekend of passion was the best thing Tad McFarland had ever done. Surely they'd be able to work out the details concerning their marriage, but they never dreamed that the first pesky little detail would be to have to make room for a baby....

Look for THE BABY GAME on sale in December 2000.

HARLEQUIN®
Makes any time special ™

Visit us at www.eHarlequin.com

PBR2TBG

This Christmas, experience
the love, warmth and magic that
only Harlequin can provide with

Mistletoe Magic

a charming collection from

BETTY NEELS
MARGARET WAY   REBECCA WINTERS

Available November 2000

HARLEQUIN®
Makes any time special ™

Visit us at www.eHarlequin.com   PHMAGIC

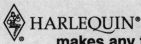

HARLEQUIN®
makes any time special—online...

eHARLEQUIN.com

your romantic
books

♥ **Shop online!** Visit Shop eHarlequin and discover a wide selection of new releases and classic favorites at great discounted prices.

♥ **Read** our daily and weekly Internet exclusive serials, and participate in our interactive novel in the reading room.

♥ **Ever dreamed of being a writer?** Enter your chapter for a chance to become a featured author in our Writing Round Robin novel.

your romantic
life

♥ **Check out** our feature articles on dating, flirting and other important romance topics and get your daily love dose with tips on how to keep the romance alive every day.

your
community

♥ **Have a Heart-to-Heart** with other members about the latest books and meet your favorite authors.

♥ **Discuss** your romantic dilemma in the Tales from the Heart message board.

your romantic
escapes

♥ **Learn** what the stars have in store for you with our daily Passionscopes and weekly Erotiscopes.

♥ **Get the latest scoop** on your favorite royals in Royal Romance.

HINTA1

CELEBRATE VALENTINE'S DAY WITH HARLEQUIN®'S LATEST TITLE— Stolen Memories

Available in trade-size format, this collector's edition contains three full-length novels by *New York Times* bestselling authors Jayne Ann Krentz and Tess Gerritsen, along with national bestselling author Stella Cameron.

TEST OF TIME by **Jayne Ann Krentz**—
He married for the best reason.... She married for the only reason.... Did they stand a chance at making the only reason the real reason to share a lifetime?

THIEF OF HEARTS by **Tess Gerritsen**—
Their distrust of each other was only as strong as their desire. And Jordan began to fear that Diana was more than just a thief of hearts.

MOONTIDE by **Stella Cameron**—
For Andrew, Greer's return is a miracle. It had broken his heart to let her go. Now fate has brought them back together. And he won't lose her again...

Make this Valentine's Day one to remember!

Look for this exciting collector's edition on sale January 2001 at your favorite retail outlet.

HARLEQUIN®
Makes any time special ™

Visit us at www.eHarlequin.com

PHSM

HARLEQUIN®
INTRIGUE

opens the case files on:

TOP SECRET
BABIES

Unwrap the mystery!

January 2001
#597 THE BODYGUARD'S BABY
Debra Webb

February 2001
#601 SAVING HIS SON
Rita Herron

March 2001
#605 THE HUNT FOR HAWKE'S DAUGHTER
Jean Barrett

April 2001
#609 UNDERCOVER BABY
Adrianne Lee

May 2001
#613 CONCEPTION COVER-UP
Karen Lawton Barrett

Follow the clues to your favorite retail outlet.

HARLEQUIN®
Makes any time special ™

Visit us at www.eHarlequin.com

HITSB